Immortal Danger

Immortal Danger

CYNTHIA EDEN

BRAVA

KENSINGTON PUBLISHING CORP.
www.kensingtonbooks.com

Battle not with monsters, lest ye become a monster.
—Friedrich Nietzsche

Prologue

So this is what death feels like.

Maya Black struggled for breath, struggled to fight the creeping cold that swept through her body. *Jesus.* She hadn't wanted to go out like this. Hadn't wanted to die in some damn dirty, stinking alley.

She'd been born in an alley like this, and she sure as hell hadn't planned to die in one.

"Ummm, you taste so good." The sick monster above her licked his fangs, *freaking fangs,* and she noticed that her blood coated his lips. "Poor little cop, I think I've drained you dry."

Her heart was slowing, the hollow beat barely echoing in her ears. The ground was hard beneath her, the moon shining brightly over her. And hell looked back at her from the creature's eyes.

A vampire. She knew what he was. She'd seen his kind before. Others thought things like him were just myths, but she knew better. She knew demons were real, knew the devil was real. Evil lurked in the world, she'd known that fact for years.

"Beg me," the vampire whispered, leaning over her and gazing at her with his soulless black eyes. "Beg me to change you, beg me to let you live."

To change you. No, oh, hell, no. She didn't want to become a monster. And she would never, *never* beg.

Not again.

He slashed his wrist open with the edge of his fangs. Shoved the wound to her mouth.

No!

She turned her head away, trying to spit out the blood. Her hands fumbled in the trash beside her. Where was her weapon? The vampire had jumped her, thrown her against the wall, sank those razor-sharp fangs into her throat, and then had her on the ground in less than a minute.

She'd dropped her gun. Where was it? Where—

Her fingers closed over the barrel of her Glock. She pulled, struggling to bring the weapon closer. It felt so heavy in her hand, so—

He laughed at her. Actually laughed. Then he grabbed the gun. Her fingers swiped out, clenched around the butt. He pushed the barrel dead-center against his chest and whispered, "Do it."

Without a moment's hesitation, she pulled the trigger.

The bullet shot straight through his chest. He smiled at her.

And her heart stuttered. The beat was slowing, *slowing.*

"You can't kill me, bitch, not with your weak bullets, not with—"

He broke off, gasping, and he stumbled away from her, raising a hand to his chest. Smoke rose from the wound, a long, thin trail of smoke. The scent of burnt flesh filled the air, combined with the stench of rotten food in the alley.

Maya's lips curled as she stared at him.

"Wh-what—" He fell to his knees, holding his chest. "Wh-what d-did y-you do?"

She'd covered her bullets in holy water. She'd been doing that since she joined the force ten years ago. Since her first night, when a vampire had attacked her while she was patrolling the park. She'd barely gotten away from him. Maya had kicked, bit, fought with every ounce of strength she had. In the end, she'd been lucky. She'd managed to keep fighting him until her partner arrived to help her.

She'd survived.

But tonight would be different, she knew that. There was no backup for her tonight. She'd been working the case alone. Following a lead.

Following death.

The vampire lunged for her, grabbed her hair, and jerked her head back. His black eyes were rimmed with red. Tears of blood leaked down his cheeks.

His teeth ripped across her neck, but she didn't scream. Didn't have the strength to scream anymore.

Her finger jerked on the trigger, firing again, again, again—

But he didn't stop. Didn't stop biting her, drinking from her, killing her.

So this is what death feels like.

Darkness surrounded her. Complete, suffocating darkness.

"What the hell do you think got a hold of her?" A man's voice, shaken.

"Dunno." A woman, she sounded like she truly didn't give a shit.

Her body was lifted. Pushed. A door slammed.

Silence.

Two more doors slammed.

An engine started.

"Did you see the blood?" The man's voice again. "That whole freaking alley was covered with her blood."

"Um." The woman.

"Had to be an animal, right? I mean, nothing else could have done that to her throat."

Maya frowned. Her throat didn't hurt anymore. In fact, nothing hurt. But she still felt cold.

And it was so dark.

What had happened to the moonlight?

A crackle of static, then a hard voice blasted, "Second ambulance en route. Got a body three streets over—a shooting victim . . ."

Shooting victim. The vamp? She hoped she'd killed his ass. Maybe he'd crawled away and died.

But what the hell had happened to her?

She tried to move, tried to lift her hands, but something surrounded her, trapped her.

A growl of frustration and fear rumbled in her throat.

"Did you hear that?" The guy's voice was nearly a shriek. Maya winced.

"No, I didn't hear a damn thing." But the woman's heart was suddenly beating faster.

How the hell can I hear her heart?

"Let's just hurry up and drop her ass off at the morgue, okay?" Mr. Shrill and Scared. "I swear, I-I think I saw the bag move."

The morgue. The bag.

Shit. Suddenly, Maya knew exactly what was happening. Those idiots had tagged her, had thought she was dead. She'd even thought so, too, for a time. She'd thought for certain she felt the icy touch of death.

But she was still alive. She'd fought, and she was still alive. Still— *"I'm alive!"* Her voice emerged as a scream.

The squeal of brakes followed her cry. The vehicle swerved, fishtailed, then screeched to a stop.

Maya squirmed, fighting the darkness that surrounded her. Her nails caught a thick, hard fabric, dug in, ripped, slashed.

"Jesus Christ!" A jerk of a zipper. Then light, bright, blinding light spilled onto her. She blinked against the light and against the sudden, sharp stab of pain in her eyes.

Then she saw the man. Young, with sandy blond hair and dark, wire-framed glasses. He was thin, lanky. The woman stood looking just over his shoulder. Her red hair flared around her and her green eyes were so wide they seemed to swallow her face.

"Y-you y-you . . ." The chick's mouth opened and closed like a fish's. Her pulse beat madly in her throat. The thudding filled Maya's ears, made her mouth water.

She shoved out of the bag, *a damn body bag,* and leapt from the back of the ambulance. She wound up soaring ten feet into the air and then she came back down to the ground with a thud.

The woman screamed. Maya glanced back just in time to see the redhead's eyes roll back into her head as she fainted.

The man's face turned completely white as the color bleached from his skin. *"Wh-what are you?"*

As his heartbeat filled her ears, that tempting, wonderful beat, her canines lengthened, burned.

And Maya realized she hadn't survived her attack.

No, she hadn't survived it at all . . .

Chapter 1

Five years later . . .

Adam Brody kept his eyes on his prey as she moved down the street. Her hair, dark, midnight black, gleamed in the moonlight, skimming just past her shoulders. Her body, slender but strong, moved fluidly as she ran through the night.

He had been watching her for days now. Watching as she prowled the streets at night. Watching as she fed. As she fought. Even as she killed.

Maya Black.

There had been whispers about her for years. Tales of the vampire who hunted her own kind.

The vampire who fought demons, shifters, vamps—any damn thing that got in her way.

There was a price on her head. But for five years, no one had been able to collect that bounty.

Because Maya was one tough bitch to stake.

She approached a ramshackle building, a building with boarded windows and red gang tags shining on the exterior walls. Her hand lifted, banged on the door.

A man wrenched open the metal door. He took one look at Maya and stepped back, letting her inside.

Adam caught the scent of blood on the wind.

His body stiffened as understanding dawned. She'd just gone into a feeding room. One of the safe houses for vamps.

A place to drink, to fuck, to do whatever the hell the vamps wanted with the humans who were unlucky enough to be inside. Often, the humans stumbled into the feeding room by mistake. They thought they'd just gone into a new bar, a trendy, secret spot. Then the vamps got then. Once the vamps took their blood, it was over for the humans. A vamp could link with his victim. It was so easy to slip into a human's mind after the bite.

The bitten humans never thought about turning on the vamps, or revealing the feeding rooms to the authorities. They were too addicted to the vampire's power, and too under the vamp's control.

Not that revealing a feeding room to the authorities would do much good, anyway. The cops had learned long ago how to hide the supernatural activities from the larger society. And the vamps . . . they were so good at blending in—hiding in plain sight.

So they took their blood and they fucked, and they didn't care how many humans they hurt.

He'd wondered when Maya would feed again. It had been two days since he'd watched her drink from a man. Two days since she'd pushed a young dumbass up against a wall and locked those red lips of hers onto his neck and shoved those sharp teeth into his throat. Even from fifty yards away, he'd heard the man's cry of ecstasy as Maya fed.

He'd expected Maya to drain the man dry. To slash his throat and leave him dead on the street. But she'd lowered the guy onto the curb, whispered to him, and walked away.

She'd left her prey alive.

Damn odd for a vampire.

Of course, the same night she'd cut the head off a level-five demon who'd made the mistake of jumping her.

He sauntered slowly down the street, keeping his gaze on the feeding room, but listening intently for every sound on the block.

Adam had never thought that he'd willingly offer himself up as food for a fucking parasite, but it looked like this might be the only way he could get close to Maya. And he needed to get close to her, for now.

She kept her prey alive.

So, it looked like he'd have to become her prey.

He reached the black door. Didn't bother glancing at the red splashes of spray paint. He lifted his fist and pounded against the cold metal.

A big, bald, ugly-as-hell guy with a twisted nose and a scar sliding down his left cheek, jerked open the door. "What the 'ell do ye want?" A thick Irish brogue marked his words.

The scent of blood was stronger now. Moans whispered in the air, the faint pounding of drums, the light strum of a guitar. And then a scream.

Irish put one meaty hand on Adam's chest and shoved back. "This ain't yer place, mate."

Adam glanced down at the hand, thought about breaking it. Just one quick snap. He took a deep breath and glanced back up into Irish's beady green eyes. "I'm here for the woman."

"No woman 'ere." His lips curled into a snarl. "Now get your arse out of—"

The hand was still on his chest, pressing a bit too hard, and it was really pissing Adam off. So he grabbed the jerk's wrist, twisted—*not enough to break, not yet*—and shoved Irish back against the door. "The woman you just let inside," he whispered. "I want her."

Irish shook his head. "Ye don't want 'er." He jerked his hand back, clenched his fingers into a fist.

"Oh, but I do." And he wasn't leaving without her. Adam waited for the guy to attack. Waited—

A hard crack of laughter filled the air. "Dumb bastard." Irish stepped back, motioned him inside. "Yer funeral."

Adam walked down the long, dark hallway. Small, sputtering candles were on the floor, providing just enough light to see the passage, but shadowing the blood he could smell all around him.

The hall ended in a large room. A band played on a small,

wooden stage. A drummer. A woman who sang as she strummed the guitar. Adam could see the blood trailing lightly down their necks. Could tell by the glazed expression in their eyes that they were the slaves of the vamps.

Damn. He fucking hated vampires.

Parasites.

His back teeth clenched as he glanced around the room. Doors led off in every direction. He already knew where all those doors would take him. To hell.

But he needed to find Maya, so he'd have to go—

"Don't screw with me, Armand!" A woman's voice, hard, ice cold. Maya.

He turned, found her leaning over the bar, her hand wrapped around the bartender's throat.

"I want to know who went after Sean, and I want to know *now.*" He saw her fingernails stretch into claws, and he watched as those claws sank into the man's neck.

"I-I d-don't k-know." The guy looked like he might faint at any moment. Definitely human. Vamps were always so pale it looked like they might faint. But this guy, he'd looked pretty normal until Maya clawed him.

"Find out!" She threw him against a wall of drinks.

Adam stalked toward her, reached her side just as she spun around, claws up.

He stilled.

She glared at him. "What the hell do you want?" She snarled, and he could see the faint edge of her fangs gleaming behind her plump lips.

It was his first time to get a good look at her face. He'd seen her from a distance before, judged her to be pretty, hadn't bothered to think much beyond that.

He blinked as he stared at her. Damn, the woman looked like some kind of fallen angel.

Her thick black hair framed her perfect, heart-shaped face. Her cheeks were high, glass sharp. Her nose was small, straight. Her eyes were wide and currently the black of a vampire in hunting mode. And her lips, well, she might have the face of an angel, but she had lips made for sin.

Adam felt his cock stir, *for a vampire.*

He shuddered in revulsion.

Oh, hell, no. The woman was so not his type.

Her scent surrounded him. Not the rancid, rotting stench of death he'd smelled around others of her kind. But a light, fragrant scent, almost like flowers.

What in the hell? How could she—

Maya growled and shoved him away from her, muttering something under her breath about idiots with death wishes.

Then she walked away from him.

For a moment, he just studied her. Maya wasn't exactly his idea of an über-vamp. She was small, too damn small for his taste. The woman was barely five foot seven. Her body was slender, with almost boyish hips. Her legs were encased in an old, faded pair of jeans, and the black T-shirt she wore clung tightly to her frame.

He liked women with more meat on their bones. Liked a woman with curves. A woman with round, lush hips that he could hold while he thrust deep into her.

But, well, he wasn't interested in screwing Maya. Not with her too-thin body. Her too-pale skin. No, he didn't want to screw her.

He just planned to use her.

Adam took two quick strides forward, grabbed her arm, and swung her back toward him.

The eyes that had relaxed to a bright blue shade instantly flashed black. Vamps' eyes always changed to black when they fought or when they fucked.

Sometimes folks made the mistake of confusing vamps with demons, because a demon's eyes, well, they could go black, too. Actually, Adam knew that a demon's eyes were *always* black, and for the demons, every damn part of their eyes went black. Even the sclera. With the vamps, just the iris changed.

Usually demons were smart enough to hide the true color of their eyes. But the vamps, they didn't seem to give a flying shit who saw the change. If a human happened to see the eye shift, it was generally too late for the poor bastard, anyway, because by then, he was prey.

Gazing into Maya's relentless black eyes, Adam had a true inkling of just how those said poor bastards must have felt.

A growl rumbled in her throat, then she snapped, "Slick, you're screwing with the wrong woman tonight."

No, she was the right woman. Whether he liked the fact or not.

So he clenched his teeth, swallowed his pride, and in the midst of hell, admitted, "I need your help."

She snorted. "What the hell do I look like? The freaking Red Cross?" Her gaze held his as she bared her teeth. Her extremely sharp teeth. "I am *not* a helper. Now get your hand off me before I have to hurt you."

As if she could.

"Playing with your prey, Maya?" A male voice drawled from the shadows.

Adam's head jerked to the left as a tall, skeletally thin man stepped forward. The guy had bright red hair and a face that looked like it had been smashed by a shovel. His twisted smile showcased his glistening fangs.

Maya swore.

"Ah, sweet, is that any way to greet an old friend?"

She moved in a flash, lunging across the room and wrapping her fingers around his throat. "You," she told him, her voice colder than ice, "are not my friend."

Rage sparked in his black eyes, but, to Adam's surprise, he didn't try to fight her. "Armand . . . told me . . . about Sean."

She slanted a quick glance back at the bartender and a satisfied smile curved her lips. "Ah, I knew he could get some information for me if he just tried."

Armand swallowed and lowered his head.

Adam didn't move. The tension in the air was suddenly, dangerously thick. The bar was quiet now. The guitarist had stopped strumming. There were no more whispers, no more moans. It was as if everyone were waiting, watching to see what would happen next.

Because that's exactly what they were all doing.

"Someone attacked my day watcher," Maya said, never releasing her hold on the vampire. "And let me tell you, Stephan, that really pisses me off." She drew back her right hand, and Adam saw her razor-sharp claws.

Why didn't the other vampire attack her? Why didn't they all jump her? Adam glanced around the room, confused as hell. Sure, the whispers and rumors held that Maya had woken to the undead world with almost abnormal vampire strength, but, hell, she was only one woman.

She couldn't be *that* strong.

"I-I've heard . . . talk." Stephan licked his lips.

"And?" She lifted him up, holding him in the air with one hand.

Adam wasn't particularly impressed.

"Wasn't a vampire. Not one of us."

"Then who was it?"

"*It was me.*" A huge guy stood just beyond the stage. Thick claws extended from his fingers, and unless Adam was very much mistaken, the fellow appeared to have horns in the middle of his wild mass of black hair.

"Ah, hell." Maya dropped the vampire and turned to face her new threat. "What is the deal? First that guy—" She jerked her thumb toward Adam, "and now you. Has Hugh gone mad-ass crazy and he's letting just any jerk inside who wants to come and play with the vamps?"

The man—*no, couldn't be a man*—smiled. Adam expected to see fangs. And he did. Each tooth the guy had—and he had a lot—was a sharpened fang.

Interesting.

He stepped back, not because he was afraid, but because he wanted to watch Maya work. He figured this would be a good test for her.

Unless he missed his guess, he was staring at a level-ten

demon. A very old level ten. An ancient. The baddest of his kind.

There were ten levels of demons in the known world. The first three levels, well, they weren't anything to worry about. Sure, they could control a small flame, or make the wind dance. Not exactly earth-shattering.

Fours to eights—they were stronger. They could hypnotize humans. Control more of the elements. They were hard to kill. To slay 'em, the head had to generally be severed.

Level nines and level tens—those guys were the demons that folks really feared. The demons of the sort mentioned in the Bible. Monsters who slaughtered women and children for fun, bathed in blood, had unbelievable strength, and could sometimes live forever—provided, of course, that the demon didn't lose his head. The oldest of these demons had tails, horns, claws, and skin that couldn't be pierced with human weapons. Considering that fun fact, the level nines and level tens really didn't have to worry too much about a beheading.

That's why the bastards got to live and kill for so long.

In the supernatural world, they were considered the bad-asses. They feared no one.

Sure as hell not a slip of a vampire, Adam thought.

Maya circled the demon and the other vampires backed away, going *way back*.

The bleeding humans even seemed to finally sense that things had taken a deadly turn in the feeding bar. They hurried to the corners, shrinking back and gazing around with lost eyes.

"Hugh?" The demon spoke the name slowly, tilting his head to the side. "Oh, would that be the man who *was* guarding the door?" He held up his hands and Adam could see the blood dripping from the demon's claws. "He didn't want to let me in, so I had to convince him."

A faint tremble shook Maya's body. If Adam hadn't been watching her so closely, he would have missed it.

"You bastard. I *liked* Hugh, and I don't like many people." She stood in front of the demon now, barely five steps away. Legs braced shoulder-width apart, hands relaxed at her sides.

"And you killed Hydan, you bitch!"

Hydan. The light dawned. That had been the demon Maya had beheaded two nights back. A rogue who'd slashed a prostitute's face and then started on her body. Adam had been following Maya when she'd stumbled onto him, alerted by the other woman's screams.

Adam moved slightly, creeping around the bar so that he could get a better view. Ah, that was it. Now he could see Maya's face.

The woman was smiling. "Yeah, I killed him. And you know what? I'd do it again."

The demon's teeth snapped together. "I'm going to enjoy ripping you open, vampire."

"Um, are we gonna talk all night?" She lifted one dark brow. "Or is someone going to die?"

Her words seemed to push the demon over some invisible edge. He roared and launched forward, beefy arms raised and his mouth open.

Maya didn't move. She stood there, looking fragile, too vulnerable, as the seven-foot demon attacked.

Adam stepped forward, an instinctual move, because she looked so *damn helpless.*

A level-ten demon was too strong. She'd never survive, and if she got her heart ripped out and her head chopped off—a surefire way to kill a vamp—she'd never be able to help him find—

Maya's hands lifted at the last second. She grabbed the demon's claws, jerked his left hand back, and then drove his own claws straight into his throat.

Blood gushed down his chest, poured onto Maya, and covered the floor.

The demon began twisting, snarling, howling. His right hand raked her side, slashing deep and ripping her skin wide open.

She never eased her hold on him.

Adam saw her fingers tighten around the demon's wrist,

then she yanked his hand to the left, to the right—and she cut the demon's head off.

With his own damn hand.

The head fell to the floor with a thud. The body stood stiffly for a moment. Swayed. Then the knees buckled and the demon's chest slammed toward the wooden floor.

Maya jumped back, barely avoiding being taken down by the headless corpse.

She stared at the demon's remains, her chest rising and falling rapidly, her fangs bared.

Now, I'm impressed.

Apparently, the rumors were true. Maya Black was truly one badass vampire.

Maya gazed down at the body, trying to swallow back the nausea rising in her throat.

Shit. The damn thing is still twitching.

She drew a deep breath, smelled his blood.

He wasn't human. I didn't kill a human.

But she'd killed.

And he would have killed me. He'd already attacked Sean, left him for dead. Murdered Hugh.

The demon had deserved to die.

A demon, not a man. She just had to remember that fact.

She lifted her head, deliberately drawing her gaze from the demon. The room around her was quiet, too quiet. She knew everyone had been watching her. Some, if not all, hoping that she'd be the one who wound up on the floor.

Luckily for her, that hadn't been her first encounter with an L10. No, she'd gone against a level-ten demon three months after her change. She'd learned the hard way that the legend about the mortal weapons not being able to pierce their flesh was true. She'd been about ten seconds away from her second and final death when she'd managed to shove the demon's claws back against his chest.

When the blood had begun to flow, Maya had known instantly what she had to do.

Kill or be killed. It was the new law, the only law, she followed these days.

Stephan sauntered up to her side. He was smiling. The guy was *always* smiling. "That'll teach 'em to come into our territory."

A rumble of agreement.

Great. Now the vampires were going to act like they'd just won some kind of pissing contest with the demons.

"So that's how you kill 'em, huh?" He bent down, dipped a finger in the L10's blood. "I'll have to remember that." He brought the fingertip to his lips, then frowned.

Level-ten demon blood was sour as hell.

The music started again then. The strumming of the guitar was light at first, tentative. Then louder, stronger as the vampires and humans began to drift from the shadows.

Maya stepped over the demon. His body would be taken care of. She knew Armand had a policy of destroying the dead left in his bar.

She'd settled her score. Now it was time for her to leave.

She hated the killing.

He wasn't a man.

He'd been a monster. Evil. Deadly.

A monster.

Just like she was.

Maya shoved open the door, stepping into the night. She didn't look down at Hugh. She couldn't bear to, not then, but she knew he was dead. She could no longer hear his heart beating.

Human. Hugh had been a human, a watcher of sorts, just like Sean. He'd always been civil to her.

The guy had also never tried to kill her, a definite mark in his favor.

Footsteps thundered behind her. Eager whispers reached her ears.

She froze. Didn't glance over her shoulder. "Don't even think about drinking from him." The scavengers drank from the dead.

But she didn't want anyone drinking from Hugh.

"Bury him. Get him a priest. *But don't drink from him.*" Now she did turn back, looking at each vampire in turn. "Or I'll come back for you."

The fear that flashed on their faces told her that they believed her. Good. Because she'd hate to have to hunt them down.

Too much work.

Maya inclined her head, then stalked down the road. Every step, the air became a little cleaner. The stench of death faded. She could almost pretend that she hadn't just been in hell.

She'd easily traveled ten blocks before she realized that she was being followed. It was the faintest of sounds that alerted her. A soft sigh. Could have been a whisper of breath or a scuff of a shoe on the pavement.

But Maya knew she wasn't alone on the dark street.

Her nostrils flared slightly as she inhaled. Since her change, all of her senses had grown stronger. Hearing. Smell. Sight.

Especially sight. She could see perfectly in the dark. When she hunted, it was like she was using some kind of heat vision. She could see the warm red glow of her prey. Could stalk and hunt easily for miles.

Normally, she could also smell with the detection of an animal. She could pick up scents, even identify different people from miles away.

But tonight, she didn't smell any trace of her pursuer.

Just as earlier, when the human had approached her, she hadn't detected his scent. Which was damn odd. Humans always carried a scent. Perfume. Cigarettes. Soap. Something. But that guy, the tall, dark guy who'd approached her in the feeding room, he'd had no scent.

Maya rolled her shoulders, stood in the middle of the street, and waited.

It didn't take a genius to understand who was on her trail. She really, *really* wasn't in the mood for any more shit right then.

"You're starting to get on my bad side," she said, and her voice carried easily in the night.

Silence.

One moment.

Two.

Then, footsteps. Slow. Steady. The guy wasn't trying to hide anymore. Good.

Maya turned on her heel and watched as her stalker approached. It was him, of course. She could tell by the strong, muscular shape of his body.

He stepped under a streetlight, and the fluorescent glow shone down on his black hair. Maya studied him a moment, frowning. The guy was big. Not especially tall. She gauged him to be a bit over six feet, but he was solidly muscled—every inch of him.

He wore a black jacket over his shirt. Loose jeans encased his long legs, and a scuffed pair of boots covered his feet.

The guy wasn't handsome. Not in the cover-boy style that most humans found so popular these days. His face was hard, *rugged*. His cheekbones were sharp, his nose a little too long. He had a strong, square jawline and a faint cleft in his chin. His lips were firm, a bit thin, and currently pressed into a tight line.

And his eyes . . . She'd never seen eyes quite like his before. The green was so deep, so dark. *Emerald*. He had emerald eyes.

Those eyes of his, they made her nervous. Very nervous.

Something was off about the guy, and as he closed the final distance between them, her body went on alert.

"Wanna tell me why you're following me, Slick?" Did the man have some kind of death wish? He'd seen what she'd done to the demon—*that* should have been a big clue for him to stay the hell away from her.

"My name"—his voice rumbled from deep in his chest—"is Adam. Adam Brody." No accent marked the words.

Maya grunted. She didn't really care about his name. She

just wanted him to leave her alone. "You didn't answer my question."

"I told you before, *Maya*, I need your help."

He knew her name. She wasn't sure if she was supposed to be impressed by that fact or worried. After considering the situation for three seconds, she decided she was neither.

Most of the supernaturals in Los Angeles knew who she was. She hadn't exactly made a habit of hiding her identity. She didn't know if Adam Brody fell into the supernatural category or if he was just a well-informed human, but either way, she didn't really care that he knew her identity.

And the guy was still singing his song about needing help. She sighed, then muttered, "I told you, I'm not into helping people." Killing, that was another matter. "Do yourself a favor. Stay away from me." Her gaze darted to the night sky, gauging the location of the moon. She needed to hurry if she was going to make it to the hospital before dawn.

Maya turned to go—

Adam grabbed her arm.

She stared at his hand a moment. The long, tanned fingers. His flesh felt warm against her.

When was the last time a guy had chosen to touch her? Without, of course, the intent to kill?

Her life was so screwed up.

"Let go," she ordered.

"No."

Now that had her jerking back to face him fully, her brows lifted. "Who are you?"

His eyes narrowed. "I told you, I'm Adam Brody, and I—"

"No." That wasn't what she meant. Time to try again. "*What* are you?"

He blinked. "A man who needs help."

A man. Maya wasn't sure she believed that. "For a human, you seem awful relaxed to be here, talking with me."

He shrugged. "So you're a vampire. I've met your kind before."

Oh, she'd just bet he had. Adam Brody was holding out on

her, and she was no one's fool. "I'm not just a vampire," she whispered, watching closely for his response as she stepped toward him and brushed her body against his. Mmm, she liked the way he felt. Liked the hard steel of his muscles. "I'm a very *hungry* vampire." Her hand lifted and Maya trailed her fingers down his throat.

She expected him to back away. To flinch in revulsion. *Something.* But the guy didn't so much as bat an eyelash.

Her fingers were over his pulse now. She could feel the blood drumming beneath her touch.

No empty threat. She realized that she *was* hungry.

The wound on her side had yet to close—it'd be several hours before she healed completely. She was still bleeding, and she'd already lost too much blood.

Blood loss weakened her. It weakened all vamps. If they lost too much, they could die.

Her fingertips stroked his skin and her canines began to stretch and sharpen. *Just a bite.* After all, he'd been the one to come looking for her. Just a quick bite, and she'd send him on his way.

Maya rose onto her toes. Her breath blew over his skin. Her heart began to drum faster as anticipation filled her. She could almost taste him.

Her lips pressed against his throat. Kissed the flesh. Her tongue snaked out, licked a light trail over his pounding pulse.

Adam's hand was still wrapped around her arm. His fingers tightened and she heard him draw in a sudden, sharp breath.

It was always so easy to make the prey want the bite. She'd discovered after her change that it wasn't necessary to force humans to submit to her. She could usually seduce men into offering their throats to her.

At first, she was just a woman to them. She looked human. Her body *seemed* human. She breathed. Her heart beat. Her blood pumped through her. The prey didn't realize until too late what she really was.

But by that point, her teeth were already in their throats, and for the men she'd tasted, well, they'd found it to be a highly pleasurable experience.

She made it a habit not to hurt humans unless she had to do so.

Now, monsters, well, they were a different matter.

Maya lightly scraped the edge of her teeth over Adam's throat. His pulse raced faster now, pounding harder beneath her mouth.

Just a taste.

He pushed her back and stared down at her with eyes that blazed with fury. "You want to drink from me, then you agree to help me."

Her teeth snapped together as she fought the blood hunger. He was a persistent one, she'd give him that. And now he was starting to make her curious.

A man willing to exchange his blood. For what?

"What is it that you need from me?" She was really almost afraid to find out. *Don't get involved.* She had enough problems to deal with and—

"My niece. Vampires took her." His fingers dug into her arm. "I've got to get her back."

Hell. "How long has she been gone?" Another question she shouldn't have asked. Because the more she learned, the harder it would be to turn away.

I'm not a helper. She'd told him the truth when she said those words earlier. Maya had tried that whole helping bit while she was still human. It had gotten her killed in an alley days after her thirty-first birthday.

"They took her two weeks ago."

Two weeks. She shook her head, and told him the truth, "She's dead."

A muscle flexed along his jaw. "You don't kill your prey."

How did he know that? But she didn't deny it, there'd be no point in lying. "Yeah, well, I'm not your average vampire, either." Most of her kind were sadistic bastards and bitches who liked to play with their food, then kill it, painfully. "If they've had her that long, she's dead. Mourn her, then move on."

The bloodlust in her had cooled at his words. With one last look at him, she spun around and began walking down the street.

She'd taken five steps when his voice stopped her cold.

"She's a child, Maya. Only nine years old."

Hell.

Her eyes squeezed shut. Vampires with a kid. Sick fucks.

"I have to find her. I *will* find her. With or without your help."

Doubtful.

A kid. Why'd it have to be a kid?

"A Born Master sent his pack after her. Bastard named Nassor."

Her body tensed. *Nassor.*

"You've helped others. I *know* you have. You've hunted down demons, shifters."

Yes, she'd gone on the hunt. For a price.

But a kid. With Nassor. He'd rip her apart.

Damn. Her shoulders fell. There wasn't much of a choice for her anymore.

Maya started walking again. Her Harley Sportster motorcycle waited for her just a few feet away.

"So that's it?" He shouted. "You're just going to leave? Going to turn your back on me and—"

She reached the bike. Climbed on. Revved the engine and felt her baby purr beneath her. Her fingers tightened around the handlebars as she glanced over her shoulder and drawled, "You comin' or are you gonna scream all night?" The guy must have some strong lungs on him.

He shook his head and then a full smile split his lips. "You'll help me?"

"Maybe." Because she was the world's biggest idiot. Her gaze held his. "But there's gonna be a price." Nothing came free. Especially not a life.

His smile faded. "Isn't there always?"

Ah, but he'd never had to pay a vampire. She'd bet her undead life on that fact. If Adam Brody wanted her to track a pack of vamps and try to rescue a kid, well, he was going to have to pay a heavy price, indeed.

He'd have to pay it in blood.

The motorcycle's engine growled. "Get on," she ordered. "There's a helmet on the back."

In seconds, he was behind her, climbing onto the bike and sliding those long, strong legs behind hers.

"Hold on."

His hands wrapped around her waist. His chest pressed flush against her back.

Damn, but the guy was *warm*.

And he felt good.

The cycle shot away from the street corner, flying straight into the night.

Adam's hold tightened. "Where are we going?"

"I've got a stop to make." Until they worked out their exchange, she wasn't letting him out of her sight.

"We need to find Cammie, we have to—"

"Slick, there's no damn way we're finding her tonight." They had barely an hour before dawn. She raised her voice over the cycle's snarl. "But there is somebody I've got to see."

She felt the sudden tautness of his body. So he wasn't happy with her plans. Tough.

A man had nearly died for her; the least she owed him was a visit.

After she settled that debt, then she'd begin her bargain with Adam Brody.

She wondered how he'd taste.

Chapter 2

The nurses and doctors on duty swarmed Maya the minute she shoved open the emergency room doors at Memorial Grove Hospital, and she realized too late that she probably looked like death.

The demon's blood still covered her. It had dried, dark red, on her arms and she could feel a faint stiffness from the blood on her neck. The blood from her own wounds had soaked her shirt and coated her jeans. But at least the gashes weren't hurting so much anymore.

Yeah, it was understandable that the folks thought they had a severe trauma patient on their hands.

If only they'd been there five years ago . . .

"I'm all right, *I'm all right!*" She snapped when they tried to force her onto a stretcher. "The blood's not mine." Well, not all of it, anyway.

But her comment made the hospital staff freeze. Then they began looking at each other, faces tense, fear flickering in their eyes.

"And where is the victim?" This came from one of the doctors. A young guy, with intense gray eyes and a stethoscope dangling around his neck.

Knowing the vampires, the "victim" was probably in lots of tiny pieces someplace. Not that she'd tell the pale doctor that.

She shrugged. "An ambulance picked him up." Her eyes

widened as she glanced at Adam. He'd followed her inside. Now, she deliberately pitched her voice low and threaded a note of worry in her words as she said, "Honey, I guess we beat them here."

His lips pursed. "I'm sure the ambulance will be along any minute, darling."

Just then, an ambulance lurched to a stop behind the glass entrance doors, sirens blaring, lights flashing. The nurses and doctors seemed to fly to the door.

Maya grabbed Adam's hand and ran down the corridor with him. They took the stairs to the third floor, and by the time they exited the stairwell, Maya's steps had begun to slow.

Damn but she was getting weak. She'd have to get some blood, and fast. She'd fed days before, and normally wouldn't have to drink again for about a month. But a wound, well, that always changed things. The longer she bled, the weaker she became.

Her gaze darted to Adam's throat and she licked her lips. Fresh blood would make her heal faster, but the way she was feeling, well, the hunger was just too strong.

She couldn't risk losing control and taking too much.

She'd have to find another source. Lucky for her, she was in a hospital. Sources all around.

Sean's room was on the right. The door stood partially open, and Maya paused for just a moment.

Adam watched her, that green gaze too intent. "Who's in there?"

Day watcher. Friend. The guy she'd nearly gotten killed.

Her shoulders stiffened and she pushed open the door.

Machines beeped inside, a steady, insistent *duh duh duh* that seemed to rake across her brain. On the bed, his face nearly as white as the sheet, lay Sean.

His body was wrapped tightly in gauze and bandages. He'd been cut, slashed with claws and teeth, and left to bleed out on the street in front of her safe house.

Safe house. There was no safe place for her anymore. She'd have to find another secret shelter.

Very slowly, Maya crept toward the bed. Her hand lifted, hesitated over Sean's disheveled mass of blond hair.

She could feel Adam behind her, watching, waiting.

Her fingers fisted. "You realize—this could be you."

He didn't respond.

Her gaze darted to the hospital tray near the bed. Someone had put flowers on the tray. Roses. Sean's glasses were next to the vase. Lenses repaired now, black frames in perfect condition.

She'd gotten his glasses fixed yesterday. She wanted them there, waiting for him, when he woke up.

"The demon did this." Not a question.

Maya nodded anyway and then she leaned in close to the bed. Her mouth was inches from Sean's ear when she whispered, "I got him. I wanted you to know, I—I found him." *He won't ever hurt you or anyone else, again.*

For an instant, she thought she saw his eyelashes flutter and her breath caught in her chest. "Sean?"

His eyes didn't open. Hadn't opened, not for two days. At least he was out of the Intensive Care unit. The doctors had told her that he *would* get better.

Sean had barely escaped death.

Now it was time for him to stay the hell away from her.

Maya backed away from the bed. Turned her attention to Adam. "Take a good look at him," she said, her voice hard. "Because this could happen to you. If we go after those vampires, and they attack—"

"I'm not worried about getting hurt." His gaze didn't drift toward the bed. The intense stare stayed locked on her. "You don't need to warn me. I know exactly what I'm doing."

"Do you?" Heavy doubt coated the words.

"Yeah, I do."

He'd been warned. Maya shrugged. "Sean was my day watcher. Had been for the last five years." Despite what most people thought, sunlight couldn't actually kill a vampire. That was just some crazy legend that had been circulating thanks in large part to Hollywood.

Bram Stoker had hit closer to the truth about vampires and daylight. Vamps were weaker during the day, basically only having strength equal to that of a human. Sure, they could still shift their fingernails into claws and drink from prey, but rousing the energy for those acts was a major drain. Because of that weakness, most of her kind had decided to rest in the daylight hours and hunt and play during the night.

Maya generally followed that rule. But she liked to have someone around, watching her back while she rested.

With Sean out of commission, she'd be on her own.

She cast one last look down at Sean's still face. *Shouldn't have happened like this.* She should have protected him.

Maya turned and left the room.

Adam didn't speak until the door closed behind them. "You were avenging him. Earlier tonight, that's what you were doing at the feeding room."

Didn't take a genius to figure that out. It wasn't like she normally hung out in the feeding rooms. Those places, oh, shit, they were hellish. The humans, twisting, moaning, *begging* for the bites. It made her sick.

And the vampires . . . Hurting their prey. Enjoying the pain.

Monsters.

Since she was a vampire, Maya knew she fell in the same category.

Monster.

"We need to get a few things straight," she told him, casually resting her arm against the wall. While her pose was relaxed, she was actually starting to feel a bit dizzy and she needed the support. "If I help you—"

"*If?*" He growled, shoulders stiffening.

She ignored the interruption. "Then I'm the one in charge, got it? You might think you know vampires because you've stumbled onto one or two in the dark and lived to spread your tales, but believe me, you have no idea how vicious some of those bastards can be."

"Oh, I think you'd be surprised by what I know."

Maya sucked in a quick breath, then lunged, grabbing Adam and shoving him against the wall on the other side of the corridor. "Shut up, Slick, and listen. Vampires kill. It's what they do. Most don't do it quickly, either. They like to play with prey. Make the humans cry, beg. Then the vamps rip them apart."

Her right elbow pressed against his chest. Adam stared down at her, eyes glittering with anger. No, not anger. *Rage.*

"I'm strong enough to fight them," she said. *Well, usually.* When she hadn't been bleeding out all night. "They'd make a meal of you."

She wanted him to understand. This wasn't some kind of game. If they went after the ones who'd taken his niece, he could die.

He had to follow her orders. To. The. Letter.

His teeth clenched as he gritted, "I'll do what you say."

So he wasn't pleased with that deal. Too damn bad. "I've taken on retrieval jobs in the past." She hadn't been helping anyone or doing the jobs out of the kindness of her heart. Because there wasn't any kindness left in there.

She'd done it for the cash. Even vamps needed money. There was the little matter of needing money to pay for the safe houses.

Ah, money. "My fee is two hundred grand."

"Done."

Maya blinked. Okay, so she had a rich boy on her hands. Now for the second payment requirement. "And I'll need your blood." No sense in her having to go out and hunt for food when she had a perfect source right in front of her. If he wanted her help, well, then he'd have to bleed for it.

Now there was hesitation. And struggle. She saw it in his eyes.

Doesn't like the idea of a vampire tasting him.

Not that she particularly blamed him. Back in her human days, the idea of a vampire tasting her blood hadn't been on her top ten list, either.

But times had changed. She had to keep her strength up if she was going to be chasing vampires—especially considering the fact that those vampires would have access to fresh blood.

"How much?"

Maya lowered her arm, but didn't step back. Even this close to him, she still couldn't catch his scent. Damn odd. "As much as I need." She didn't plan to drain him, or even take enough to weaken him. "Don't worry. You won't even notice it's gone."

His head jerked in a brief nod.

Maya took that for the agreement it was. "You'll have to stay with me," she said, already making plans. "And I'll need to know every detail about the vampires who took your—"

"Why do I have to stay with you?"

The man sure liked to interrupt. An annoying trait. "For your safety, of course." He probably didn't realize it, but just by going into that feeding room and talking to her, he'd already captured the attention of many in the vampire realm. If one of the vampires who'd taken his niece happened to find out about their connection, well, then they'd both be in for a bloody fight.

"Um, of course."

She waited for him to argue, but he just said, "I'll need to stop by my hotel. Pick up some things."

Whatever. As long as they were fast, he could pick up his goodies.

She stepped back.

Adam rubbed his chest. "I'm surprised."

"By what?" Maya's head cocked to the right.

"I mean, I'm surprised you trust me enough to bring me into your home."

Home. Right. She didn't have a home. They were going to

the last safe spot she knew, and the place was closer to a hovel than a home.

But she knew what he really meant. Taking him with her was a big step. Generally, she trusted two humans in the world, and one of them was currently unconscious back in his hospital room. But, once she'd tasted Adam's blood, she'd be linked to him.

Trust wouldn't be an issue then.

"Before I sleep, I'm gonna need to drink from you." Her mouth grew dry at the thought. "After that, trust won't really matter." Because if she wanted to, then she could control him through their blood link.

He nodded once, curtly.

"Don't worry. I promise, it won't hurt . . . much."

His gaze fell to her lips. Lingered.

A curl of heat rose in her stomach.

What the hell?

Maya shook her head. She was covered in blood. Weak with hunger. And the sun would be rising soon.

Time to go.

"Come on. I need blood."

His hand lifted to his throat.

She growled. "Tempting. Very tempting. But if I drink from you now, I'll drain you." Since she hadn't actually drained anyone dry, *yet*, she'd rather try another option.

They were in a hospital. Blood was nearby, right down the hall, actually. Just waiting for her.

Time to break into the blood bank.

Adam stalked the small interior of Maya's safe house. The place was shabby, too small, and covered in dust.

She'd taken him there after their brief pit stop at his hotel. She'd driven too fast, speeding over the deserted streets and traveling past the edge of town.

This wasn't the house she'd used when he'd watched her for the last few days.

This place was a dump.

But a very, very secure dump.

There were a grand total of three rooms in the house, but the whole place was wired with state-of-the-art security. Cameras outside the house. Motion sensors. Steel doors and windows with automatic locking shutters.

The little vampire obviously believed in being prepared.

He figured as far as backup houses went, it could be worse.

It could also be a hell of a lot better.

The shower stopped, the crashing of the water dwindling to a faint trickle. He heard a rustle of sound. Muttering. Then Maya opened the bathroom door and stalked toward him.

Adam stared at her, a bit surprised. She'd finally gotten rid of all the blood. Her smooth skin was shining, glistening with drops of water. She'd secured a white towel loosely between her breasts. The bottom of the towel barely skimmed her thighs. When she moved, the terry cloth shifted, revealing and concealing in tempting flashes.

Adam swallowed and realized with a bit of shock that he was getting aroused *by a vampire.*

When she'd touched him on the street, rubbing her body against his and drifting her fingers over his throat, he'd felt a stirring in his groin. When she'd put those red lips on his flesh and licked, his cock had jerked to attention.

Now, all it took was a flash of thigh, and the lust he felt stirred to life.

A vampire.

What was happening to him? This wasn't part of his plan.

Screwing a vampire definitely hadn't been on his agenda. No matter how soft her skin looked or how red her lips were or how—

Maya walked past him. Her bare shoulder brushed his arm, and the contact seemed to send an electric current through him.

She stopped at the bed. Dropped the towel and treated him to one fine view of her ass.

And of the black dragon tattoo that blew flames at the base of her spine.

He blinked.

His lust seemed to double.

Oh, he hadn't been expecting that.

His hands lifted and he stepped toward her. The need to touch her suddenly burned through him. The lady obviously wasn't the modest sort and if she hadn't wanted him to play, she wouldn't have stripped.

She had a good ass. Tight. Firm. Just the right size for his hands to grip and caress.

His fingers skimmed over her flesh.

Maya jerked on a T-shirt that he hadn't even noticed lying on the bed. Then she spun around and caught his hand. "I don't remember giving you permission to touch, Slick."

He swallowed. His cock pressed hard against the edge of his zipper. "Thought the striptease was an invitation."

She snorted. "When I give an invitation, you'll know it."

He clenched his teeth and fought to rein in his desire.

She pushed him back. Reached behind her, maneuvered a bit, and pulled up a thin scrap of lace.

Probably supposed to be some kind of underwear.

His control slipped, just a bit. Now it was his turn to grab her, to wrap his hands around the silken skin of her upper arms and to yank her against him. "You like teasing men?"

Her chin lifted. "This place is the size of a shoebox. It's not like either one of us will get privacy while we're here."

But she could have changed in the bathroom. That walk across the room, the falling towel, the bare ass, it had all been designed to get to him.

To turn him on.

"Baby, if you wanna fuck, all you have to do is say so."

Her mouth tightened. "I'll remember that lovely little tidbit."

Well, shit.

Adam drew a deep breath, smelled her. *Damn flowers.* How did she do it? No other vampire had ever carried a scent like—

"It's time."

He blinked.

"Dawn's coming."

Understanding hit. The little vampire wanted her drink.

She thought she could control him that way. Thought she'd be able to look into his mind, link with him.

Drinking from a human gave a vampire enormous power over the victim. Enough power to glimpse into the victim's mind. To see memories. To touch dreams.

Once a vampire drank, well, she'd have control over the prey. She'd be able to get him to do whatever she wanted.

No wonder Maya wasn't too worried about trust being an issue.

If he'd been human, well, she would have been right to think that way.

But since he wasn't, all bets were off.

There'd be no control. Unless he was the one doing the dominating.

"You've probably heard talk about what happens when blood's exchanged."

Not really an exchange if he didn't get to taste her. Not that he was particularly into that, but—

Her eyes met his directly. Blue, not hunter black. Not yet. "I'll just take enough now for a bond. That way, if you get into any kind of trouble while we're working together, I'll know."

If only he believed her.

Adam had never met a vampire who didn't lie. He tilted his head back. Gazed up at the cracks in the ceiling and muttered, "Take your drink." *For all the good it will do you.*

She rose against him. Her breath blew over his skin.

He should have been repulsed. Ashamed. He'd never given

his blood to one like her before. Never offered his throat in submission.

Never been a fool.

Never been prey.

Until now.

His choices were nonexistent. If he wanted to find Cammie, Maya was his only hope.

"Relax. I told you, I not planning to hurt you."

Actually, he believed the woman had said she wasn't going to hurt him . . . *much*. The pain wasn't an issue, though. He could deal with pain. He'd managed easily enough in the past.

But it burned in his gut that she was already lying to him. While he'd never been food for a vampire, he'd heard the stories from the lucky few who'd managed to survive. Ripping, slashing pain. Teeth that cut, severed.

Mental screams that were never voiced because by then, it was too late. The vampire was already in the prey's head.

He remembered the foolish humans he'd seen at the feeding room. Eyes glazed over. Blood trickling down their throats. Had they tried to scream when they realized—*too late*—that it wasn't all dark fantasies and passion? In that last second before the vampires took control, had they been afraid?

Her lips were on his throat now. Soft lips. Pressing gently. His hands clenched into fists. "Get it over with," he growled.

"If that's what you want." A faint whisper.

He stared up at those cracks—like spiderwebs in the ceiling.

Her tongue swept over him, a warm, wet caress that caused his cock to jerk in reaction.

He was sick. No other explanation.

The edge of her teeth pressed into his neck. The pressure was hard, and he prepared for the piercing pain as—

Heat exploded through him, a blinding flash that shook his body. For a moment, he worried that he'd lost his control, worried that the beast was free, that it would destroy Maya—

The ecstasy hit him. Waves of pleasure, the feelings so intense he shuddered—and wanted more.

His hands locked around her. One hand held her head to him, forcing her mouth tight against his neck. The other hand clenched around the curve of her ass, pressing her against his swollen flesh.

No pain. They'd been wrong. There wasn't pain, just—

Pleasure.

She could drink from him all day, he didn't care. The feel of her mouth, sucking on his neck, licking, was one of the most erotic things he'd ever experienced.

Better than sex. Stronger, harder, so much bet—

Her head pushed against his hand. She wanted to stop.

No.

His fingers tightened. He could make her keep drinking. There was no danger to him. He could—

What am I doing?

His hands dropped from her. He stepped back.

And immediately missed the press of her mouth.

But the haze was clearing from his eyes. The lust still blazed through his body, the remembered pleasure seared his nerves, but at least his sanity was returning.

His fingers touched the wound on his throat. The skin was tender, but he knew the wound would heal soon.

His gaze locked on Maya's face. She licked her lips, and her eyes slowly faded from black to blue.

Then that stare narrowed on him. "You don't taste like a human."

His heart was racing. Arousal, not fear. "Oh? And just what do I taste like?"

She didn't answer. Just stared at him a moment longer as if trying to figure out some sort of puzzle.

Good luck with that one. He'd keep his secrets from her until he was damn good and ready to reveal them.

His cock was so hard and thick that he was pretty sure the zipper of his jeans might be leaving a permanent impression on his flesh.

He'd just gotten turned on by a vampire's bite.

Impossible.

Or so he'd thought.

His gaze dropped to the front of Maya's T-shirt. Her nipples poked against the fabric, sharp, tight peaks.

She'd been aroused by the exchange.

Good. So he wasn't the only one being driven to the edge.

"We'll talk about your niece at dusk. Figure out a game plan." She was obviously dismissing him for the time being and ignoring the tension between them, and her own need.

Interesting.

He found he wasn't quite as capable of ignoring the need. The lust pumped through his blood, driving a hunger he'd never expected to feel.

If her bite felt that good, he couldn't help but wonder, *how would it feel to fuck her*?

She walked toward the wall. She punched in a series of codes, and a faint *whur* filled the air. There was a soft *clank* as the shutters locked into place.

"What are those for?" he asked, and his voice was harder, deeper than he intended. She had control. If she could fight the desire, so could he.

Maybe.

Control had never really been his strong suit.

He tried again, clearing his throat and deliberately not looking at the bare expanse of her pale legs. But he bet they'd feel good wrapped around him. "I thought the sun didn't hurt you." He knew it didn't. He'd once tied a vampire to a tree and waited for the sun to rise and the fire to start.

Nothing had happened.

Lucky for him, it had been easy enough to start a fire another way.

"The shutters don't just keep out the sun," she said, yawning a little and heading toward the bed. "They keep the monsters out, too. They're made of reinforced steel. It'd take someone with a hell of a lot of strength—more strength than a vamp has—to get past 'em during the daylight."

The lady sure believed in being prepared.

She pushed back the covers, climbed into the bed. Then she threw a pillow at him. Hard. "You should fit on the sofa in the den."

The den? His fingers curled into the lumpy pillow. Since when did the place have a den? There was a bathroom the size of a closet, a miniscule bedroom, and he'd been pretty sure when they entered the house they'd walked through a kitchen.

Huh. Now that he thought about it, he did remember seeing a rather ragged green couch in the kitchen.

And there was really no way he was going to fit on it. "I think I'd prefer the bed."

She stretched out. "Um, I'm sure you would." Another yawn, one she made no attempt to cover. "But you're getting the sofa. Or the floor. Your choice."

What a fine choice it was.

"There's food in the cabinets, if you get hungry. Pay to . . . keep it stocked." Her eyelids began to lower.

"Uh, Maya?" Surely this wasn't it. The great vampire was just going to curl up now and go to sleep?

And he was going to stay up, horny, all damn day long?

What about the bite? Did she think they were linked now, that she could trust him?

A long sigh filled the room. "Slick, I've been hunting all night. I killed a demon, got my body ripped open, and had to deal with *you.*" She drew out the last, making it seem as if his presence had been the most stressful part of her night.

Adam frowned.

"Now, I'm tired, and apparently, I've got one hell of a hunt planned for tomorrow."

But he hadn't even told her all the details about Nassor and his pack yet.

"So I'm going to bed."

"You need to—"

Her eyes closed. "We'll talk tomorrow." Her voice had started to slur.

Well, damn. The vampire was dismissing him.

Just curling up and going to sleep.

He spun and stomped toward the door.

"Brody." No sleepiness in her voice now.

Glancing back over his shoulder, he found her stare trained on him.

"I've got you in me now. Got your taste." Her eyes were wide open as she told him, "We're linked. Don't think about lying to me or betraying me. I told you that I'd help you find the girl, and I will."

But only after she'd gotten her beauty sleep.

Adam bit back his impatience. Just because he didn't need sleep didn't mean that she could stay awake and be strong.

Even the undead had to rest.

He gave a curt nod.

"Turn on me, and I'll kill you." Her eyes flashed black for just the briefest of moments. "Believe me, if you even *think* about betraying me, I'll know."

No, she wouldn't. She had his blood, yeah, and though she didn't realize the fact yet, it would give her more strength than she'd ever possessed.

Maya would need that strength in the nights to come.

Yet other than the physical power the blood gave her, there was no other connection. If he wanted, he could let her into his mind. But only if he allowed it.

The vampire kept applying human rules to him.

A serious mistake. Human rules had never applied to him.

Not in all the centuries of his existence.

"Sleep well, vampire. You can trust me this day." For the day, she could. After that, well, they'd just have to see.

Her gaze bored into him and he knew she was trying to test their blood link. He could feel her power stirring in the air around him. Deliberately, he projected a calm, steady presence back to her.

She nodded her head slowly. Settled back against the bed and closed her eyes, apparently satisfied that she didn't have to worry about him while she slept.

Adam stared at her, emotions, needs churning in him. Maya Black wasn't quite what he'd expected.

She was making him feel. Making him want.

Not an ideal situation for one of his kind. Because when creatures like him wanted something, well, they took it.

After all, they were the strongest of the beasts that roamed the land.

Yeah, if he wanted something, he took it.

And, usually, he killed anything that got in his way.

Chapter 3

"Tell me about the kid."

Adam looked up at Maya. She stood in the doorway, clad in a pair of faded jeans and a white T-shirt.

The sun had set less than twenty minutes ago. As it had dipped beneath the horizon, he'd heard Maya stirring in the next room. He'd stayed on the couch, not moving, too leery of finding another strip show if he walked into the bedroom.

Because what would he do then? He'd already spent the better part of the day trying to forget what the woman felt like beneath his fingers. He didn't need another visual tease to stir him up.

Maya sauntered across the room and stared down at him. "I need to know everything about her."

He licked his lips. "Her name's Camellia. Cammie. She's nine." But he'd already told her that.

"What does she look like?" Her gaze drifted to his hair. "Dark, like you?"

He nodded. "Same hair color, but she's got curls. Same eyes. She's kinda fragile, and small."

"What, is she your sister's kid or—"

"My brother's. But I'm her guardian." Protecting her had been his responsibility, and he'd failed her.

He'd just wanted her to feel normal. Going to a sleepover at a friend's house had seemed so innocent.

So human.

But Cammie wasn't normal. Never would be.

The vamps knew it. That was why they'd taken her.

"Why isn't your brother the one looking for her?"

"Because he's dead." Jon had passed years ago. Taken his own life, right after Cammie's mother died.

"Must be tough on the kid. Not having a father."

"Or a mother." Hell, he hadn't meant to tell her that.

Her lips pulled down. "So it's just the two of you, huh, Slick?"

"Yeah."

"And where's home for you and Cammie?" Maya drawled. "I get the feeling you aren't from L.A."

No, he definitely was not. "Maine. Small town. Cotter's Ridge." At least that's where they'd been living when his niece was taken.

"Um." She sat on the couch beside him, her knee brushing his. "And you came all the way to L.A. in order to find little old me?"

Yeah, he had. Because Maya could lead him to Nassor.

"How do you know that it was Nassor's pack that took her?"

"A witness told me. She saw the vampires, heard them mention his name." Nassor wasn't exactly a name that could be forgotten. Those who knew of the supernatural world, well, they usually knew of Nassor.

The vampire was old. Maybe one of *the* oldest of his kind. Writings of him began in the time of ancient Egypt.

According to the legends, he'd been favored by his gods. Granted immortality.

The bastard had been raising hell ever since.

Maya rubbed her index finger down the bridge of her nose. "Nassor's men don't usually leave witnesses behind."

"They thought she was dead." He still wasn't sure how Karen had managed to hold on until he'd gotten there. Sometimes, humans could surprise him. "Karen—Cammie's nanny—managed to tell me what happened."

Maya reached for his hand. "Show me."

He hesitated. *The bond.* She wanted in his mind. Wanted to peer at his memories.

Maybe she wanted to test him. To see if the story of his niece was true.

But he could show her this.

Only this.

He took her fingers. Held tight, and opened his mind to the vampire.

Instinct took him out into the night. A gut feeling that something was wrong.

He'd sent Cammie out in the limo. The nanny had gone with her. Two guards.

He couldn't keep the girl in a cage. She needed her freedom.

Going to the party—he'd thought there would be no harm in the simple trip.

Then he'd begun to fear.

He found the car first. The hood had slammed into a light pole. The limo's doors were open. He smelled the blood as he ran forward, then he saw the guards. Throats ripped open, eyes staring sightlessly ahead.

But no Cammie.

"Cammie!"

A gasp. Soft, pain-filled. Adam ran as fast as he could toward the sound.

He found her in the street, tears streaming down her face, blood pooled beneath her body. The nanny. Not Cammie, not his Cammie.

"Karen!" He reached her, dropping to his knees beside her and touching her cold flesh. He could hear the faint rasp of her breathing. He could feel death around them, waiting. So hungry.

Her eyes met his. Full of pain. Fear. "A-Adam . . ." She choked on her blood, barely able to get the words out.

"It's all right." But it wasn't. Wouldn't be, not for her. The wounds in her chest were too deep. The blood loss too se-

vere. He squeezed her hand tightly. "You're safe now." Fear knifed through him, filling his veins, his every thought. Where was Cammie?

"T-took . . . her."

His heart stopped, then began a frantic rhythm, thudding in his chest. "Cammie? Someone took Cammie?"

She tried to nod. Her head moved just a fraction and a groan burst from her lips. Her lashes began to flutter closed.

Death crept closer.

"No! Karen, dammit, no! Talk to me!" She couldn't go, not yet. "Who took Cammie?"

"C-cl-aws, t-teeth . . . like . . ." Blood gurgled past her lips, "a-animals."

Karen wasn't like him. She didn't know about the supernatural beings that roamed the earth.

Or, rather, she hadn't known, until they attacked her.

Claws and teeth. Had it been shifters? Vampires? Demons?

"L-laughed." She was shaking now. "B-bit me and l-laughed."

The full moon shone brightly down on them. He could see the marks on her arms, her legs. Her neck. Very gently, he turned her head to the side.

He knew that bite.

Vampire.

"Did they say anything?" he demanded as the fear turned to rage. "Anything?"

"Th-that . . . she'd . . . g-gif-t . . . N-Nas-sor . . ."

Her gaze drifted from his. Her eyes looked up at the moon. At the heavens. "F-forgi . . ." Her words ended in a final gasp for breath.

Her eyes were open when she met death.

"No!"

Maya dropped Adam's hand. Dammit, she'd hadn't wanted to see that woman's last moments.

They were too much like her own.

Only the bastard who'd attacked her had managed to get a few drops of his blood into her mouth. She'd tried to spit them out, but, well, since she was now one of the undead, that hadn't exactly worked for her.

"I've been telling you the truth." Adam's voice was calm.

She gave a jerky nod. She hadn't really thought the guy was lying, not about the girl anyway, but she'd needed to test their link.

"Did you see enough?" He gritted.

"Yeah." Enough to know they were going to have one hell of a fight on their hands. *Nassor. Sonofabitch.* She'd hoped Adam had been wrong about him.

There weren't many things in this world that scared her, but Nassor was at the top of her list.

She'd been aware of him from the moment she'd woken as a vampire. It had started as a vague stirring in the back of her mind. A need to go somewhere, to search.

To find him.

In vampire land, the hierarchy was simple. The Born vampires, those rare bastards who'd been born with a thirst for blood and a curse of immortality, were the rulers. The strongest. The Born or the Blood because the power of vampirism was literally in their blood. Physically, psychically, they were the alphas. No one fucked with them—not L10s, not shifters. No one.

You didn't mess with a Born unless you wanted to die. Slowly. Very, very painfully.

The Born were the ones who'd spread the disease of vampirism. Because, yeah, she thought of it as a disease. Made her feel less like a horror movie freak. They'd bitten, exchanged blood, and infected thousands.

But the thing about the Born, whenever they created a new vampire, a Taken, well, that vamp was tied to the Born Master. And so was that Taken's next changed human, and the next and the next. . . .

New vampires discovered that in addition to the perk of

living forever, they had a not-so-nice voice whispering in their heads. The Master's voice. They could *feel* the Master. Feel him calling when he wanted them.

So far, Maya had been able to ignore that call.

She had a feeling that was about to change. "You know about me, don't you?" she asked Adam. "You know Nassor created the bastard who changed me." Tyrus. He'd been the one to attack her in that alley. He'd been old, according to the gossip she'd heard. Two centuries. And one of Nassor's favored assassins.

"Yes." That deep emerald stare of his never wavered. "I know you can take me to him."

"Not that simple, Slick." Oh, if only. "Nassor's been in the ground for the last couple of years."

A faint line appeared between his brows. "What?"

"He's in the ground. Healing." Or so the whispers said. "The guy was injured, pretty damn bad from all accounts, a little less than five years ago." If the rumors were true, he'd gotten a stake through the heart and his head had been partially severed by a hunter.

He'd lived through the attack and killed the hunter. And the hunter's family.

Nassor scared her. A lot.

"His injuries were so severe," and well-deserved in her book, "that human blood wouldn't heal him. He had to seek the darkness." Total darkness. Deep in the earth. "His body's been regenerating since the attack." So the tales went.

"Are you certain? Absolutely certain?"

"Yeah." Because the moment the ground had sealed over him, that damn call in her head had dulled to the faintest of drones and she'd been able to stop fighting the near constant need to head east.

To go to him.

Not that she was planning to ever just priss over and join his psychotic little army. Sure, she felt the call, but Maya had promised herself that if she ever gave in to the summons, she'd go to kill Nassor, not to pay homage to him like some mindless sycophant.

"You can find him, though, can't you? You can track him. Find his resting place."

"Yeah."

He exhaled.

"But it'll be guarded by his best assassins, and I don't think it will do us any good—"

"What the hell? He's got Cammie! We can—"

"He doesn't have her yet." She knew what the vampires in the vision had meant when they'd referred to Cammie as a gift. Every Born Master awakening was a sacred event in the vampire world.

Such an event would deserve a very fine gift.

What finer gift was there than the innocent blood of a child?

"The vampires that attacked, they haven't delivered the girl to him yet." Because the bastard was still entombed in the ground.

But she had an unfortunate feeling he'd be rising, soon.

That droning in her head, it had started to get the tiniest bit louder.

Not a good sign.

But, on the plus side, at least the girl was probably still alive. Maya really hadn't been expecting that development. Plans began to race through her mind.

"How do you know that he doesn't have her?" Adam asked quietly.

"Because I know he's still sleeping." Getting stronger, more powerful every day. "And that's a very good thing for us."

Adam shook his head. "How the hell is that a good thing? You can't track the other vampires—"

"Sure I can." Who did he think he was talking to? Some rank amateur? "I can't feel them muttering in my head, but, believe me, there is one thing in this world that I know how to do very well . . . and that's hunt."

For a moment, hope flashed across his face. It was followed immediately by doubt. "You really think you can find them?"

For a guy who was paying her two hundred grand, he sure seemed to be lacking faith in her. "I know I can." But while she was thinking about the cash . . . Maya pulled her cell phone out of her back pocket and tossed it to him. "Before we track down those vamps, there's the little matter of my fee."

He'd caught the phone automatically in his left hand.

Maya held up a slip of paper. "I need those funds transferred to this account." *Then* they'd go hunting.

"Promise me that you aren't bullshitting me." The edge of desperation that she heard in his voice gave her pause. "Promise me that you can help me track those bastards and find Cammie."

"Don't worry, Slick. I've got connections."

The guy still didn't look reassured.

"I'm your best bet." So true. Without her, well, he'd just be screwing around in the dark. But she wasn't going to promise him that they'd find the girl. She wasn't sure that was a promise she could keep. She'd try. Try her damnedest.

But she wouldn't promise.

Besides, the guy should really know better than to trust the word of a vampire.

Her fingers tapped on the sofa's armrest. "You're wasting time. If you want my help, then make the call."

His gaze drifted to her lips. "I thought you wanted more than money."

Ah, she did. Maya smiled. "I'll take that payment, too, *later.*" She'd fed well the night before. The bagged, ice-cold blood from the hospital had been more than enough to sustain her. Sure, it hadn't given her the wild rush that came from the blood taken straight from a source's neck, but she'd gotten that rush when she'd sampled Adam.

The man's taste—*Hot, rich.* She'd never had anything like it.

His blood, the tangy flavor, the power.

Emotions and needs had ripped through her when the first drop of his blood spilled onto her tongue. Hunger. Lust.

Sex. Orgasm.

Life.

She had a feeing that Adam's blood could prove to be addictive.

She wondered if the second taste would be as good as the first.

Watching her, Adam slowly lifted the phone. Punched in the numbers and, after a few moments, ordered the transaction.

Maya smiled.

Time for the hunt.

"What the hell are we doing here?" Adam snapped, climbing slowly off the back of the motorcycle and glaring up at the elaborate building with its gleaming glass windows and sweeping arches.

"I need to meet a friend." Okay, so "friend" wasn't quite the term she should be using. Maya knew Josette wasn't exactly going to be thrilled to see her, but she needed to ask the lady a question.

The art gallery's parking lot was full of fancy cars. Big ones, with shiny rims and perfectly polished exteriors. Through the gallery's front windows, she could see men and women in formal attire, talking and laughing.

Josette had sure as hell come a long way in the last six years.

Homeless to high society.

Maya admired her.

Josette pretty much hated her.

Such was fate.

Maya marched up the stone walkway, her head high. The valet approached her, frowning.

"Miss—"

"The bike stays put, dude. We'll only be here a min—"

"You'll be here less than that," Josette said, her voice still tinged with the faint southern drawl she'd acquired while living in New Orleans. She stepped away from the gallery's entrance and into the soft lantern lighting.

"Ah, Ms. Dusean, should I—"

Josette strode forward until she was approximately ten feet away from Maya. Then she stopped and ordered the valet, "Leave us alone."

Maya eyed the distance between her and Josette. The woman had always been like that. Not wanting to get too close to the vampire.

Can't blame her, not with her history.

But that didn't mean she had to like the woman's attitude. Hell, just for sport, Maya was tempted to bite her right on her elegant neck.

Josette was a beautiful woman, no getting around it. The soft lighting made her look all the more stunning. Perfectly defined cheekbones. Wide, red mouth. Eyes the color of the night. Skin a dark cream.

"You going to stare all night, vampire? Or are you here for a reason?"

Beautiful, but the lady sure could be a bitch.

"You didn't have to walk outside to meet me," Maya murmured softly, aware of Adam's silent presence behind her. "I was planning to come in and find you."

Josette's lips thinned. "I bet you were."

"You've come a long way." The gallery was Josette's. The fancy pictures. Everything was hers. Not bad for an immigrant from Haiti who'd barely spoken English when she'd arrived in the U.S.

Josette didn't respond. Just stared with ice-cold eyes.

Maya tucked her hands into her back pockets. "How'd you know I was here, Josie?"

"Could feel you." Her stare drifted to Adam. "You always know when evil's around."

No, most people didn't know, but Josette did. And so did her grandmother.

So as fun as this walk down memory lane was . . . "I need to find Marie."

Josette stiffened.

"Where is she?"

"How the hell should I know?" Josette turned away. "Get out of here and—"

Maya lunged forward and grabbed her arm, holding tight. Adam never moved.

Josette shuddered at her touch.

"I need to find her. It's very, *very* important." Josette might have turned her back on the old ways, but Marie hadn't. She never would.

"*Rete!* Let go." The words were gritted between clenched teeth.

Maya dropped her hand, but didn't step back.

Josette glared at her. "I haven't talked to *grand-mere* in months. I have no idea where she is—"

"Bullshit." Sure, Josie might have stopped the visits and the phone calls to protect her new image, but Maya didn't buy for one minute that she didn't know where Marie was. "You're probably sending rent money to her. All I need is the address."

Adam stalked forward, and Maya was suddenly, fiercely aware of him at her side.

Josette stumbled back a step, her eyes widening.

"Josie. . . ." Shit, she didn't have all night.

"Mythlin Street. 208." Another hurried step back.

Jeez. Had that been so hard? Maya waved to a guy in a tuxedo who'd poked his head out of the gallery's entrance.

"Josette?" Uh, oh. Mr. Elegance looked worried.

"I'll be right there, Martin." Cool, calm tone. Wild, desperate eyes. Josette lowered her voice and said, "You cannot come here again, understand? I am out of that life now. All of it. I don't want demons, vampires," those wild eyes darted to Adam, "*anything* coming around. I want to be normal, okay?"

Normal. Check. "You won't be seeing me again."

Her breath caught. "We're even?"

Not really, but Maya nodded.

Her chin lifted, some of the hard arrogance coming back. "Then get the hell off my property, vampire."

"Charming friend you have," Adam drawled as they made their way back to the bike.

Maya grunted.

His anger spiked. Adam grabbed her arm, jerking her around and against his chest. He had the feeling she was dicking around with him, and he didn't like it. "Why the hell did we come here?" The way he saw it, they were wasting valuable time. They needed to be out there, tracking down the vampires who'd taken Cammie.

Not screwing away time at some gallery.

Maya's teeth snapped together. Her hands balled into fists and pressed against his chest.

He should have let her go then, but he didn't. Her eyes were wide, swimming with emotion, and damn if he didn't want to kiss her.

She'd gotten her taste of him last night. Now he wanted his turn.

She smelled of roses instead of death.

What would she taste like?

"You're overstepping your bounds, Slick." Her voice was a warning growl.

Oh, the vampire was getting angry. Good. He liked to see her with some kind of passion in her eyes.

The valet lifted a hand as he approached them. Adam stared at him, let the fool see the rage he carried.

The young guy nearly tripped running away.

Maya wasn't struggling within his hold. Her breath came hard and fast, but she wasn't trying to break free.

Good thing that. Because the mood he was in, he'd just hold her tighter, vampire strength be damned.

Then she'd know he wasn't just a man.

Her chin lifted as she stared up at him. "Do you know,"

she began quietly, "just how many vampires there are in the world?"

Too fucking many.

"Hundreds of thousands," she gritted. "And they are *every-where*. In every country that you know and even in those small-ass ones you don't. They hide in plain sight. Drink when they want. Kill when they want." Her fangs glinted.

She wasn't telling him anything he didn't know. His fingers tightened around her. "Your point?"

"My point is that finding them can be like hunting in the dark. You don't know what's out there until it's too late." She shook her head. "I wanna know what's waiting. *Who* is waiting."

"And this Marie—she's going to tell you?"

"I think she will."

His hand fell away. "Fine. Then I'll trust you, *for now*." But he didn't want to waste any more time.

"Hey, you came looking for me, remember? If you don't like my methods, hit the road."

The woman truly didn't understand that she was playing with fire.

He caught her chin in his hand. Soft flesh. Tender. Her mouth was close to his. Just inches away. Such a full, tempting mouth.

And one that could spew insults so quickly.

"I'm not leaving you yet." Not until Cammie was safe. Because he truly didn't doubt that Maya could find her.

He just knew that Maya was going to keep pissing him off along the way.

His thumb brushed over her bottom lip.

"Wh-what are you doing?" Her breath feathered against him. No more belligerence in her voice. Confusion filled her eyes.

He wasn't sure. He was furious, impatient, and . . . hungry. For her.

Just a taste.

One taste, that was all he'd need, and then this ridiculous hunger for a vampire would disappear. She wouldn't taste sweet. He wouldn't like the touch of her lips against his. Her teeth—they would repel him.

Yes, just one taste. That was all he'd need. And this insanity would end.

"Adam . . ."

Her mouth was open. Perfect.

His lips covered hers.

She gasped softly into his mouth and he stole her breath, locking his mouth onto hers and feeling the soft press of her lips beneath his.

His tongue pushed inside, swept against hers and—

Her taste. Adam shuddered *Her taste was unlike any other.*

His mouth tightened on hers in sudden demand.

Not bitter, dammit. *Good. So fucking good.*

Sweet like honey. Rich like wine. And the flavor of her—it was making him drunk. Making him crave. More.

More.

His fingers locked around her waist, and he pulled her tight against him so that he could feel her nipples pressing into his chest.

Her tongue met his. Just as hungry. Just as wild.

Mistake. The word blasted through the growing fog of lust in his mind. Tasting the vampire had been a serious mistake.

Because now he wanted more. A hell of a lot more.

Fuck, he was so screwed.

Fighting his instincts, struggling for control, Adam managed to lift his head and step away from her. Her scent, roses and aroused woman, tickled his nose and made his cock jerk.

Maya's lips were still parted. She swallowed, staring up at him.

He figured she was about to rip him a new one, but she stared at him, looking a little lost.

And damn if he didn't want to put his arms around her and just hold the woman.

So. Screwed.

Then that chin of hers shot into the air and her index finger jabbed into his chest. "I don't remember asking to be kissed, Slick." She barred those fangs. "Try that again and you might just get bit."

His breath expelled in a hard rush. "I'll keep that in mind." Because he sure as hell planned to try *that* again. That, and a whole lot more.

She frowned at him, then straightened her shoulders and stalked toward the bike. For a moment, he admired the sway of her ass in those jeans.

The woman knew how to move.

He followed her slowly back to the waiting bike. Maya glanced over her shoulder, not to look at him, but to stare at the glowing lights of the gallery.

Her lips curved down, just the tiniest bit.

He balled his hands into fists so he wouldn't give in to the urge to touch those lips. Not again. Not yet. Adam cleared his throat, and tried to figure out how to get back on neutral ground and away from his building lust. He looked toward the gallery, saw the outline of a tall woman in black gazing out of the window. Staring at him.

Huh. She'd been watching them.

He glanced back at Maya. "How'd you meet her?" And just what was going on between them?

Maya turned toward the motorcycle. "I found her in the middle of a gang war."

Not the answer he'd been expecting.

"One of the assholes had a knife at her throat. She was up against the wall, bleeding, not making a damn sound. And he was laughing."

He studied her profile. Heard the anger in her voice. "What'd you do?"

She shot a hard stare toward him. "I was still a cop back then. I told him to drop his weapon. To stand down."

"Did he?"

"Hell, no. He came at me, blade flying."

His stomach knotted. When she'd been a cop, she'd been human.

Humans were so weak.

They died too easily.

A slow smile spread across her lips. "Then I beat the hell out of him. Necessary force, you know."

He should have known. Adam shook his head and grabbed the black helmet. "So your friend's pissed because you saved her life?" She was still watching them. He could *feel* her stare.

"Nah, she's pissed because I'm a vampire. Josette was fine when I was human, but when I changed—" A shrug. "Let's just say her family doesn't have the best track record with supernaturals."

The woman, Josette, had power. He'd felt the lick of her magic in the air. She wasn't strong. But *something* had been there.

She'd known he wasn't human.

"Josie's mom was killed by a vampire. So she pretty much thinks we're all bloodsucking bastards or bitches."

Ah, well, no wonder the woman hadn't greeted them warmly. "Will this Marie have the same feelings? Will she talk to you?"

"Yeah, Marie'll talk."

And she'd better have something interesting to say. The news that Nassor didn't yet have Cammie had thrown him and made a rush of excitement leap in his blood. If they could find her before he awoke—

But he couldn't hope yet. Maya had said that she could track the vampires who'd taken Cammie. So far, the only thing she'd done was take him to an art gallery.

He hoped her next stop proved more helpful.

It had better.

"Josie's turning away from the old ways," Maya said, climbing onto the bike. "She's seen too much darkness in her life, and now she wants to try to pretend it doesn't exist— that things like me don't exist."

Maya wasn't a thing. He frowned, holding the helmet. What did she mean about the old ways?

"The lady tends to get pissed off when she's reminded that things on Earth aren't all caviar parties and cocktail dresses."

The cycle's engine roared to life. "No matter how much she might wish they were."

"Sometimes people need their illusions." That was why so many refused to accept the reality of demons. Vampires.

"Guess they do."

Adam climbed onto the motorcycle behind her, his body stiff. He was getting rather tired of being her tag-along. It wasn't a position he was used to, but he knew he had to play the role for now.

But later . . .

"So why is it so important to find Marie?" He had to shout over the roar of the bike.

Maya laughed. He could barely hear the soft sound and her equally soft reply. "You'll see, Slick. You'll see."

He clenched his teeth. The lady could only try his patience so far. Adam wrapped his arms around her waist, holding on tight. His cock pressed hard against her perfect ass, a deliberate move on his part. He was still horny as hell, and feeling her ass against him, holding her to his chest, well, it was the closest thing to relief he was going to get.

He had to suffer the indignity of riding behind her.

But at least he got the benefit of her soft body.

And when the ride was long, he sure as hell did enjoy her.

Maya had no trouble finding 208 Mythlin Street. The bike bounced down the old pothole-filled road. Drove past the ramshackle buildings. Stopped at the two-story brick house that was nearly hidden by twisted trees.

Maya parked her bike and they stepped onto the broken sidewalk. It wasn't quite midnight, but the yard was full of people. Men, women. All dressed in white.

Five tall, muscled men with skin a deep brown and bodies humming with tension, immediately walked toward them.

Maya raised her hand. "I'm here to see the *Mambo*."

Mambo.

The word was familiar to him. He struggled, trying to remember where he'd heard it before.

The men looked back toward the house. Silence stretched across the yard.

"Maya." A whisper. Could have been the wind. Could have been a woman's voice. Adam wasn't sure, but the men stepped back, eased into the shadows.

He stared at the house then. It wasn't like the others on the street. No disrepair. No neglect. Strong bricks. Long, wraparound porch. White windows open to the night.

The house didn't belong on this road.

There was something off about the place. About the people who watched them walk forward and whispered quietly, their eyes knowing.

Lights burned brightly from inside the house.

The porch steps creaked as Maya climbed them. She didn't look nervous. Hell, so far, he hadn't seen her look nervous at all, not even when the L10 had gone after her.

But he was getting a bad feeling. Every instinct went on full alert as his body tensed.

The front door was open. Waiting.

Inviting?

Maya stepped over the threshold.

Adam froze.

He glanced down and saw the red dust. The thin line that went all the way across the entranceway.

Shit.

Mambo.

Maya glanced back at him, brows lifted.

His jaw locking, Adam gritted, "This Marie, just what is she?" Why had Maya wanted so badly to see her?

The power from the house, from Marie, swept around him.

Hell, no.

Josette's power had been weak, but she'd still sensed his deception.

This woman, Marie—she was too strong for him to fool.

A man's laugh rang from the darkness.

Maya wet her lips. Her own gaze fell to the line of dust. "Don't you know?"

Yeah, he did.

The woman was a voodoo priestess.

Sonofabitch.

"Let's get out of here." His skin was prickling, the hair on his nape rising.

"No, you don't understand." She leaned back over that line. "Marie knows things. She might be able to tell us which vampires took Cammie."

"Yeah, and we can also just go and find some feeding rooms and start kicking ass until we round up the vamps who know." Going into the *mambo's* house—that wasn't an option for him.

And he didn't want Maya out of his sight.

A half-smile curved her lips. "That's plan B, Slick. The slow plan. For Plan A, I wanna see what Marie knows."

A growl rumbled in his throat. The men around them slipped back even further into the shadows.

Shit. This hadn't been part of *his* plan. "Next time, you go over Plan A with me, fucking thoroughly, before you act." When she went in the house, he wouldn't be able to protect her.

And since when did she need protecting? He shook his head, but couldn't shake the feeling that he needed to watch over her.

Bullshit. Utter bullshit.

Maya didn't need anyone's protection.

So why did he want to shield her?

"Go in," he finally snarled, fighting to control the rage coursing through his veins. He'd never be able to cross that red line, but if he sensed any trouble, if he so much as heard Maya cry out—

He'd tear the house down.

Then no damn magic line would keep him out.

The beast within him began to roar.

Chapter 4

Marie Dusean could have been anywhere from fifty to a hundred. Her face was lined, but eerily beautiful in the flickering candlelight.

She stood when Maya approached, holding out her hands. "Child, it's been too long." The sound of her native Haiti flowed richly in her voice.

Maya took her hands, felt the delicate bones, the fragile skin.

"You've fed well." Marie's eyes swept over her. "And you still look so young."

Maya stared back into Marie's faint, crystal blue eyes. Eyes that were completely covered by cataracts, and had been, for as long as Maya had known the priestess.

She forced a laugh. "Gonna keep looking that way, Marie. We both know things aren't gonna be changing for me."

Unlike Josette, Marie didn't hate all vampires. Or, at least, she didn't hate Maya.

Back when she'd been human, Marie had even tried to warn Maya about the fate that waited for her.

That first night, when she'd brought Josette back home and found Marie waiting with her pale eyes and knowing voice, the lady had whispered, "Beware of the night, child. He'll wait for you, hiding a monster, behind the face of man. He'll take you. Change you. Destroy what you've been."

She hadn't listened to Marie's words. Hell, she'd thought

the lady was crazy. She remembered mumbling something and trying to get the hell away from Marie as fast as she could.

It was only later—*too late*—that her words had made sense.

Marie Dusean was a very special woman. Maya didn't doubt her powers even for a minute. Marie *knew* things—things no human should know.

Very slowly, Marie lowered into a faded red velvet chair. Her eyes never left Maya's face. "You've come about the child."

She nodded.

Marie's hands flattened on the round table before her. "Dreamed of her. Child of light, taken by the dark."

Tension tightened her body as Maya leaned forward. "Her uncle thinks she's being used as a gift for Nassor."

Marie hissed at the name, and her fingers curled into gnarled fists. "Rises soon."

"Yeah, I thought he might." *Dammit.* "So the vampires who took her, where are they? Have they already gone back to his—"

The mambo's hand shot across the table, grabbed Maya's. "You will have to choose, child. Life or death."

Well, shit. Wasn't she already dead? Well, undead? Her heart had stopped during that fateful attack. She'd seen the faintest glimpse of another world—then she'd been yanked back to hell. "I already chose once." She wasn't particularly in the mood to do so again.

"The desert. Seek the vampires there." Her nails dug into Maya's wrist. "Hiding where the rocks have bled."

Where the rocks have bled. Excitement pumped through her.

"They keep the girl, waiting." Marie's voice lowered to a whisper. "Not much time before the Born Master rises."

Then the shit would hit the fan.

A hard sigh shook Marie's chest and her hand slipped away as her body sagged against the chair.

Maya knew their talk was at an end. The Mambo's strength

wasn't what it used to be. "Thank you, Mambo," she said softly and reached into the right front pocket of her jeans. Carefully, she pulled out a small ring. A ring of pale gold, crowned with a delicate oval ruby.

Marie's lips trembled. She lifted her hand. "*Carline.*" Grief choked her voice.

Maya pushed the ring across the table. "Thought you might want this back."

Marie's trembling fingers closed over the ring. A lone tear slid down her cheek. "It is done?"

"Yeah, it's done." She'd had to track the vampire to Louisiana. He'd stayed on his hunting grounds all these years. She'd tracked him, found him with his necklace of trophies—rings, earrings, jewels of all sorts. He'd had his next victim in his hands, a girl, barely eighteen. Her blood had been on the ground.

Blood was precious. It wasn't to be wasted in a slaughter by a beast who'd long since lost touch with good and evil.

But the beast wouldn't hurt anyone else, she'd made sure of it.

The pale eyes closed for just a moment. Marie brought the ring to her heart. "It is I who owe you now, child."

Shaking her head, Maya rose to her feet. "No, you don't owe me a damn thing." Marie had been the one to help her after the change. The one who taught her how to survive.

The wooden floor creaked beneath her feet as Maya walked across the room. She stopped in the doorway, glanced back. A question had been nagging at the back of her mind. "Mambo, I brought a man with me. Why wouldn't he come in?"

Marie's head was bent over the ring. She was rocking back and forth slowly. But at Maya's question, her head lifted. "Evil—it cannot cross my line."

The red line of dust.

But that didn't make sense. "No. Adam's not evil. He's looking for his niece, he's not—"

Her head lowered again, and the rocking continued.

He wasn't evil. *Was he?*

But Maya couldn't just dismiss Marie's words. She'd done that once before, and had her life stolen as a result. She turned away, her hand gripping the doorframe. "I should have listened to you all those years ago. Things could have been so different for me."

A soft laugh floated in the air. "Ah, child, now whatever made you think I was talking about the vampire?"

Her heart kicked into a furious rhythm. If not the vampire, then who? She turned around, the question on her lips.

But Marie was gone. The red velvet chair sat empty, and the ruby ring glinted on the table.

Maya stormed out of the house moments later. The yard was empty—all the men and women in white had disappeared.

Where the hell was Adam?

Evil—it cannot cross my line.

She stepped off the porch—

And was jerked against a hard male chest.

Her claws lifted and a snarl curled her lips.

"Easy, vampire. It's just me." Adam's arms tightened around her as his breath fanned over her cheek.

She glanced over his shoulder. "Where did everybody go?"

"Don't know. Just seemed to disappear right before you came barreling out of the house."

That wasn't a good sign. Why would they all leave? Unless—*hell.* "We need to get out of here." She shoved away from him. Noticed the utter silence of the yard.

Oh, no, not good.

She'd left her gun with the bike, not wanting Marie's guards to think she was a threat.

Marie had enough threats in her life—that was why the mambo had to move locations every few months.

Fucking stupid.

"Why do—"

She took off running for the bike. Her nostrils flared as she moved, drinking in the scents of the night. Human flesh. Decayed vegetation. Dank earth. Wisps of smoke. Animal.

Wolf.

She heard the growls just as she touched the cold metal of the motorcycle. She reached into her saddlebag, locked her fingers around the butt of the gun.

Over the years, she'd learned a few important facts.

Fact one. Bullets soaked in holy water could kill a vampire—if they pierced his heart. She'd been lucky enough to learn that one while she was still alive. Well, sort of.

Fact two. The bullets could be made of any metal to work on a vamp, but if she was going up against shifters, particularly those damn vicious wolf shifters, she needed to make absolutely sure the bullets were made out of silver.

Fact three. A silver bullet/holy water combination could really save her ass.

A howl sounded to the right.

Maya spun around, weapon ready.

"What the hell was—" Adam jerked to a stop beside her, his chest rising and falling quickly.

"Get on the bike." She could smell the wolves, hear the soft pad of their paws as they closed in.

How many? Three? Four?

Damn. Six?

More?

When the wolf shifters tracked in packs, they were nearly unstoppable. The fact that they could communicate telepathically while in animal form, well, that just made it all the easier for them to hunt.

And they were very, very good at hunting.

Definitely time to leave.

She heard him draw in a deep breath. "Shit. Why are the wolves stalking us?"

"'Cause they're probably working for Nassor's men." She'd seen it before. Vamps using the wolves as hunting dogs. But now wasn't the time to talk about how easily some of the wolves' allegiance could be bought.

Now was, quite simply, the time to run.

Talk could come later.

In the darkness, she saw a pair of glowing eyes staring back at her.

Then another.

Another.

"Get on the bike!" The growls and snarls were louder now. *Had* to be at least six of them. Maybe more.

Adam got on the bike.

The wolves stalked from the shadows, bodies hugging the ground, mouths open, fangs dripping with saliva.

The lead wolf, a big black beast missing half of his right ear, kept his eerie stare locked on her.

His muscles bunched.

Shit.

Maya jumped on the back of the motorcycle, wrapped her left arm around Adam's muscled waist. With her right hand, she lifted the gun, aimed—

The wolf sprang forward

"Go!" She screamed and pulled the trigger.

The bullet fired, blasting straight toward the snarling beast.

The wolf twisted, jerking to the left, and the bullet slammed into his flesh. The bastard fell to the ground, a long whimper of pain gurgling in his throat.

Not a heart shot. Or a head shot. Sonofabitch. He'd live.

The motorcycle's engine fired to life, and the bike shot forward, snarling like a demon straight from hell.

The rest of the pack sprang forward, jaws snapping.

Adam and Maya flew past them, but she felt a flash of burning pain sear her thigh.

One of the wolves had clawed her.

She jerked around, fired one shot. Another.

The wolves were chasing them, their big, powerful bodies eating up the road nearly as fast as the motorcycle.

She couldn't aim for shit while the bike was swerving all over the road.

Hell. "Faster!" If he didn't get them out of there within the next thirty seconds, the wolves would tear them apart.

The motor growled. Adam leaned forward, curling his body into the bike. Maya held on with one hand, and kept trying to aim with the other.

With a sudden burst of speed, the motorcycle raced forward.

The wolves couldn't keep the pace.

Finally.

Maya tucked the gun into the back of her jeans. Her palm smoothed over her thigh. Touched blood. She hissed out a breath at the pain.

Damn. It was deep.

But she'd heal. She always did.

She pressed her head against Adam's back, drawing in a hard breath. Wolf shifters. Fucking *werewolves*. She hated those animals.

They'd kill anyone, anything. Conscienceless, predatory. They were the worst kinds of monsters. Psychotic.

And now the wolves were on their trail.

The fact that the wolves were after her, when they'd pretty much stayed the hell out of her way before, was no coincidence. She'd *never* believed in coincidences. Someone—probably that spineless Stephan—had reported to Nassor's men about her little meeting with Adam, and the vamps had called in the dogs.

"Maya?" Adam's voice shouted over the roaring motor.

"It's okay." She licked her lips, then said, louder, "We've lost them."

For now. But wolves never gave up on a hunt.

They'd be back. She just had to make certain she was ready for them.

The bones snapped, crunched. The fur melted from his body and the beast that had prowled on four legs slowly stood upright.

Blood dripped in long, slow rivulets down Lucas Simone's shoulder.

The bitch had shot him. With a silver bullet.

The poison was in his body. He could feel it, eating away at him.

He lifted his right hand. The tips of his nails stretched into three-inch-long claws. Clenching his teeth, he drove the claws straight into his wounded shoulder.

His pack gathered around him, heads low, bodies shaking.

The blood poured faster now.

He ripped away the skin, the muscle. Found the bullet. Jerked it from his shoulder.

The silver burned his fingers and he threw it, tossing the bullet far into the night.

In the distance, he could hear the roar of the motorcycle, fading now as the vampire fled.

She hadn't been his prey. He'd wanted the man.

The rules of the game had changed now.

"We find them," he said, his voice ringing loud and clear. The wolves around him stiffened, stared with unblinking eyes. "I don't care how fucking long it takes, but *we find them.*" There would be no safe place for the vampire and the man.

The wolves began to growl.

He held up his hand. Skin and blood coated his claws. "The vampire is mine." Blood for blood. The others needed to know the kill would be his.

Only his.

Lucas threw back his head, rage racing through his body, and howled his fury to the night.

Adam drove hard and fast through the city. The motorcycle slid easily into the curves, then shot past the cars and trucks on the highway.

Maya held on tight as they streaked forward. She'd directed him to the busiest part of town deliberately. If they were followed, well, the werewolves would have to take their human form. Even they wouldn't be stupid enough to risk running around the town as giant, furry wolves.

Hiding in plain sight was one thing.

Terrorizing the humans by charging through the city in full-on shifter mode was a whole different matter.

No, even they wouldn't be that stupid.

She hoped.

"Stop here!" She leaned in close and since he'd never put on his helmet—another human with a death wish—she spoke the words directly into his ear.

He pulled the bike over to the curb. Shut off the engine. They were in the nightclub district, and the streets were jammed with traffic and people partying.

Fancy dresses. Perfect hair. The women were laughing, the men were drinking. Long lines of human bodies circled some of the clubs as the folks waited for their chance to enter the "in" places.

Maya's gaze scanned the street.

Adam's body shifted in front of her, and she eased back automatically, making room for him to climb off the bike. He turned back toward her almost immediately, his features tight. "Where the hell are you hurt?"

She'd almost forgotten about the leg. The throbbing had eased and the skin just felt strangely tight now.

Her hand touched her thigh.

His jaw clenched and he reached for her.

Her hand caught his. "How'd you know I was hurt?" She hadn't said anything to him about the wolf clipping her. There hadn't been a point, really. It was only a matter of time until the injury would heal and she'd be as good as new.

He pushed her hand away. "I could smell your blood." And he sounded incredibly pissed about that fact.

She blinked. For a human, the guy had a well-developed nose. But then, she was becoming increasingly convinced that there was more, much more, to Adam Brody than met the eye.

His hands were on her thigh, jerking an even larger hole in her favorite pair of jeans. They were parked underneath a streetlight and the bright glow easily showed the blood caked on the denim.

Adam swore.

"Ah, Slick. Relax. It's not as bad as it looks."

Another jerk and the hole in her jeans expanded a couple more inches. Then his fingers were on her skin. Warm, strong fingers pressing lightly against her inner thigh.

A shiver of awareness worked its way down her spine.

He knelt before her, his gaze on the wound. Maya swallowed over the sudden dryness in her throat and craned to see over his shoulder. "Really, the wound will heal—"

His head tilted back. "It already has."

No damn way. She was a fast healer, but not *that* fast. "Impossible." She'd gotten the gash less than an hour ago.

But the skin had already closed. The flesh was a bright pink now, and soon, she knew the hue would fade to her normal too-pale complexion.

Her gaze lifted to his face. She found him watching her with that deep stare of his. His fingers were still on her thigh, moving lightly, almost stroking her. Around them, people brushed by and the sounds of laughter and voices drifted on the wind.

Maya wet her lips. "I shouldn't have—the marks shouldn't have faded so fast." She had to stop thinking about how good the man's hand felt on her and focus on the fact that her body had just done the impossible. Healing in less than an hour's time.

His fingers caressed her flesh once more.

Her nipples tightened.

Down, girl.

Adam's hand fell away from her as he rose to his feet.

Damn.

"Maybe you're getting stronger," he said, his voice perfectly calm. "Vampires do that, right? Get stronger as they age?"

Not after just five years. But, well, maybe the wound hadn't been as bad as she'd thought. When the wolf's claws had pierced her, she'd thought the flesh ripped open all the way down to the bone.

Perhaps she'd just been confused. A hell of a lot had been going on at the time. The wound could have been shallow and not nearly as deep as she'd feared. Yeah, that was possible.

Screw it. They didn't have time for her to waste worrying over a cut.

Maya swung her left leg over the bike. "We need to get rid of this bike." Fast. "If the wolves put a tracker on us," and they probably had, the bastards, "then he'll be out there now, following the scent."

"The scent?"

Well, not his scent because the man didn't have one—but she did. And the bike did. If they ditched the bike, sent it in another direction, it would buy them time to get out of the city.

Luckily, she knew someone in the area.

She studied the long line of well-dressed men and women waiting to get inside Heaven and Hell, the bar at the end of the block. A glance at her ripped and bloody jeans told her that she wasn't going to be blending well with them.

Then again, she'd never been particularly interested in blending.

She headed for the bar.

Adam's hand caught her wrist. "What did the priestess say?"

That you could be evil. Her head tilted to the right. Not the time to lay her cards on the table. "She told me where to look for those vamps—and as soon as I get us a new ride, we'll get the hell out of here and start tracking them." *Hint, hint*—he was holding her up and they could play the question-and-answer game later.

"She said that Cammie's still alive?"

It was the desperation in his voice that got to her. She gave a quick nod. *They keep the girl, waiting.* Maya had no idea if the vamps had tasted the kid, or if they'd been playing a nice game of Torture-The-Girlie. Some vamps really got off on things like that. But the kid was alive, that much reassurance she could give him.

Adam swallowed. Maya deliberately looked down at his hand. "Now are you gonna keep grabbing me or are you gonna let me do what I was hired to do?" Because if he wanted, they'd just stand there all night. Sure, the wolves would come after them and then they'd have to fight and all the humans would scream and run and chaos would ensue.

But it was an option.

She quirked a brow and waited.

"Do your job," he growled.

Maya led the way to Heaven and Hell.

She didn't bother with the line—she'd learned long ago she wasn't a good waiter. Besides, they didn't have the time to piss away.

Pushing through the crowd, ignoring the mutters behind her, she headed for the door. The bouncer, a tall, muscular red-head, smiled when she saw Maya. Maya smiled right back. She liked Ronnie—the woman was hard as nails and didn't take shit from anyone.

"Hungry tonight?" the bouncer asked.

Since she didn't like the traditional feeding rooms, Maya had visited bars like this one before. Feeding—that was how she'd met the owner, Tim.

The man's blood was sweet. Not as good as Adam's, but—

No one's was.

"Maybe," she finally drawled in answer to Ronnie's question.

A laugh rumbled in the woman's chest. Ronnie wasn't afraid of vampires or demons or, well, anything that Maya knew of. Another mark in the woman's favor.

But Ronnie's laughter faded when she caught sight of Adam. Her eyes narrowed in suspicion and her body stiffened. "He with you?"

"Yeah." And as much fun as chatting with the chick was, they needed to hurry. "Tim inside?"

Ronnie's gaze raked down Adam's body.

"Ronnie? Is Tim inside?" The woman's expression shifted and she started to look . . . interested.

Maya found she didn't like that look. She could still feel Adam's touch on her thigh, feel the warmth of his fingers, and *she didn't like the way Ronnie was staring at him.*

The redhead finally glanced back at her. "He's in there, but why do you need him? You've got a fine man right here."

Maya bared her teeth, knowing her fangs would show. "Sometimes, a gal just can't have too many men." Then she brushed by the bouncer and pushed open the swinging doors of Heaven and Hell.

The music hit her first. The loud, pounding beat. Spotlights circled over the crowd, shining on toned legs, tight asses, breasts that were exposed by low-cut tops. Dancers writhed and twisted in front of the stage. Couples huddled together in the shadows.

Yeah, it was a great place for feeding. So easy to seduce those who were already high from the booze—or from the drugs passed secretly in the back to those with enough money or fame to get a hit.

"Not your kind of place, is it?" Adam murmured, his body close behind hers. His breath stirred the hair on her nape.

When she'd been living, hell, no, she never would have stepped a foot inside the high-priced door.

But she wasn't in a position to be so choosy anymore.

She shoved her way through the crowd, heading for the long, twisting spiral staircase that led up to the VIP area. Tim would be up there. Behind the tinted windows. Watching the crowd.

Tim had always liked to watch.

A thickly muscled man in a perfectly fitting black suit stepped in front of the stairs and blocked her path. His eyes, dark brown, swept over her dismissively. "The area's not for you, lady."

"It's the jeans isn't it?" she murmured and deliberately locked her eyes with his. "They just don't make me look stylish."

His stare held hers. She wished that she could use the Thrall on him. That lovely psychic power that the elders of her kind possessed. One look and the victim was under the vamp's total control.

If only.

She would've used that handy trick on Adam.

Since she didn't possess that magic—maybe in another hundred years or so—well, she'd have to do things the old-fashioned way.

Maya licked her lips and leaned forward.

The bouncer's eyes narrowed, but she could hear the sudden, fast race of his heart. "Lady, uh, you can't—"

She wrapped her fingers around his throat and jerked him up into the air. "Trust me, I can. I can do just about any damn thing I want."

He tried to swing at her then, sending a big, meaty fist right toward her face. Her right hand tightened around his throat, and her left caught that flying bear claw in a death grip. Then she squeezed his fingers, hard.

All of the color bleached from the guy's face.

Behind her, Adam swore and then muttered, "Subtle, Maya, real—"

She didn't have time to play subtle. And damn, but it seemed a little too easy to lift this guy. Usually there was a bit of a strain when the prey weighed over two hundred and fifty pounds, but it felt like this fellow was as light as a feather and—

"Ah, Maya, do you mind putting my guard down?" A drawling male voice asked.

She turned her head just a few inches to the right. Saw the man with the sandy hair and the devilish grin. *Tim Largent.* Just the guy she wanted.

Very slowly, he began to descend the stairs. "Myles is generally good at his job, you know. I'd hate to lose him."

Myles was starting to shake in her grasp. She sighed and sat him back on his feet. Then she smiled at him, flashed her fangs and said, "Boo."

The bouncer jumped.

Tim laughed. "Let the lady pass, Myles. She's my . . . special guest."

The guy nearly tripped trying to get out of her way.

Hmm. Had to be his first time with a vamp.

Amateur.

She'd expected Tim to be better staffed. Ah, well. Lesson learned for his man. Just because the foe is smaller, it doesn't mean she can't kick your ass.

Maya sauntered up the stairs, stopped on the step just below Tim. The man was as good-looking as she remembered.

Too damn good-looking.

Perfect face. Sensual lips. Eyes that sparkled.

And a soul as black as the night.

"Been a long time," he murmured, staring at her. His hand lifted, then trailed down her cheek. "I've missed you."

If he weren't such a bastard, she would have missed him, too.

The guy was very good in bed.

He was also funny.

Smart.

But as deceitful as they came.

She was counting on that deceit right now.

Maya looked into his perfect eyes. So gold. So deep.

His mouth lowered toward hers. His lips pressed lightly against hers—

"What the fuck?" Adam grabbed her arm and jerked her down three steps. He stepped forward, putting his body between her and Tim.

Tim stared at him, and for just a moment, his pretty-boy face didn't look quite so perfect.

Rage.

Then the emotion smoothed away and he looked over at Maya, one golden brow quirked. "Got a new friend, do you, love?"

"You can never have too many friends." She cleared her throat. The pounding music was starting to make her head ache. "We need to talk. Privately." Away from the avid humans with the curious eyes.

"Send the new toy away and we can talk . . . privately for as long as you want."

"No, sorry, that's not the way it's going to—" Maya broke off, nose twitching. What the hell? Was that sulfur she smelled?

It was an unusual scent, one she remembered back from her days in high school when a chemistry experiment had gone dismally wrong.

Sulfur. She touched Adam's arm. What would cause . . . ?

He drew in a deep breath, seemed to relax a bit.

The scent faded as abruptly as it had appeared.

"The *lady*," Adam spoke in a hard, tight tone, "doesn't go anywhere without me."

Tim grunted but turned and climbed back up the stairs. "We can go to my office." He tossed a knowing glance back at Maya. "You remember where my place is, don't you, love?"

"Vaguely," she muttered. She'd fed from him there once. On the black leather couch.

She'd been a vampire only six months then, and she'd still been fighting against hunting humans.

Since Tim wasn't exactly human and he knew the score from the start, she'd felt safe with him.

Stupid mistake.

One she wouldn't make again.

Adam stopped in front of the gold-lettered door marked VIP. He leaned in toward her as she passed him, caught her hand. "What are we doing here?"

Tim had good hearing, *very good*, and she didn't want to give away her plan. "Trust me," she barely breathed the words to him as she passed, but her fingers clung tightly to his.

His jaw tightened, but he didn't question her again. He followed her inside, slamming the door shut behind them.

Tim walked over to the leather couch. Lowered his body onto the plush cushions. "That's better." He smiled again, this time flashing a perfect set of dimples. "Now tell me, what brings you to my side of Hell tonight?" The whites of his eyes began to darken.

The darkness of the demon, usually hidden by glamour. Or in Tim's case, half-demon.

"I need a favor," she said baldly, meeting that cloudy stare head-on.

"Hmmm. I don't usually offer favors."

No, he didn't. But in this case—"Help me, and you'll get the chance to screw over a pack of wolf shifters."

His smile stretched another inch. "Tell me more."

"Six are on our trail." *Could be more, but not really the point.* "I need to ditch my bike. Get a new ride and go as far and as fast out of this city as I can."

His fingers began to stroke the leather arm of the couch. "Running, Maya? I didn't think that was your style."

Adam didn't speak—a very good thing right then—but she could feel his tension. "I'm not running from them."

"Running *to* something, are you?" His fingers began to *tap, tap, tap,* on the couch. "Must be something important if a wolf pack's involved."

"Um." He didn't need to know any more about that.

His stare flickered to Adam. "Why do I think this 'something' has to do with your new friend?"

"'Cause you're a fucking genius?" Adam drawled.

Tap. Tap. Tap. His nails began to grow. His attention drifted back to Maya. "Where are you heading?"

"Texas. The border." The lie came easily. They always did.

Adam's head jerked toward her. "Is that where she—"

Luckily, she still had ahold of his hand. Her claws dug into him.

He got the message and shut up, fast.

But she knew the damage had been done.

"The border." Tim nodded. *Tap. Tap.* "All right. For old times' sake, I'll help you." Another smile—this time, one that showed a lot of sharp teeth. "And I'll enjoy the hell out of screwing over a pack."

He stood, walked over to a desk, and jerked open the top drawer. He tossed Maya a set of keys. "The black Jag down the street. Garage 812, slot 13."

Her fingers closed around the keys. "And my bike?" She hated to lose her baby, but there wasn't a choice.

"I'll take care of her."

She freed Adam's hand and walked across the room. "I knew I could count on you."

His fingers brushed down her cheek. He always did that. Always stroked her cheek with the back of his hand. A tender caress.

So it seemed.

"We need to go, Maya," Adam said, his voice cracking like a whip.

Tim's eyes began to lighten. "When you get tired of the new toy, come back for a visit. I'll be here."

Adam lunged across the room, got toe-to-toe with Tim. "She's not coming back, demon."

But Tim just flashed those dimples again. "We'll see."

Adam growled and spun on his heel. He didn't speak again until they were out of the bar and once again on the crowded street.

He stopped at the edge of the building, casting her a hard stare. "You've had sex with him."

Ah, hell, so not the time.

He blocked her path, used his body to trap her against the cold brick wall, but he didn't actually touch her. Not yet. "You screwed him, didn't you?"

"How is this your business?" she snapped. They had more important things to deal with at the moment. Her ex-lover was really low on the totem pole of priorities and—

Adam kissed her. A hard, deep, demanding kiss. His tongue thrust into her mouth, claimed hers, even as his hands clamped around her waist and jerked her against the thick heat of his arousal.

And the man was most definitely aroused. She felt every hot inch of his cock pressing against her.

Her sex began to cream.

He tore his mouth from hers. "This is why," he growled,

his forehead resting against hers for a moment, "because I can't even breathe anymore *without wanting you*."

Oh. Pretty good reason.

"I don't care what you are," he said, his voice rasping and his breath blowing lightly over her sensitive lips. "I just want you, naked, beneath me."

"Adam . . ." Maya began, not really sure if she was going to protest or offer to strip.

His tongue licked her bottom lip.

Her knees trembled. *Strip.*

It had been too long. She'd tried to push aside the needs of her body, but, damn—she wanted.

She wanted him.

Her lips opened for him and she drew his tongue into her mouth, sucking lightly. Then she let her hunger have free rein. A moan rumbled in the back of her throat as she lifted her arms and pulled him closer.

Not the time or the place. The warning drifted through her head, but she didn't stop. Didn't want to stop.

The fingers of his right hand curled over her ass, squeezing lightly, and she parted her thighs just enough to feel the brush of his cock against her sex.

Too long.

Adam's mouth began to kiss a path down her neck. Her nipples tightened to sharp points—her neck had always been her weak spot, and if he kissed just under her left ear—

His tongue slipped over her, licking in—*ah, just the perfect spot.*

Her hips jerked against his.

Her panties were wet now. She could feel the damp fabric brushing against the folds of her sex.

And she knew she was moments away from having sex with Adam.

Wolves were on their trail.

Not the damn time.

Her fingers curled around his shoulders and she pushed

against him. "Adam, no." So hard to say. Her voice emerged as a whisper.

His hold on her tightened. His dark head lifted and he gazed down at her, his eyes burning with lust. "You want me."

It'd be stupid to lie. Every fiber of her being was screaming with hungry desire. "This isn't the place—"

His nostrils flared and he licked his lips. "I can smell your arousal. Damn, you're sweet—I need a taste."

An image of Adam having that taste jumped into her mind. *Oh, yes.*

Two men walked past, eyeing Maya with knowing stares and twisted lips.

But not here. Not now.

She pushed against him again, this time using her enhanced strength.

He took a step back. A muscle flexed along his jaw as he dropped his hands. "I'm gonna be having my taste, vampire. Very soon."

How had the need between them gotten so wild, so desperate, so fast?

"We can't do this now," she said, wishing that her voice was stronger and didn't sound so husky. But she could still taste *him* in her mouth and she wanted more. "The adrenaline is pumping through us, making us crazy and—"

He shook his head. "Not the adrenaline. *I want you.*" He didn't look particularly pleased about that fact.

Well, she wasn't exactly over the moon to find her body breaking free of her control. The man made her feel hot, hungry, and desperate for his touch.

She had to get her control back. A vampire who let go in the heat of the moment, one who went wild—that wasn't a good vampire to be around.

Lust could make her kind very dangerous.

"We're going to finish this," Adam said clearly, those eyes of his seeming to look right into her soul. "When we're alone, when it's safe, I will have you."

Maya knew the words were a promise.

She sure as hell hoped the man was good at keeping promises. Because she was desperate to have *him*.

Tim watched them through the tinted glass of his second-story office. Watched the kiss. The touches. Felt the need and arousal burning from the couple.

His fingers tightened into fists.

So Maya was fucking her new toy. He'd figured as much when he'd seen the predatory look in the guy's eyes.

There had been lust there.

Possession.

Once upon a time, he'd possessed Maya. Had all that hot, rich power in his hands.

Sex with a vampire—it was one of the best pleasures on earth.

And the most dangerous.

They were walking away now. Hurrying down the street toward the promised Jag.

His fingers uncurled and his left hand rose toward the phone that waited on his desk. *Tap. Tap. Tap.* His nails clicked against the back of the plastic receiver.

Maya.

He'd cared about her, once. As much as he could care.

Of course, he'd still tried to kill her, but she didn't know that. Didn't know that he'd been paid a hundred grand to set her up.

When the choice fell between love and money . . . to him there really *wasn't* a choice then.

He didn't know how she'd survived that demon attack in the alley that night.

The woman was too good at cheating death.

But no one's luck lasted forever.

Tap. Tap.

They'd disappeared. Gone into the garage.

His gaze remained locked on the street. He'd give Maya a few more minutes. At least allow her to get the car on the road.

She deserved a bit more time. The woman had been the best fuck of his life.

Tap.

Ah, there it was. The black Jag streaked down the street, barely braking as it rounded the corner and disappeared into the night.

That should be enough of a head start.

Tim picked up the phone. Punched in the numbers for his call and waited patiently.

The phone was answered on the third ring. He heard the faint sound of breathing, but no one spoke.

"Maya Black was just here to see me," he murmured. "Apparently, some wolves are on her tail."

Silence.

"For a hundred grand," that was the price he'd accepted last time, so he figured it was still fair, "I can tell you where she's going, and I'll even activate the GPS tracking unit so you can hunt her car." Now surely that was a deal too good to pass up.

A sharp inhalation of air. "You'll have the money in an hour, demon."

"Good, and you'll have your vampire." He ended the call and glanced back out the window. The street was swarming with humans. Foolish, weak humans.

There wasn't any sign of Maya now. But it would be easy, too easy really, for her to be tracked.

"Sorry, love," he murmured, "guess there won't be a next time for us, after all."

Pity.

But business was business.

Chapter 5

"Uh, wanna tell me why you just paid that kid a hundred bucks to take our car?" Adam asked, wondering if he had just missed something very important. "You do have a backup plan for getting us the hell out of the city, right?"

"Sure I do," Maya said and stalked over to a nearby SUV. Her lips pursed as she eyed the car. Then she shrugged, walked past the driver's side door and paused next to the back door. She lifted her fist—and drove her hand right through the window.

A shrill, screaming alarm immediately echoed through the garage and the headlights and taillights of the SUV flashed in a sickening blur.

Adam swore.

Maya pushed her hand through the jagged hole, unlocked the door, and jumped into the backseat. Then she shimmied up to the front and Adam saw her crawl under the dashboard.

In seconds, blessed silence filled the garage.

Maya's head popped up and he could see the smile that stretched across her face.

Damn, but the woman was cute. And apparently, something of a thief.

But still cute.

For a vampire.

Adam drew in a deep breath.

"You gonna stand there all night, Slick?" The engine started with a rumble of sound. "Or are you ready to find Cammie?"

Cammie.

He ran to the passenger side. Maya had the door open and waiting for him. He jumped inside. As they shot through the garage, circling down the spiral ramp, he had to ask, "If you were planning to steal a car all along, then why'd we have to waste our time with the demon?" And he knew the guy, Tim, had been a demon. No mistaking those eyes.

Shit, if the rumors were true, way, way back in their family tree, the vamps and the demons were related. That's why they both had those dark eyes.

If the rumors were true.

Those same rumors said that once, long ago, the very first Born had done something to piss off a very, very powerful force. A force some called God—a betrayal had been made, and as punishment, the Born had been cursed—an eternity of darkness. The fact that holy water burned the vamps, yeah, that just made the rumors ring true.

But demons didn't have a holy water weakness. The strong ones had pretty much *no* weaknesses.

He'd never trusted demons. They weren't the fire-and-brimstone, Devil's-helpers, like most folks thoughts. They were actually a whole separate race of humans, maybe even offspring from the original Fallen.

They were good at magic, mind control, and deceit.

Most of 'em were outright bastards.

Like Tim.

"We weren't wasting time," Maya snapped, sounding annoyed. Instead of heading for the exit, she spun the car around and drove for the entrance on the opposite side of the building. "We were throwing the wolves off our scent."

Thus the whole stealing the SUV bit, but why go in that loud, overpriced bar?

A horn beeped as another car had to swerve to avoid a head-on collision with Maya.

She didn't even flinch, but she did flip off the other driver.

Then they were outside, pushing hard toward eighty and speeding away from the snarls of traffic.

"Interesting thing about Tim," she finally said, "the guy set me up to die a few years back."

His head jerked toward her as rage pumped through his veins. "And why," he asked softly, voice deadly, "in the hell did we just prance into the asshole's den?"

Her small nostrils flared. "Do you smell that? I swear it's like someone just opened a damn pack of matches in here and started a fire."

"Why'd we see him?" he demanded, ignoring her words. If he'd known the truth about Tim back when they'd been in that bar, he would have made certain to give the guy exactly what he deserved.

A slow, painful death.

Maya didn't speak for a moment, but he saw her fingers tighten just the briefest bit around the steering wheel. The streets and buildings passed them in a blur.

"Do you know," she shot him a quick glance, "just what Tim is doing right now?"

Probably screwing one of his scantily clad waitresses when he should have been bleeding all over the floor and begging for mercy.

"He got on the phone the minute we left, most likely with someone in the local wolf pack, and he offered to sell us out."

Bastard. "Nice ex you got there."

Her lips firmed. "There was probably some kind of tracking system on his car, and I imagine good old Tim is making arrangements to activate the GPS or at the very least, he's telling the pack to head for Mexico."

"Uh, we're not planning on traveling down to the border, are we?" He asked, feeling slow for not having recognized that fact sooner.

"No, we're not."

His anger kicked up another notch and he had to fight the urge to grab the woman. "Since we're talking about my niece's

life here, do you mind telling me just where we're headed?"
Or did the woman intend to keep leading him around in the
dark?

"The Mojave Desert, near Vegas. We're gonna stop by the
safe house first, load up on weapons and gear, then start
tracking."

Finally. "Are you sure she's there?"

"No."

His lips parted in surprise at her quick answer. "What?"
Then why were they going to waste time driving out—

"Marie's sure, and that's good enough for me."

Marie. "The voodoo priestess? Is she always right?" He
knew women like her had gifts, but he didn't want to take a
chance with Cammie's life.

"Always?" Maya sighed then muttered, "I sure hope not."

He frowned.

"Relax. She's right about this." She braked for a traffic
light. "We're going to find the girl."

And she'd better be *alive.*

But Maya didn't promise that, because he knew she *couldn't*
promise that.

"Just get me to her," he said. If he could just find Cammie,
shield her—"I'll take care of the rest."

"You and your army, huh?"

He didn't know what the woman was talking about.
"What?"

"Forget it, Slick. Just sit back and enjoy the ride—because
this party of ours is going to be heading straight to hell soon."

He'd thought they'd just left hell. Or had it been heaven?
Hard to say about Tim's bar.

Nah, for him it had definitely been hell.

The bastard had been with Maya. Touched her. Tasted her.

His hands fisted.

Tried to kill her.

And she'd just casually walked up to the guy and let him
put his hands on her again, his mouth.

The woman had ice in her veins. "I can't believe you're just letting him get away with it."

"Huh?"

"Tim." He snarled the word. "I can't believe that you're just gonna let that demon get away with trying to kill you."

She laughed them. A real, honest laugh that seemed to echo right in his heart. "Adam, I'm not letting him get away with anything." Another traffic light. Another quick brake. She flashed him a smile. "Just what do you think is gonna happen to our demon friend when the wolves find out that he can't deliver as promised?"

A soundless whistle slipped past his lips.

Her smile widened. "Tim didn't get away with a damn thing. I was just biding my time. Now *his* time, well, it's about to end."

And the guy had dug his own grave.

They drove until just before sunset, heading northeast along the long and empty interstate. They'd stopped by the safe house only long enough to grab supplies and clothes and then they'd been on the road again.

Maya could feel the change in the air that always signaled the rise of the sun. The faint shift, the slow drain on her energy.

They'd made good time, though, and even now, she could see the glitter of the Vegas strip shining through the waning night.

"We'll get a room," she said, her hands gripping the steering wheel hard. "Get some sleep, and then—"

"We can go after them now!" Adam said. "The vampires will be weak, we can take them, get her—"

"*I'm* weak, and you have to be dead on your feet." The night had been hellishly long. They'd stopped twice along the route and switched license plates with other SUVs to make certain they didn't have to worry about the cops bothering them.

But with the wolf attack . . .

The car theft . . .

The driving . . .

They both needed to rest before they went up against a gang of vamps.

"Look," she told him, turning the SUV toward one of the small motels near the highway, a place that boasted a bright red vacancy sign. "We'll leave before dusk, before those guys have stirred, and we'll arrive just as they wake." And just as her full strength kicked in. "We'll get the girl. Trust me."

He gave a jerky nod.

He was not a happy camper, but there was no way they could go traipsing through the desert right then. If the vamps had any kind of guards out there—more wolf shifters or demons—she and Adam would be dead in seconds.

She'd never enjoyed being easy pickings.

They checked into the motel, made sure the SUV was parked out of sight, and then Maya pushed open the old wooden door to their room just as the first rays of the sun streaked across the sky.

Damn. It had definitely been one hell of a night.

She hoped her day was better.

Maya was in the bathroom. He could hear the faint spray of the shower through the paper thin walls.

Tension kept his body tight as he paced the small confines of their room.

The place was a piece of shit. Sagging bed. Carpet worn through in places. A nightstand that was missing a leg and in its place had a pile of three stacked phone books. An ugly armchair and a couch that sagged so low it touched the floor.

When Maya had seen the room, she'd just shrugged those thin shoulders of hers and muttered, "I've seen worse." Then she'd stripped—yanking off her T-shirt so that he caught a glimpse of the long, smooth line of her back as she'd walked into the bathroom—and slammed the door shut.

Now he was stuck with a hard-on, anger pumping through him, and the same desperate need he'd felt before.

Closing his eyes, he imagined her. Saw Maya standing under the rush of water. Watched the liquid pour over her nipples and trickle down between her thighs.

Shit.

He understood why they couldn't go after the vamps right then. The bastards would have hidden well during the daylight and no doubt set guards around their precious prize.

He'd need Maya's help to fight them, and if she wasn't at full strength—and he knew by the tightness around her mouth and the stiffness of her body that she'd been weakening—then they wouldn't have as good of a chance at saving Cammie.

Yeah, he understood waiting. He just didn't like it.

And the fact that he was horny as hell just pissed him off more.

What was it about Maya? Why did he want her so much? He'd always hated her kind.

But she wasn't like the others.

Wasn't like anyone he'd ever met before.

His eyes opened and he stared at the bathroom door. Such a weak barrier, really. He could hear every move she made behind that wooden door. Could catch the scent of soap, of woman.

Adam was at the door before he even realized his own intention. He lifted his hand, touched the wood.

She'd wanted him earlier. Had kissed him back with a hunger to match his.

They'd stopped because it hadn't been the time. Or the place.

The time was different now. So was the place. He had to get this damn desperate lust out of his system so that he could focus on the attack plans. He couldn't afford a distraction, not while his niece's life was in danger.

His hand dropped to rest on the doorknob. *If she says no, I'll walk away.* It'd be one of the hardest things he'd ever done, but he'd walk away.

If she says no.

But what if she said yes?

His cock jerked in anticipation, and he opened the door.

Steam filled the small bathroom, fogging the mirror and drifting lazily in the air. Maya stood in the shower, a thin curtain both concealing and revealing her body. He could see the outline of her breasts. Firm, round. The flare of her hips. The sleek expanse of her thighs.

He wanted those thighs wrapped around him. Wanted his hands tight on her hips. And those breasts. He wanted to taste them. Wanted her pink nipples in his mouth, on his tongue.

Adam licked his lips, already tasting her.

"Are you gonna stand there all day?" Maya's mocking voice rang out as she pushed aside the curtain and met his stare with a raised brow. "Or are you planning to join me?"

Her nipples were tight, the pink tips hard and flushed. His gaze drifted over her, hungry for the sight of her flesh. Such sweet flesh. Flat stomach, round hips, a small thatch of dark hair shielding her core. He glimpsed the plump folds of her sex, flushed the same pink as her nipples.

He'd like to taste her there. Taste her cream and hear her moan.

Very slowly, never taking his gaze off her body, he jerked off his shirt. Threw it to the floor. Kicked off his shoes and socks. Stripped off his jeans and the boxers he'd worn.

He felt her stare on his body. First on his chest. Then down, to the thick cock that sprang from the hair at his groin.

Damn, but he couldn't wait to drive inside her.

He took a step toward the shower. Saw the swift rise of her chest.

She had the prettiest nipples.

The water sprayed on her, dripping down her body, trickling onto the tiled floor.

He stood in front of Maya, waiting, fighting to hold onto the control that weakened with every breath he took. Because he could smell her arousal now. The rich, heady scent filled his nostrils and made the beast inside him desperate for release.

"I'm not going to stop this time," he told her, his voice a hard rumble of sound.

Her hand reached out toward him, touched the center of his chest. "I don't want you to stop." Her gaze, bright blue, but occasionally starting to flicker black, met his. "I want you to fuck me."

Her words pumped a fire of need and lust through his veins. He stepped into the shower, grabbed her, and pushed her back against the tiled wall.

The water poured on his back. Hot.

His mouth locked on hers. His tongue drove deep as he tasted her. He loved the way she tasted. Loved the wet, warm feel of her body against his. He held her hands chained to the wall, and her body twisted and pressed against his.

Her nipples raked across his chest. Her smooth thighs brushed against his.

Fuck.

He pushed her arms higher and used one hand to hold her wrists tight. He wanted to be the one to touch and play this time. He wanted the control.

He wanted her. Blind with pleasure, screaming his name.

His right hand slipped down her body as he kissed her. Found her breast, fondled the tight peak, squeezed. Maya moaned into his mouth and her hips shifted urgently against him.

Adam ripped his mouth from hers. Gazed down at her breasts. Then took one ripe mound into his mouth, laving his tongue over the sweet flesh and enjoying the shiver that worked its way over her body.

He sucked on her breast, drawing strongly on the nipple, then easing back to tease the peak with his tongue. He loved the sounds she was making. Low, husky moans. Panting breaths. He knew she could break free of his hold at any moment, knew, too, that she was enjoying the pleasure he was giving her—and because of that, she wouldn't break free, not yet.

His hand skimmed down her stomach and stopped at the

juncture of her thighs. "Let me in," he breathed the words against her breast.

Her thighs parted, giving him perfect access to her core. His fingers eased between her spread legs. Her delicate folds were soft and slick from the shower and her own arousal. Adam touched her lightly at first, barely skimming his fingertips over the heated button of her need, then brushing the entrance of her sex.

"Don't play," Maya growled. "I'm not the light and easy type."

Neither was he. He had a stranglehold on the beast raging inside of him, but if Maya wanted fire and passion, he'd be more than happy to give it to her.

He pressed against her clit. Rubbed. Gently bit against the tender underside of her breast.

Then he drove one finger deep into her waiting sex.

Maya gasped, rising on her tiptoes.

The water pounded down over them.

His cock was swollen, heavy with the lust that poured through him. Her sex was tight around his finger, squeezing—so fucking good—and he couldn't wait to drive his shaft into her. Hard and deep. Just the way they both wanted it.

But first, he had to make certain his vampire was ready for the demands he'd make on her.

He pulled his finger back, deliberately raked his thumb over her clit, then thrust his hand against her, rocking his palm against her sensitive folds and then pushing two fingers deep into her.

Her head tilted back against the wall. The delicate muscles of her sex quivered around him.

Her scent drove him to the brink.

Adam pulled back his hand, raised his head, and gazed down at her. He licked the cream from his fingers, savoring her taste.

And knew that he wanted more.

Adam dropped to his knees before her. Pushed those slim thighs apart even more to open her wide for his eyes.

Her hands were free now, and her fingers immediately clamped around his shoulders, her claws digging into the skin.

But her intent wasn't to stop him. No, when he glanced up, he could tell by the hunger shining in the darkness of her eyes—she wanted more.

Just as he did.

His mouth found her, kissing her through the cascading water. Taking her essence onto his tongue as he licked the pink flesh between her thighs. He found her clit, stroked once, a long, thorough lick, then he sucked the button, pulling it into his mouth.

He felt her tremble around him. His hands locked around her thighs and he lifted her legs. He held her easily, barely feeling her weight as he kissed and licked her. Her taste was so *fucking good.*

Her breath came faster now. Harder. Her body was tight, and the quiver of her sex—oh, yeah, he could feel it. She was—

"Adam!" She cried out his name, her thighs tightening as she came. He felt the ripples of her release on his tongue. Tasted her pleasure.

And still wanted more.

He eased her legs down. Rose with the taste of her cream in his mouth and his cock all but ready to burst. His hand reached out, snapped off the flow of water. He grabbed Maya, lifting her into his arms and striding from the shower.

He took her to the bed. He didn't give a damn that they were both soaking wet.

He had to get inside her.

The bed squeaked when he placed her on the mattress, groaned when his body came down on top of hers.

He reached for her, ready to thrust deep into her.

Maya grabbed his hand. Met his stare with eyes a coal black. "My game now, Slick."

Then he was on his back, with Maya on top of him. She pinned his arms to the mattress. Her legs straddled him. Her sex was open, teasing him, just above his cock. The soft down of her black curls rubbed against him.

Maya leaned close. Her breath feathered over his lips. "Did you enjoy your taste?"

Hell, yes.

Her tongue snaked out, lightly licked his lips. "'Cause it's only fair that I get a taste, too."

Her lips brushed over his chin. Pressed against his jaw. Whispered down his throat. Adam expected her to bite him. Expected to feel the sting of her teeth and the rush of pleasure he'd known before.

But she just licked him. Long, slow licks that caused every muscle in his body to quiver.

His hands lifted, to pull her closer—but she shoved his wrists back against the bed.

"My game, remember?"

Damn, but she was beautiful.

He clenched his teeth, managed to grit, "For now." But if the vampire didn't get moving, he'd take control.

Dawn had come. Maya was weak, but the sun had never held sway over him.

Maya lifted her hips. Pushed down. Her creamy sex brushed against the length of his cock.

She curled over him. Her right hand released him. Her fingers caressed his chest. Touched his nipples. Her mouth followed the path, licking, sucking. When her lips closed around his nipple, Adam's heels dug into the bedding.

Her mouth . . .

He growled at the lust ripping though him.

Her left hand eased away from his, began to stroke him. To tease.

His fingers clenched into fists as he fought the urge to grab her and force her underneath his body.

Lower, *lower*. She moved down his body. Licked his abdomen. Kissed his flesh.

Her thighs shifted around him as she moved her body and he instantly missed the touch of her sex against his. "*Maya.*"

Her hair fanned over his stomach.

Her breath blew against his cock.

The sound of his heartbeat, the fast, desperate drumming, filled his ears as he waited for that hot mouth to close around his cock.

Her lips touched him first. Brushed over the tip. His shaft jerked and her soft laughter rumbled against him.

Then her tongue touched him. Licked away the drop of moisture that had beaded on the head of his cock and slowly moved down his erect length.

Her hand wrapped tight around the base of his shaft. Began to pump as she licked.

Sonofabitch.

His muscles were taut. His heart slammed against his chest. He could smell her, was breathing her in—and he had to take her.

Her mouth closed over his cock.

His control shattered.

With a snarl, Adam locked his arms around her and jerked her back up the length of his body. He kissed her. Hard. Deep. Then he rolled her under his body, pinning her beneath him.

Her legs spread immediately for him.

Her gaze met his. Hunger blazed in her eyes, a hunger to match his own.

He parted her folds, pushed his cock against her moist opening—

And drove balls-deep in one long, swift thrust.

Her legs clamped around him, her heels brushing his ass, and she bucked against him.

"More." One word, husky with need, slipped past her lips.

Adam withdrew, pulled to the very entrance of her body, and thrust inside. Again, again, again.

She met him each time, her hips rising to drive against his as they fought for release.

The bed squeaked beneath them, the harsh sound blending with their moans and ragged breathing, and seeming to drive the passion even higher.

More. The order had been hers, but the need was his. He wanted to feel more of her, to taste more, to have more.

To have everything.

Her nipples pressed against his chest and he just had to taste her breasts again. Her back arched when he tongued her nipple, then he drew it deep into his mouth.

And he thrust. Plunged deep. Withdrew.

Her fingers raked down his back. Her hips bucked beneath his.

The base of Adam's spine began to tingle. His balls drew tight against his body as his orgasm approached in a powerful, driving wave.

His fingers pushed between their bodies. Found her clit. Rubbed, tugged.

Her sex clenched around him in a spasm of release as she cried out, shuddering beneath him.

Adam drove into her one final time and stiffened. His release barreled through him, stronger, harder, than anything he'd ever experienced. Pleasure exploded, singeing his nerves and rippling through his muscles.

When the climax ended, when the haze of lust and need finally cleared from his eyes, he looked down at Maya.

She gazed back at him, a faint furrow between her brows and a wet tear track sliding from the corner of her right eye.

He stared at her, not sure what to say or do. His cock was still cradled in her moist heat, already stirring again.

Slowly, the furrow smoothed away and a slow smile stretched her lips. She said, simply, "More."

He was only too happy to oblige.

When she slept, she turned from him. Curled onto her side and faced the pale blue wall.

He didn't like that.

Adam gazed at Maya's back, aware of a simmering sense of discontent within him.

His body was replete, the voracious hunger for Maya temporarily satisfied. But . . .

It seemed as if something were missing.

Because she'd turned from me.

Curled in on herself. Hunched her shoulders and drifted away from him.

He didn't know how to pull her back.

His hand lifted, stroked a lock of her hair.

She didn't stir.

His fingers clenched into a fist.

Sleep pulled at her, but Maya's eyes were open as she stared at the peeling wall. Her sex still quivered with little aftershocks of pleasure. She clenched her thighs together, enjoying the feeling.

As she'd enjoyed Adam.

He was touching her now. Stroking her hair. She held carefully still when she felt that tentative touch, aware of a sudden yearning to turn toward him, to curl against that muscled chest and sleep cradled in his arms.

Ridiculous, of course.

She didn't need to be held to sleep. Never had.

They'd just had great sex—pretty amazing sex, actually, but just sex. She didn't need anything more from him.

Didn't need anything more from anyone.

She closed her eyes and deliberately pushed Adam's image from her mind. A battle waited ahead of her. She needed all the sleep she could get.

She pictured darkness, complete and empty in her mind. It was an old trick, one she'd perfected as a child when the sounds from the room next door grew too loud and she had to shut them out to sleep.

To stay sane.

Darkness. Always the darkness.

She pictured the darkness closing around her. Shielding her.

Darkness.

Silence.

Her breath began to slow. Her body to relax.

She went into the darkness.

"Bitch!"

At first, Maya thought she was dreaming. Or remembering. Sometimes the dreams and the memories got all twisted together.

Luckily, she didn't dream much.

Just saw her blessed darkness.

"I'll fucking kill you!" A man's voice. Screaming with rage.

A loud crash sounded and a woman began to cry, harsh, gulping sobs.

Memory.

She'd hoped that being a vampire would have at least come with the perk of uninterrupted sleep. In all the movies, Dracula climbed into his coffin, closed his eyes—and wham— the guy pretty much died until sunset.

Maya figured you didn't have to battle nightmares and memories if you were dead during the day.

Unfortunately for her, a vampire's day sleep was all too normal.

She couldn't hide from her past while she slept.

Dammit.

"*No, Chuck, don't! I-I'm sorry!*" A woman's voice. Thick with a southern accent and shaking with fear.

What the hell?

Maya's eyes flew open.

Her mother didn't have a southern accent. She'd been born and bred on the streets of L.A.

A thud shook the wall behind her, sending a tremble through the bed.

"*No, please!*"

"Fucking bitch!"

Breaking glass. A scream.

Not a dream.

Not a memory.

Maya jerked up in bed, glanced to the right. A faint imprint on the mattress was the only sign of Adam's presence.

Where the hell had he gone?

"You'll be sorry for playin' me, Rosie."

A whimper, barely discernable through the thin walls.

She grabbed her clothes. Jerked on the jeans and shirt, didn't even bother with shoes. The asshole was hurting the woman, and if she didn't stop him—

A woman lying twisted on the floor. Mouth bloody. Bruises around her eyes—eyes that stared up at nothing.

Damn memories. She *hated* them.

She ran for the door, yanked it open, and immediately had her eyes flooded with blinding light.

Figured. The sun would still be high and she'd be weak as hell.

Another scream.

Maya pounded on room 206, slamming her fist hard against the door. "Open up!"

Silence.

Her fist thudded into the door. "I said," she snarled, "open this damn door!"

The door was jerked open. A big, fat, bull of a man with a pug nose, beady brown eyes, and a thick bald head glared down at her. "What the fuck do you want?"

Maya drew in a deep breath. "I'm trying to sleep next door, and the fact that you're trying to beat your woman to death is keeping me awake." Her fingers clenched into fists as she prepared herself for a fight. Without her vampire enhancements, she was going to have to do this the old-fashioned way.

Stupid sun. Why couldn't it just set already so she could give this guy the ass-whipping he so desperately deserved?

His eyes raked over her, lingering on her breasts and hips. He licked his lips and damn if a smug smile didn't stretch across his face, revealing a missing front tooth. "You're a pretty little thing, aren't you? Wanna come inside and play with old Chuck?"

Why were the bullies always the biggest idiots in the world? "Chuck, I don't think you're going to like the way I play." Oh, she could almost guarantee it. "Now why don't you step aside and let the woman come out." If she was even still alive. The guy's knuckles were bruised and she could smell the blood on his hands, literally.

"Rosie don't wanna come out, bitch." He put one of his beefy hands on her chest and shoved her back, hard. "Now go mind your own fuckin' business!"

"Mama?" A child's voice. High-pitched, desperate with fear.

Oh, hell, no. The bastard had a kid in there.

And blood on his hands.

She stepped forward, still feeling the imprint of his hand on her chest. A big guy like that—she didn't even want to think about what he could do to a kid. "Let me see the woman *and* the child." She wasn't leaving until—

He tried to slam the door, but she had her foot in the doorway and the old wooden door just flew back.

"Wrong move," Maya whispered and rammed the bald badass back as she forced her way fully into the room.

Chapter 6

The door to room 204 was open. *Shit*. Adam glanced up at the sky, saw the sun sitting bright and heavy between the clouds.

Maya wasn't in the room anymore. He knew it without having to take a step inside, but her scent lingered around him—actually, it was—

"*I told you not to fucking touch me again!*" Maya's voice, filled with fury, and coming from the room next door.

Adam dropped his food. He didn't stop at the closed door, just kicked it in—and then drew up short at the sight before him.

Maya had a man, a human, shoved up against the wall. The fingers of her right hand were wrapped around his beefy throat. In her left hand, she held a broken beer bottle—and that bottle was currently pushed up against the guy's side.

"You don't touch me, you don't touch Rosie," Maya continued, her voice hard and mean. She hadn't so much as glanced over at the sound of the door shattering beneath his fists. "And you sure as hell *never* touch that kid, got it?" The jagged edges of the bottle cut into his stomach.

Rosie? Adam's gaze darted around the room. Found a thin woman with bright red hair and a face stained with bruises huddled in the corner. The woman's skirt fluttered, just a bit, and Adam saw the bright eye of a child peeking from behind her.

"You're gonna walk out of here—and you're gonna keep walking, *Chuck*. You're never gonna bother Rosie or her kid again—"

"Fucking whore!" He spat. "Just like *you*." He tried to lunge forward, but Maya caught him and slammed him back against the wall.

Adam frowned. The guy was big, too big for her to be handling during the day. He stepped toward her, then caught a glimpse of fang.

"I'm not a whore," Maya murmured, bringing her face in close to the man's. "I'm something much, much worse." Her lips were parted. Her teeth bared.

Blood began to trickle from the guy's neck—where her claws had buried themselves deep in his flesh.

The guy whimpered.

Maya stood on her toes and licked away a rivulet of blood. "I've got your taste now, Chuck," she said, "so I can find you, anywhere, anytime." The beer bottle fell to the floor. "And I won't need glass to kill you if I come hunting." Her teeth snapped together. "I'll rip you apart with teeth and claws."

The guy, Chuck, had turned white. "You're some . . . kinda devil."

She laughed at that. "Yeah, and I've come to take you to hell."

He started to shake then.

Maya released him, but kept her eyes glued to his. "Get out before I kill you."

Adam didn't doubt that she would. There was something different about her at that moment. A rage was in her—one he hadn't seen before.

The human ran from the room, leaving drops of blood on the floor to mark his wake.

Maya turned to him then, finally acknowledging his presence. "Give me a minute, Slick." There were lines of tension around her mouth.

He nodded, prepared to watch and wait.

Slowly, Maya walked toward the woman and child. She studied the woman first, then said, "Where are you from, Rosie?"

"B-Barlow, A-Alabama." Rosie stared at the floor while big, fat teardrops rained down her cheeks.

Maya crouched in front of her and held out her hand. "And who are you?" she asked the black-haired child who peered around his mama's skirt with big, wide eyes.

"Jake." A faint whisper.

But Adam heard it, and Maya's equally soft reply.

"It's good to meet you, Jake." She still held out her hand. After a minute, two, the little boy's fingers lifted to touch her.

Rosie gasped then and jerked the boy back. "Don't you be hurtin' him!"

Maya glanced up at her. "I won't."

Rosie swallowed. "You gonna . . . hurt me?"

From the looks of things, Adam thought the woman had been hurt enough.

Maya stood, swayed just the faintest bit. "Not if you do what I say."

Her eyes doubling in size, Rosie nodded.

"I want you to take Jake and get the hell out of town. I want you to go back home to Barlow."

The tears fell faster as Rosie's head bobbed in quick agreement.

"Good."

Maya moved toward him.

"I-I'm not a-a whore." Rosie's chin was lifted, her shoulders struggling to straighten.

Maya didn't glance back at her. "I know."

"You—you're not a devil, a monster, either—are you?"

Now she did look back and Adam wished that he could have seen her expression as she said, "Sorry, Rosie, but I'm both."

She didn't speak until they were back in room 204 and the door was firmly shut behind them. Her shoulders sagged and her feet shuffled slowly across the floor.

"Hate assholes like that," she muttered heading for the bed. "Think they can do anything they want to a woman."

She turned toward him, her chin raised, and he caught sight of the faint blue bruise along her jaw.

The bastard had hit her.

He reached for her, but she was already turning away from him. "Had to watch jerks like that with my mom. So many fucking bruises."

Like the one she now wore?

"Wasn't gonna let another woman die, not just gonna stand around and let it happen again."

She stood before the bed, hands clenched into fists at her sides.

"Another woman?"

Her back was stiff, her voice gruff as she said, "My mother."

Damn. No wonder she'd run to the other room when she heard old Chuck threatening the woman.

She climbed into the bed, fully dressed, and pulled the covers up to her chin. She met his stare with a glare. "I'm not talking about this, about her. Not now, not later."

Stubborn vampire. He bit back the questions that sprang to his lips and managed a nod.

A heavy sigh slipped past her lips. "I'm not like her," she whispered and her eyelids began to flicker. "Never was."

He sat on the edge of the bed and watched in silence until her breathing smoothed out and sleep claimed her again.

After a moment, he brushed the hair from her face. "You lied to me," he whispered, and realized that it shouldn't change anything. *It shouldn't.* "You helped that woman, that kid."

I'm not a helper, Slick.

Bullshit.

There was more to Maya than just the monster she carried. A hell of a lot more.

Just as there was more to him.

* * *

"You lied to me."

Tim Largent jerked awake at the angry snarl, blinking the sleep from his eyes and gazing around his office in dazed confusion.

He'd fallen asleep on the couch after a rather enjoyable, if tame, bout of sex with—Karen? Michelle?

He just couldn't remember—

"I don't take well to liars."

Tim swallowed, rising slowly to his feet. He realized that Karen and Michelle didn't really matter right then.

The thing that mattered—it, *he* would be the giant wolf shifter standing in his doorway.

Lucas Simone snapped his fingers and four other men walked into the room. "Neither does my pack."

Fear began to ice Tim's veins. The packs—they were vicious. They'd been known to rip men *and* demons apart.

"I-I didn't lie to you," he managed, putting the heavy desk between them. Shit, where were his bodyguards when he needed them?

One of Lucas's men dropped a small, dented, black box-like object onto the desk.

Tim got a really, really bad feeling in the pit of his gut. "What's that?" But he already knew.

GPS. The tracking box.

"Funny thing," Lucas murmured. "We found that car you told us about, but there was no sign of the vampire or her companion."

His mouth went desert dry. "She was going to Mexico, I told you—"

"The coyotes have been looking for her, guarding the border." Tim knew the coyote shifters had long since taken over Mexico. "But they haven't so much as caught a whiff of her scent."

The lying bitch. "Maya set me up." How had she known what he was planning? *How?*

Lucas rubbed the tattered edge of his right ear. "Or you set us up." He jerked his thumb toward the door and a young, dark-haired shifter hurried to seal the room. "Something you should know about me," he said, and his fingernails began to lengthen into claws. "I get angry—*real angry*—when some asshole tries to play me for a fool." His claws raked across the desk, leaving deep grooves in the wood.

Tim was very much afraid those claws would soon be used on something softer than the wood. He swallowed. "I'll give the money back." He didn't need it, not really, and he had the cash in the office, right there in his safe.

A smile curved the alpha's thin lips. "Oh, you'll most definitely give it back."

His hands slick with sweat, Tim turned to the wall safe, fumbled with the dial, and managed to open the lock. He tossed the still-bagged money to Lucas. "Take it, and get the hell out of here."

The shifter didn't look at the money as he caught the bag. His stare was on Tim, and his teeth were sharpening. "Not quite ready to leave yet."

Tim's gaze darted to the circle of wolf shifters closing in on him. "Wh-what do you want?"

The pack leader's eyes were colder than death as he said, "Our pound of flesh. Demon flesh."

The pack began to growl in hungry anticipation.

He woke her an hour before sunset. They didn't speak about the incident in room 206. Not then.

Before they left the room, Maya used one of the disposable cell phones she'd picked up to call L.A.—to check in on Sean again.

He was awake, but not making much sense. She promised to call and check in with him again later.

Adam drove the SUV, following her directions to Red Rock Canyon. The sun's rays looked like streaks of fire, blazing across the horizon.

Streaks of fire.

Or streaks of blood.

The vampires had long since claimed the canyon as part of their territory. Humans didn't realize it, but tunnels criss-crossed the canyon. Hidden deep in the ground and stone, the vampires had created a near-impenetrable lair.

Blood Rock, that's what they called it. Maya had heard whispers about the canyon before. She'd overheard tales in feeding rooms about the dark deeds committed beneath the heavy stones.

The caverns were said to be lined with skeletons.

The way Maya figured it, she was about to find out if all the gossip was true.

And, with any luck, find the girl.

They stopped a few miles from the canyon. Maya climbed from the SUV, her eyes squinting against the sun's fading rays.

"You all right?" Adam asked, moving almost soundlessly to her side.

The sun had already half-settled beneath the horizon. She managed a nod. "Getting better every minute." And she was. Her strength was returning. Her power. She hated the curse of the sun. She couldn't stand being so weak. So . . . human.

They started trekking through the desert, moving quickly, but quietly. She'd already warned Adam that the vamps could have human guards stationed in the area.

She wasn't the only one of her kind to use a day watcher.

As they traveled, the sun inched even farther below the horizon. Maya opened her senses fully, straining to hear every sound in the desert and to catch any unusual scent.

But so far, she didn't hear or smell anything out of the ordinary.

And that fact had her body tensing.

The twisted, thrusting sight of Red Rock Canyon soon greeted her. The Aztec sandstone gleamed a blood red in the light of the setting sun.

Blood Rock.

Her gaze scanned the area.

No sign of vamps. Or humans.

The hair at her nape began to tingle. "Something's off," she whispered. "There should be guards here." But the place looked completely deserted.

Maya drew her weapon, motioned for Adam to do the same. She wasn't going to take any chances. They'd find the entrance to the tunnels, grab the girl, and then run like hell.

That was her current plan, anyway.

She crept past a large outcropping of rocks. Burnished red. Weathered from time.

Adam eased behind her, but he stopped, his body stiffening. The sound of his accelerating heartbeat reached her ears.

She glanced back at him, found him staring at the rocks, a frown between his eyes. "Adam?"

He lifted his gun. Pointed it straight at the rocks. "I heard . . . something."

Was he crazy?

His gaze flashed toward hers. "We're surrounded, Maya."

What was he talking about? Her gaze searched the area, found only the hard rocks. She still didn't smell anyone, didn't hear—

Adam fired his weapon, and the bullet plunged into . . . a man. A man as red as the rock—a man who seemed to appear from nowhere, a snarl on his face and his arms raised in fury.

Shit. Understanding dawned too late as a chorus of screams erupted from the rocks. *Chameleons.* Beings who could change their skin and hair color and blend perfectly with their environments, even adapting their scents to match the—

Two red chameleons sprang at her. Maya fired fast with her gun, catching one in the shoulder, then delivering a hard kick to take the other one down.

"Hell, Adam, we . . ." Her words ended in a grunt as Maya was grabbed from behind by a pair of icy cold hands.

Not another one.

Just how many were out there?

Dammit! These bastards were reputed to be so cold-blooded they could even nearly suppress their own heart-beats.

Even with enhanced senses, it was all but impossible to pick up a chameleon's presence. Couldn't see them, couldn't smell them, and usually couldn't hear them.

She jabbed her elbow into the jerk's ribs. He grunted, and his hold on her tightened. Oh, hell, but he was strong.

Good thing she was a hell of a lot stronger. Maya twisted her body, spun around fast, and slashed her lengthening claws down his side. His blood spilled out—red, slightly darker than his flesh. He swiped at her with a fist, but she ducked the blow. Her hands shot out, caught him in an unbreakable grip, then, with a hard toss, she threw the chameleon against the rocks.

His head cracked against the stone with a sickening thud.

Maya whirled back around. The guy she'd just shot stared up at her with bulging red eyes. Then—*shit*—one eye rotated to check on his companion while the other stayed locked on her.

That was just weird. Maya slammed her gun down onto the side of his head, knocking him out and effectively closing both eyes.

The chameleon who had attacked Adam now lay on the ground, blood dripping from his side, a faint groan slipping past his lips.

She stalked toward Adam, her gun swinging in an arc to-ward the rocks. "Are there more of them?" She still didn't know how he'd realized the chameleons were around them, and she wasn't about to go looking a gift horse in the mouth. Not at that particular moment, anyway.

He shook his head. "I don't think so."

She would have preferred a resounding no, but Maya fig-ured she'd take what she could get. She grunted as she stepped over one of the prone bodies. "Guess the vamps up here have upgraded on their day watchers." Smart. Very smart.

But not smart enough.

Her gaze drifted over the rocks. She noticed a section that

was a shade lighter than the surrounding red. "There." Maya pushed against the slight indention on the hard surface of the stone.

The damn thing didn't budge.

She hated the sun.

Adam stepped beside her. Put his hands next to hers.

"On three," she muttered. "One, two, th . . ."

The rock slid inward with a groan. The corridor it revealed was pitch-black and reeked of death and decay.

They'd found the lair.

Now if they could just find the girl. "Stay behind me, Slick," she ordered, stepping into the darkness without a single hesitation. "If things go to shit, run like crazy and don't look back."

Maya wasn't sure what they'd find hidden in those tunnels, but she couldn't rule out the chance that she might not make it out.

Life had always been a gamble. So was death.

She heard the whimpers first. Slow, pain-filled cries in the dark.

Don't let that be the kid.

Adam tried to shove past her. Maya caught his arm in a steely grip. *Ah, there's the full strength. The sun must've finally set.* "Take it easy," she whispered. "We don't know what's waiting for us."

The tunnel they were in was a tall, thin corridor. Maya could see easily in the darkness and she carefully avoided stepping on the human bones that littered the floor.

So that part of the tale had been true.

Up ahead, the tunnel branched in two directions. Maya hesitated, trying to catch the scents from both the left and the right.

The whimpers were coming from the left, and she caught the faintest trace of perfume. A light, sweet scent. *Human.*

To the right, well, she didn't hear or smell a damn thing but death from the right tunnel branch.

So she stepped to the left. Crept forward, her gun ready, her heart racing.

She saw a faint light first. A flickering, pale light.

The cries were growing weaker. Not a good sign. There was an old door up ahead, the hinges literally drilled into the rock.

The human was behind that door, and unless Maya missed her guess, the human was dying.

Maya pulled in a deep breath and kicked open the door.

Her gaze swept the room, searching the shadows for any threat, but there was only one person in the cavernous room. One woman.

The blonde lay on the floor, her body curled in a fetal position. Maya knelt beside her, touched the woman's shoulder.

Ice cold.

The woman's face was turned away from her and Maya could hear the wheezing of her lungs as she fought to breathe.

It would be a very short battle.

Gently, Maya rolled the woman over, then flinched at the sight of the poor human.

Scratches lined her face, and bite marks ravaged her neck. Her right arm—damn, the flesh looked as if it had been burned in a fire, red, angry, with boils and blisters marring the length from wrist to shoulder.

But that wasn't the worst wound. No, the worst was the knife wound in her chest. The wound was deep. Too deep. Her blood soaked her clothes.

Maya stroked her face, tried to soothe the pitiful cries.

"She knows where Cammie is." Adam's voice. Cold. Hard.

What the hell? Didn't he see that the woman was dying?

"Ask her," he demanded. "Ask her about the girl."

She'd ask, but Maya doubted she'd get an answer. "I need to—"

The woman's eyes jerked open. Pale blue. "I'm . . . gonna . . . ch-change . . ."

"What?"

"B-be . . . strong . . . get . . . b-blood . . ."

Maya stared down at the woman's body, hoping she was misunderstanding. "A girl," she said, trying to keep the woman's attention. "Was there a little girl here?"

The blue eyes narrowed a moment. The cracked lips twisted into a sneer. "B-bitch . . . b-burned . . . me . . . just . . . wanted . . . taste . . ."

A taste? But the woman wasn't a vampire, not yet anyway. Maya gently touched her bleeding mouth, parting the lips.

Filed teeth. Razor sharp.

Not natural vampire canines. They were too small for that—and the edges were a bit jagged.

The woman dying before her had filed her own teeth to look like a vampire.

And, apparently, she'd tried to drink from a child.

"M-mon . . . ster . . . changed . . . b-burned . . ."

Cammie had caused the burns on her arm? The room was lit with candles, so a mild burn, yeah, maybe she could understand that, but how had the girl—

"D-deserves . . . what . . . sh-she'll . . . get . . ."

A growl rumbled behind her.

"And what will she get?" Maya asked softly. There was something in those blue eyes, something blazing brightly even as the woman faced death.

Insanity.

"Heart . . . r-ripped . . . out . . ." The battered lips widened into a bigger smile. Blood slipped down her chin. "D-drink . . . b-blood . . . for . . . Mas . . . ter . . ."

Yeah, she'd been afraid of that.

Maya's fingers closed over the hilt of the knife. The woman's heart was stuttering. If she pulled out the knife, maybe—

Icy fingers closed over her hand. "Ch-change . . . me."

The woman had lost too much blood. If Maya drank from her—and she'd have to drink before she gave the woman her own blood—the woman with the pale eyes would die instantly.

Maya figured that's exactly what the vamps who'd left her

behind had been counting on. "I-I can't." Even if she could, this woman—she was—

"P-promised! I . . . k-killed . . . many . . . f-for . . . them . . . b-brought . . . food . . ." Her lashes were closing. The wheezing in her chest easing.

"Yeah, I bet you did." And she'd held a kid captive in this hole in the earth.

A Lure. She'd bet her undead life on it. The blonde had been used as a Lure by the vamps. She'd probably brought in her friends, maybe even family first for them to drink from, and then she'd started luring strangers, humans, into the den.

Had she been sane then? At the start?

Then slowly lost her reason as she witnessed the killings? As she participated in the slaughters?

What a damn shame. All because she'd bought into the promise of living forever.

The woman's heart stopped, ended on one final, faint beat. Her chest stilled.

Maya released the hilt of the knife. She brushed a tear from the woman's face and rose—only to find Adam glaring down at the dead body.

"She knew their plans," he muttered. "That's why they killed her."

A definite possibility. Or maybe they'd just decided their Lure wasn't useful once she'd tried to attack their special prey. Maya began pacing around the room, trying to find any clue—

"She hurt Cammie."

Her gaze met his. Absolute certainty laced his words. "Looks to me like Cammie got a lick in, too." Damn, but those burns were bad. "Wanna tell me about that?"

His lips thinned.

"Didn't think so." No candle had done that. What was the girl? One of those Igniters she'd heard about? A human born with the power to control fire?

She was getting damn tired of Adam not dealing straight

with her. If he expected her to save the girl, he needed to be honest. "Look, Slick," she began.

"*Help!*" A high-pitched, desperate cry. A child's voice, echoing through the tunnels.

Adam spun around, ran from the room.

Shit. "Adam, wait for me!" She lunged forward—

And two chameleons sprang from their cover near the entrance.

They grabbed her, wrestling her to the ground. She fought, kicking, punching.

She had to get out of there, had to go after Adam.

Nothing had better happen to him.

Snarling, she twisted beneath the chameleons and drove her fist straight into the biggest one's nose.

Cammie's voice. The cry for help resonated from deep in the tunnels, sounding strangely distorted—but there was no mistaking it *was* Cammie.

Hold, on, baby. I'm coming.

He ran as fast as he could, not even trying to conceal his presence. He wanted the bastards to know he was coming.

His heart raced as he thundered through the darkness. He was so close to her now, so close.

A faint light shone from up ahead. A trickling glow of illumination, spilling from beneath a wooden door—just like the door of the last room, the door that had smelled of death.

Adam shoved open the door, chest heaving. "Cammie!"

A slow laugh came from behind him. Too late, Adam caught the stench of rotting flesh and decay.

Vampire.

He tried to spin around, but the creature jumped on him from behind, tearing his flesh with his fangs and sinking his teeth deep into Adam's throat.

The fierce agony whipped through him. *This* was what he'd expected when Maya bit him. The tearing. The slashing of flesh and the white-hot pain.

The vamp drank greedily, gulping down his blood.

Not like Maya's bite. Maya.

He'd left her in the tunnel. She was alone, she—

"No!" Adam lunged forward, managing to break free of the bastard's hold. The vampire's teeth sliced across his flesh. Blood dripped onto the ground.

Another rumble of laughter.

Adam turned to face the vampire, uncaring of the blood that trickled down his neck. "Where's Cammie?"

The vampire, a tall, thin man who looked like he was about thirty years old—and he probably *had* been thirty when he'd been turned—narrowed his black eyes. "Getting ready for Master Nassor." He licked his lips, muttered, "I thought you'd taste better. Considering what you are."

"What I am . . ." He grunted. "I'm the guy who's about to kill you in the next four seconds unless you tell me *where the hell my niece is!*"

The vampire took a step back. Another. A smile curved his lips, one that never flickered in his soulless stare. "You're not the one who is going to do the killing."

"And you actually think you can kill me?" Adam snarled. "I've been on this earth far longer than you can imagine, vampire. And I'm a hell of a lot stronger."

"But not invulnerable." Another low, sinister laugh. Another slow step back. "Even you can die, Brody."

Where was Maya? Adam had thought she'd left the last chamber right on his heels.

A new fear began to stir in his heart.

Separated. The vampires had separated them. An old ploy, all the better for an attack.

Adam took a deep breath and tried to calm his racing heart. He needed to focus. To be ready for the vampire's next move.

But he'd heard Cammie's voice. He knew it had been her. His gaze shot around the room. Landed on a still mound of clothing, blankets.

Every drop of saliva in his mouth dried away when he caught sight of Cammie's green shirt. The shirt she'd been wearing when she vanished.

"Go on," the vampire urged. "You might be surprised at what you find."

He took another look at the mound. He didn't smell Cammie, even though her shirt was right there. But scents could be cloaked. He, of all people, knew that.

His nostrils twitched as the odors of blood and death swirled around him.

The mound—it was big. Too big?

He took a step forward.

"Go on . . ."

He snarled at the vampire, but found he was nearly running for the mound. Swiping through the clothes and blankets, hoping that he wouldn't find Cammie's broken body, that he wouldn't see—

A tape recorder.

Her voice had seemed distorted.

Trap.

He was such a fucking idiot.

Adam spun around.

The vampire stood just beyond the wooden door.

He smiled. Then waved. "Good-bye."

An explosion rocked the room, shaking the floor, sending the heavy rocks that composed the ceiling and the walls tumbling right down on him.

The first chunk of rock hit him hard, catching Adam on the back of the head and sending him falling, facefirst, onto the floor. A roar filled the room as the ceiling gave way, the heavy sandstone breaking apart and plummeting down on him.

The rocks hit him, one after the other, harder, slamming into him, covering his body.

He tried to move, to get up—to run. But the rocks just kept falling, burying him in the rubble.

The candlelight had sputtered out, destroyed by the cave-in.

Adam couldn't feel his back anymore, or his legs, his arms. The rocks covered him, every inch.

He closed his eyes, struggling for breath.

Maya.

An explosion shook the tunnel. Maya swayed at the impact, grabbing the wall.

What the hell?

The answer came immediately. Booby trap. The vampires must have wired the place for protection.

Well, shit. Dumbass move on their part—the tourists really wouldn't be able to overlook an *explosion.*

She glanced back at the room she'd just left. The two chameleons were on the floor, unconscious, but alive. They'd slowed her down, though, and she didn't know how to find Adam and—

Maya.

For just a moment, she could hear his voice so clearly in her mind.

And she could hear the echo of pain.

Blinding agony, crushing him, all around—burying him alive—

Then, in an instant, their sudden connection was severed.

"Adam!" She screamed his name, not really caring if anyone—vamp, chameleon, human, whatever—heard her. Adam was in trouble.

She began running, going straight ahead, following the reverberations she felt—the shaking walls, the tumbling rocks. She knew it was crazy to run toward the cave-in, but—

But maybe she was crazy, because she was convinced that Adam was in there—that he'd been hurt.

Dust hit her. A thick rising cloud of dirt and dust. She swiped her hand through it, hurried forward. She caught the faint scent of rotting flesh, ignored the sudden prickling of her nape that told her a vamp was nearby.

Adam needed her.

It would be the vamp's lucky night—if he was smart and

stayed the hell out of her way, he'd get out of there alive, or well, undead.

But if he got in her way . . .

She found the room. Saw the horrible, thick pile of rocks, and knew, *knew* that Adam was beneath the rubble.

Their blood link was strong, she realized. She'd heard his cry, found him through the maze of darkness.

Damn strong.

Her nails lengthened into claws.

She couldn't hear his heartbeat. Couldn't hear him breathing.

Because he wasn't.

No. "Adam." His name was a whisper on her lips. He couldn't be dead. Not so fast.

"Dammit, I told you to wait for me." So many rocks. So much weight. If he were under there, he would have been crushed beyond recognition. At the very least—

Buried alive.

She climbed over the bigger rocks, crawling and fighting her way to the back of the room.

That was where the scent of blood was strongest.

Don't be dead. Dammit, Adam, hold on! The cry was in her mind, and soon, blood was streaming down her hands.

But Maya didn't stop. She pulled the rocks away, one at a time, scratched through the chunks of sandstone, dug through the rock and grime.

Hold on.

Her claws broke. Her fingertips ripped open.

But she didn't stop.

Even though she was very, very afraid of what she'd find at the bottom of that pile.

Chapter 7

The sun shone down on him, and he squinted, trying to focus against the light.

Something hard and tight was around his ribs, squeezing the breath from him.

Adam moaned, jerked, tried to fight the pressure, but the hold just tightened.

"Dammit! Would you stop?" A woman's voice. Annoyed, but . . . weak. *Maya.*

She was okay. She'd made it out of the caverns. He opened his mouth, wanting to talk to her, but a coughing fit sent spasms through his body.

"Shit, Slick, it's hard enough moving you in this damn sunlight without you fighting me, *now stop struggling!*"

But he wasn't struggling, not really. He just couldn't breathe and every part of his body hurt.

Actually, his legs didn't hurt.

He couldn't feel them.

But he knew they were dragging against the ground. He could hear the grind of his shoes on the hard earth.

Maya's hands were around him, Adam realized. His head cradled against her chest.

He would have enjoyed that, would have liked the press of her flesh cushioning his head—but he just hurt too fucking much.

Time seemed to stop as she pulled him through the desert.

He shut his eyes, trying to block out the sun. Feeling was starting to return to his legs, sharp pinpricks that quickly turned into knife points of agony.

Beep. Beep. Beep.

What was that sound? He tried to open his eyes again but found that his lashes were too heavy.

Then his body was shoved, lifted, and pushed back against something soft. A cushion?

The soft surface moved, easing back so that he was reclining.

Not a cushion, a car seat. *They were in the SUV.*

But they should have been in the tunnels, finding Cammie. *Cammie.*

"I need you to listen to me, Slick."

He tried to turn his head toward her voice. Tried and failed.

"I don't know how the hell you're still breathing, but I'm gonna get you someplace safe, okay?"

No, they couldn't leave yet. Not without Cammie.

"Just hold on for me. Just—"

"C-Cam . . ." It was all he could manage. The effort left him shaking with exhaustion.

Silence. Then, "She wasn't there. They'd already taken her."

He remembered hearing her voice, calling for help. Adam tried to shake his head. They couldn't leave, not without her.

"Dammit!" The curse exploded from her. "Fine. Hell. You just better not die on me, you got that?"

A door slammed.

Silence.

Adam stopped fighting the agony that racked his body.

Don't die.

Not a promise he could make right then.

Her eyes were tearing. No, watering. From the sun. Had to be from the sun.

How was the man still alive?

And how much longer would he stay that way?

Maya spared a glance for her hands as she hurried back over the rough terrain. At least six of her fingers were broken. Dried blood coated her hands, from fingertip to wrist.

But she'd gotten him out.

As much as she wanted to run like hell from Blood Rock and the heat of the sun, Adam wasn't going to let her leave yet.

Not without Cammie.

Maya knew Cammie was long gone. She'd found the tape recorder's broken remains under Adam's body. One look, and she'd known how the vamps set the trap for Adam.

No, Cammie wasn't in the tunnels.

But maybe she'd find someone else who could help them— and she didn't really care if that help was given willingly or not.

"Dammit, settle down in there!" Maya's voice. "I'm not going to hurt you!"

Adam jerked at the shout, then heard her snarl, "Yet."

He didn't understand. Why would Maya be threatening to hurt him?

Were they still in the tunnels? No, the car—

"It's okay, Adam." Her voice was softer now, almost soothing. That didn't make a bit of sense. When had Maya ever been soothing? Wild. Hot. Sexy. And very often dangerous. But soothing?

Not his Maya.

"We're safe, now. You hear me? Safe."

A warm, soft cloth had been pulled over his chest.

He was laying down, Adam realized. Not in the car: he didn't feel the cushions of the seat beneath him. No, this seemed more like—

"You're in bed, back at the motel," she said, almost as if she'd sensed his thoughts. Maybe she had. They were linked and—

Her fingertips stroked his cheeks, felt strangely rough against his skin. "Can you hear me?"

He tried to nod, but found he couldn't move his head. Fear rose in his throat.

"Adam?" A whisper. "Adam! *Adam!*" More demanding now. And she had fear in her voice. A fear to match his.

Since when was Maya afraid of anything?

"I need you to open your eyes. Can you do that for me? Please, Adam, just open your eyes—for a minute, okay? Let me know that you're still in there."

He was there. Right beside her. He could hear every word she said. Could feel her body so close to his. He tried to open his eyes, struggled.

Her breath caught. "Adam?"

His lashes fluttered.

"That's it, that's . . ."

He couldn't get them to open, and the effort had left him feeling hollowed out.

"You can hear me." Absolute certainly now. "Then listen up, Slick."

Slick. He'd rather liked it when she called him Adam.

"Time's running out. You're hurt bad. Real bad."

Yeah, he'd managed to work that one out for himself.

"You're not going to make it," she said softly and her fingertips rasped across his brow. "I don't even know how you're still alive now."

She was telling him—No! He wasn't dying. He—

"There's a chance, a very, very small chance . . ." She swallowed and he could hear the painful click perfectly. "Th-that I can change you."

Change him. Turn him into a vampire.

"You've lost a lot of blood," she murmured, "and the damage—it's so bad that I-I'm not sure you'll survive long enough for the exchange." She drew in a deep breath. "But it's your only chance."

No. He couldn't change. It wasn't possible for him.

"It's your choice." Her breath feathered over him and he knew she'd leaned in close. "I-I won't make this decision for you—so I need some kind of sign here, Adam. I need to know, need to see what you want me to do."

He understood what she was saying, and what she wasn't. Maya wouldn't take the option of dying away from him, as it had been taken from her.

"Give me a sign," she said, "and make it fast."

But he couldn't move. Couldn't even lift his lashes. He didn't want to die and he sure as hell didn't want to transform—becoming a vampire wasn't an option for him.

He tried to talk. Vaguely, he remembered saying something to her before, but now, all he managed was a faint moan and a choked gurgle.

"Adam!" Maya wiped his lips and he understood the moisture he felt sliding down his chin was his own blood.

Not a good sign.

Shit.

"You're dying. There isn't any time left."

He wanted to look at her. To see her face once more and to find out if she was really crying, because it sure sounded like she was.

The great Maya Black. Crying over someone like him.

"Choose, Adam. Show me something . . . *choose!*"

Her words rumbled against his right ear. Then her mouth moved down, pressed against his throat and he felt the edge of her teeth.

Choose.

There was no choice.

Gathering every bit of strength he had, Adam managed to jerk away from her, just one tiny inch.

Maya lifted her head. Gazed at his battered face.

Adam.

He was choosing death.

Her hands clenched into fists and the tears tracked down her cheeks.

Chapter 8

Maya was staring at him.

Adam frowned, pushing his body up slowly from the soft mattress.

She stood at the foot of the bed, her hands clenched at her sides, a frown pulling her brows low.

Not staring. *Glaring* at him.

He swallowed. His throat felt dust dry and hurt like a bitch.

"Water's on the table." Her voice was hard.

Adam glanced to the right. Saw a half-full pitcher of water.

A chair had been pulled to the edge of the bed. Red-stained cloths littered the floor.

He lifted his hand for the pitcher.

"Here." Maya had moved almost soundlessly. She poured the water into a cup, held it to his lips.

Adam drank greedily, the water pouring down his chin as he gulped the sweet liquid.

"Not so fast," she murmured. "Just take it easy."

He drained the glass dry. Waited for her to fill it again.

Then he noticed there were shadows under her eyes. "Have you . . . slept?"

She shrugged. "Little bit."

Sunlight trickled through the blinds. "How . . . long have I been out?" His voice was stronger.

The cup pressed against his lips. Her eye met his. "Two days."

Two days.

Three swallows and the glass was empty. "More."

For an instant, he swore her eyes heated. Then she looked away. "I-I'll go refill the pitcher."

When she stepped away, he finally found the courage to glance down at his body. He shoved the sheets away.

"You're fine." Maya had paused near the bathroom. "No cuts, no broken bones." His gaze rose and he saw her give a little shrug. "Not even so much as a bruise."

She opened the door, disappeared, and he thought he heard the faint murmur of her voice.

He glanced back at his body. She'd stripped him. Washed him. He could smell the faint scent of soap on his body and he knew that before, he'd been covered with blood and grime.

"Here." She was back by his side. Holding out the paper cup. "From the looks of you, I figure you're probably strong enough to hold it yourself."

He took the cup. His fingers brushed against hers.

A small shiver shook her body.

An answering quiver began in his groin.

Her gaze raked over him. Hot. Searching.

But he had to know. "You didn't . . . bite me again, did you?"

She licked her lips, muttered what could have been, "Don't tempt me." Maya shook her head, sending her dark mane brushing against her cheeks. "If you're trying to ask if you're a vamp, the answer is no."

He hadn't thought that he was, but it was still damned good to know. He took a long swallow from the cup, nearly draining all the water.

Maya just stared at him, a curious tenseness in her body.

"You look pretty good," she finally said softly, "for someone who should be dead."

Tipping back his head, he gulped down the last of the water and then crumpled the paper cup into a ball.

"Um, you're one to talk." The lady was undead and she'd taken his breath away from the first moment he'd seen her.

Maya grabbed his hand. Her flesh was slightly cool against his, but just that one touch had his body tightening with a sudden, fierce yearning.

"I thought you were dying on me." Something that could have been pain, but surely wasn't, lurked in her eyes.

His jaw clenched. "You dug me out." Memories were coming back to him. The falling ceiling. The pummeling rocks.

And Maya.

Her touch. Her voice. Calling to him.

Saving him.

If she hadn't pulled him out, he would have died. Pinned as he'd been, he wouldn't have been able to escape and with the constant battering pressure of the rocks on him, there would have been no chance for regeneration.

If the cave-in hadn't killed him, eventually, starvation would have.

The vamp who'd attacked him had planned well, but he obviously hadn't counted on Maya.

And, Adam realized, *he* hadn't trusted her enough.

His hand flipped over, caught hers. Linked tightly with her fingers. He stared into her bright blue gaze.

Maya Black had saved his life. She could have left him. Taken his two hundred grand and walked out of the tunnels and gone on with her life.

She just kept surprising him.

Time for trust. He owed her trust.

Time to take a risk.

He just hoped he didn't frighten her. Adam didn't want Maya to be afraid of him.

"There's something you should know," he told her, and realized that his voice had hardened to a growl. He was just so damn nervous. "Maya, I-I'm not human." *Never had been.*

Her lips thinned. One eyebrow rose. After a beat of silence, she finally murmured, "No shit, Slick."

Adam blinked. "What?"

She climbed onto the bed, eased down beside him. Kept her fingers locked with his. "I knew from the first taste that you weren't human." Her left hand lifted, traced a gentle line down his throat. "Your blood was different."

And she hadn't said anything? "Why didn't you—"

"I don't want to talk now." Her lips were close to his. "Later—later you can tell me what the hell you are."

Another hard blink.

"Right now, Adam, I just want you." Her mouth brushed over his. So soft. So easy.

So right.

"I just want you," she whispered again.

He sure as hell wanted her.

She'd seen death enough times to know what the beast looked like. The lifeless eyes of a perp. The bloodstained clothes of a victim.

The still body of a child.

Yeah, she'd seen death too many times in her life, and she'd been damn sure that she'd been seeing death steal Adam's life.

Not human. Hell, yes, she knew that. She wasn't a fucking idiot. But right then, she didn't really care *what* Adam was.

As she'd told him, she just wanted him, needed to feel his flesh against her. In her.

Needed to make damn sure this wasn't some twisted dream and that he was real.

Alive.

Because there'd been so much death in her life. Too much.

Her hand left his throat. Pressed against his lips. "You have to be quiet," she whispered. "Don't make a sound."

His brows furrowed. "What? Why?"

"Shh." They'd get to the whys later. She kissed him. A light, gentle kiss, a wet glide of her tongue past his lips.

Her legs straddled his naked hips. Her thighs pressed against his and his chest—the guy had a freaking amazing chest—pushed against her breasts.

His cock was swelling. Her hips shifted against him and

she rubbed her sex over him, hating the denim that separated her from that hard heat.

But this time, she didn't want the sex between them to be hard and fast.

Not her usual style. She wanted something . . . different.

Her tongue rubbed against his.

She'd missed his taste in the last two days.

His hands were on her now. Sliding under the edge of her T-shirt and moving up her back. Strong fingers. Warm flesh. Caressing. Stroking. Slipping around her body and cupping her breasts.

She hadn't bothered with a bra. Not much point when she'd been keeping a death vigil.

Until dawn. When the sun rose, his body had changed before her eyes. The bruises had faded. The cuts and lacerations vanished. The bones snapped back into place.

Death had disappeared from the room.

Now, she wanted to reassure herself that Adam was with her once again, completely whole.

Maya wanted to touch every inch of him.

Just to make absolutely certain.

Her lips trailed kisses over the firm line of his jaw. Sucked lightly on his throat. The temptation to bite was strong. She could almost feel his blood trickling over her tongue.

Control.

There'd be time for blood later.

"I fucking love your breasts." Adam's voice rasped.

His fingers teased her nipples. And she loved his hands.

"Taste you," he whispered. "Want your nipples in my mouth." He eased her back and jerked her shirt up. Tossed it onto the floor. Cold air swirled over her skin. Then his mouth was on her. Wet and warm. Licking and sucking her nipple and sending liquid heat straight to her groin.

She bit back the moan that sprang to her lips.

Quiet.

Her hands skimmed down his bare arms. Such strong arms. The muscles beneath his skin were corded, tight with power.

Her fingertips stroked his chest, found the hard brown nipples, and plucked.

Adam hissed out a sharp breath. "I need to be inside you. Want to fuck you so bad."

"Not yet." *Not too fast, not this time.* She pushed against him until she was sitting in his lap, chest to chest, groin to groin. "I want to touch you first." Every inch.

His hand settled on her ass. Clenched. "Don't make me wait too long." A warning.

A challenge.

A smile curved her lips as she drew her hand down the tight line of his abdomen. His body jerked beneath her touch. "Maya . . ."

"Shh. We don't want anyone to hear."

His lips closed over her throat. The edge of his teeth scored her skin. "I don't give a damn who hears."

Well, if that was the way he felt—

Her hand wedged between their bodies. Brushed against the curling thatch of black hair at the top of his thighs. "You didn't let me finish before." He'd taken her to orgasm with his mouth, turnabout would only be fair.

Besides, she wanted to savor his release on her tongue. She had a feeling it would be even sweeter than his blood. "Lay back," she ordered softly.

Adam growled, but slowly obeyed. His hair brushed against the pillow.

Her hand closed over his shaft.

The heat of his arousal nearly singed her hand.

She wanted him inside her. Thrusting, driving them both to the edge of sanity and the dark paradise of release.

Soon.

But first . . . her fist tightened and she pumped her hand up and down. Squeezing that thick length, not too hard—not too soft—but with a strong, steady pressure.

"Maya!"

He didn't care if they were overheard. Neither did she.

Up and down, she stroked. Again and again. Tightening,

releasing. His breath grew ragged. His body slickened with sweat. "Don't wanna . . . come like this . . ." he snarled. "Want in . . . side you!"

And that was what she wanted. But she hadn't touched enough yet.

She released his cock with one last, lingering stroke. He reached for her, but she slipped just out of his reach. Maya put her hands on his legs, enjoying the feel of the resilient muscle beneath her hands. Her fingertips moved over him, smoothing over his powerful thighs and down to the heels that dug into the mattress.

"*Maya.*"

She crouched between his spread thighs. His cock stretched straight into the air, the wide tip dark red and glistening with a bead of moisture. She murmured as she leaned forward, her mouth open and hungry. Her lips closed over him, greedy for that small drop.

He cursed and his fingers clenched in her hair.

Her tongue swirled over him, circling the head of his cock. Maya had known she liked the flavor of his blood, and his cum was just as good. Sweet, with a spice of tang. She sucked on his length, wanting more, *more.*

He grabbed her under the arms, pulled her up. "In . . . you." His face was red. His eyes blazed. "Not in your mouth, damn . . . tempting though it is." He swallowed and his eyes fell to the jeans she still wore. "Get out of them, and *let me in.*"

She'd wanted to savor him.

Now, she just wanted to fuck him.

Maya rolled away, darting from the bed. She needed a minute to get her control back. Just a minute . . .

Her fingers shook as she unsnapped the button at her waist and then fumbled with the zipper.

Just a minute.

The jeans hit the floor.

Her fingers caught the edge of her cotton panties.

And Adam caught her.

His hands closed over her hips, and he shoved her back against the nearby door. "Can't wait." His cock pulsed against her stomach.

Definitely healed.

Her thighs clenched.

And so did her sex as anticipation filled her.

His fingers pushed between her legs, slipped under the panties, and drove up into her core.

"Adam!" Okay, screw trying to take it slow. She wanted him inside.

"You're ready and you smell so . . . damn . . . good." His fingers withdrew, and he jerked the crotch of her panties to the side. "I need to take you, *now.*"

Her hips rocked forward.

He snarled and caught his cock in one big fist. His left hand positioned her and then that hot length drove into her.

Yes! Adam caught her legs, lifted them as he thrust his cock deep inside her.

So full.

Her legs wrapped around his hips. Her claws dug into his ass. She didn't worry about hurting him with her strength, not anymore. She knew Adam could take whatever she had to give.

Her back rapped against the door as he plunged into her. Plunging deep and forcing that cock straight to the tip of her womb.

Her inner muscles closed over him eagerly, gripping his shaft, holding tight as he thrust.

His fingers dug into her hips and he yanked her away from the door. "Deeper." She could barely understand him. Didn't really care what he was saying.

His cock slipped over her clit and she moaned.

"In . . . deeper." They fell onto the bed. His cock drove balls-deep inside her. Again, again.

She thrashed beneath him, fighting for the release that was just out of reach.

But so temptingly close.

He raised her legs, pushing her thighs against his shoulders, and shoved deep.

The bed rocked beneath them. Squeaked.

She clenched her teeth, turned her head away from him, and fought the sudden, desperate urge to bite.

His shaft withdrew, plunged. His rhythm was fast, hard.

Perfect.

Maya's orgasm hit her. White-hot pleasure blasted through every inch of her body.

She tasted blood in her mouth, realized it was her own, that her fangs had pierced her bottom lip.

Adam shuddered against her, called her name on a long, fierce groan.

As the waves of release pulsated in her sex, Maya turned her head and pressed a kiss against his cheek.

No, definitely not human.

As if there had ever been any doubt.

"So . . ." Maya began, her voice a slow drawl, "I think it might be time we had that little talk of ours."

She was lying in bed beside him, propped up on one elbow. Her eyes were blue again, not the burning black they'd changed to during her orgasm.

And, damn, but she was something else.

His heart still pounded like a drum, and his thighs actually shook.

Sex with Maya was freaking great.

The best of his very long life.

He'd never planned to get involved with her. To care.

But he'd learned long ago that great plans often went to shit.

"Adam?" A frown narrowed her eyes.

"Give me a minute," he said and decided to tell her, quite truthfully, "I'm still trying to recover."

For a moment, one brief split second in time, she smiled.

Actually smiled at him. A real smile, not one of those sarcastic, kiss-my-ass grins she usually wore. No, this smile was different. Her face softened, changed from pretty to—

Beautiful.

Oh, shit.

But then the smile vanished, disappearing as if it had never been there, and she studied him with a slightly distant expression in her eyes. "So what are you?"

A strange conversation to have in bed. Probably not the right place. They were both also still naked, which served to make him horny as hell, but when Maya heard what he had to say, well, he doubted she'd be feeling a return of her lust.

Maybe that's why I needed her so much. I wanted one more time with her, before—

"Not a demon. Although when I caught the scent of smoke around you a few times, I thought you might be an L10."

He'd learned to mask his scent over the years, but sometimes, if he became angry enough, the beast inside overpowered even the strong chemicals in his system.

"Figured at first you were a shifter. Maybe a wolf or a bear."

Adam climbed from the bed. Rifled through the closet until he found a pair of his jeans.

"Huh." He glanced over his shoulder and saw that Maya had sat up in bed. She hadn't bothered to cover her breasts or any part of her sexy little body. With an effort he managed to look at her face.

Her head tilted slightly to the left. "Must be bad if you're jumping out of bed."

No, the move had just been a way to fight the temptation to jump *her* again.

Business first.

Pleasure, if she'd have him again, later.

"I am a shifter," he told her, pacing toward the bed. "Of a sort." *A very ancient sort.*

"Go on."

He hadn't shared this secret with many. The first had been his childhood friend Richard.

The same friend who'd tried to butcher him twelve short days later.

The second, well, that had been his intended bride, Isabella. He'd shared his secret many, many years after the bloody encounter with Richard. He'd thought of not telling her, but if the woman was planning to spend every night of her life with him, he figured she'd deserved to know.

Isabella had thrown herself from the cliffs near his home. Her body had never been recovered. He'd grieved her for years. Wished he'd kept his dark secret.

No, definitely not a good track record.

But Maya wasn't really in a position to judge. She wasn't exactly normal, either.

Yet Maya had once been human. While he—

"Look, Slick, unlike you, I didn't spend the last two days sleeping." Her mouth split open into a wide yawn, one she actually tried to cover this time. "So do you think you might could hurry this little tale of yours along?"

Screw it. "I'm a Wyvern."

Her brows drew low. "What the hell is that?"

"You . . . don't know?"

A shrug.

Well, hell. So much for being the terror of the century. "I'm a dragon," he said, voice hard.

Maya snorted. "Bullshit."

He didn't quite know how to respond to that. "I assure you," he finally managed, "I'm telling the truth."

"Prove it." One brow arched. "If you're a shifter, then shift." She waved a hand before him. "Change into a dragon."

He glanced around the room. Gauged the distance from floor to ceiling. "Not enough room in here."

"'Course not." She climbed from the bed. "'Cause that'd be just too much to ask for, huh? I mean, I've only *saved* your ass here, if you don't want to trust me with the truth about yourself—"

He grabbed her arms, pulling her close. "This is the truth."

"The stories all say your kind were wiped out a long time ago. I mean, I haven't so much as heard a whisper about a dragon shifter still being around—and, you know what, Slick? I'd think it would be pretty hard to keep something as big as a dragon secret."

Not as hard as she might expect. "You're still new to the supernatural world, Maya." A baby, really. Just five years in his realm. "Trust me on this one. You need to accept the fact that there are literally *thousands* of creatures out there that you don't hear about."

Everyone knew of the vampires and the wolf shifters, *the werewolves*. Those two just couldn't seem to keep low enough profiles. Sure, most supernaturals also knew about demons—because those guys were always going around stirring up trouble.

But the really smart beings, they stayed in the shadows, and they let the vamps and the wolves draw all the fire from the humans—in their books, their movies, even in their nightmares.

"I'm new, huh? Okay, I'll buy that. But what about you, Slick? Just how new to this game are you?"

Truth time. "I'm a little over a thousand years old."

Her eyes widened. "How is that possible? Shifters age—wolves, panthers, bears. Hell, that's the reason they're always selling out to the vamps—looking for that promised you'll-live-forever magic."

He let her arms go, stepped back. Mostly because the sight of her breasts with the tight pink nipples was really distracting him at a point when he needed to stay focused. "Could you . . . get dressed?" Hard to say. So very hard. But they needed to talk, and if she didn't cover up, he figured the talking would be stopping very, very soon and the hot sex would be starting.

She frowned at him, but marched over to her bag and pulled out a black bra and another T-shirt. As he watched, helpless to look away, she covered those touch-me breasts, slipped into a matching black pair of panties, then jerked up her discarded jeans. "Satisfied?"

He had been, but—

"You were telling me how a guy who claims to be a thousand looks like he's thirty." Her foot began to tap against the carpet. "Focus here, Slick."

He swallowed. "Wyverns are different." *Ancient blood, ancient power.* "We don't age. Every time we transform, it renews us, almost as if we're regenerating." Adam hesitated. Tricky part. "Don't get me wrong, we can die." They could also heal, *fast.* "But—"

"But like the L10s, you're just tough to kill," she finished, her gaze sliding over him.

Yeah, that was pretty much the case. Because when he was in dragon form, well, he usually just toasted his enemies. *Burned them to ash.*

"So how come you're not the big bad bastards that everyone whispers about? If Wyvers—"

"Wyverns," he corrected, jaw clenched.

"Whatever. If you're so bad, then I *should* have known your kind was still out there. Everyone should."

Well, *some* did know about him. That was why Cammie had been taken.

As for everyone knowing—that was *not* what he wanted. Adam didn't want to spend his days killing fools who came to prove how powerful they were by going up against a dragon. "Let's just say that when I change, I don't exactly leave witnesses around to spread the word about me."

Maya huffed out a hard breath. "I want to believe you. I really do, but—hell, can't you do something? Breathe some fire. Grow some scales, something?"

Yeah, he could do *something.* He paced toward her. Held out his hand, palm up. "I can't change fully here, the room is too small." And, honestly, he didn't want her to see him in his true form. Not exactly sexy.

He didn't just get sharper teeth like she did. His eyes didn't go all smoky and black and his nails didn't sharpen.

He went primal.

The monster inside roared free. His entire body transformed in a maelstrom of rage and fire.

Not a very pretty sight.

He wanted Maya to keep thinking of him as a man. A man she wanted. Not some disgusting, fire-breathing beast who smelled of death.

"Uh, yeah, I see your arm." Vague impatience filled her tone.

He almost rolled his eyes. The woman just couldn't wait for anything. "Give me a second." He lowered his lashes. Looked inside the fire dwelling in his soul.

Not letting you out of the cage. Just need a sample.

"Well, damn." A little breathless.

His eyes opened. He stared down at his arm. An arm that was covered in dark green scales. Impenetrable scales that could cut through skin and bone.

Maya lifted her hand, her fingers hesitating over him.

"No, don't—"

Too late. She touched him and blood trickled from her fingertips.

She never cried out. Just kept her bloody fingers pressed against his scales.

He found her gaze. Held it.

A slow smile curved her lips. "You feel warm."

She had no idea.

"All right, dragon." Her hand lifted.

The scales vanished. Flesh and hair returned.

"I believe you." Still holding his gaze, she murmured, "And the way I figure it, this is sure as hell gonna change up our battle plans."

Their plans? Adam blinked. The woman already had new plans worked out? "You're accepting this rather well." Better than he'd expected. *Much* better than anyone else.

A little shrug. "Well, not like I can really judge, now can I? I mean, I'm a vampire and I'm a killer. I figure that pretty much makes us even."

Not even close.

"Besides, as long as you don't get all Wyver hungry—"

"*Wyvern.*"

"—and try to eat me, I figure things will be fine."

His gaze automatically dropped to her thighs and he licked his lips. So tempting.

"The girl, Cammie—she's like you, huh?"

A nod.

"I felt different after I took your blood," she said, her voice thoughtful. "Stronger. I healed faster." Her lips twisted for a moment, not into a real smile, but rather a quirking of her mouth. "I didn't realize my new power came from dragon's blood."

"My blood, Wyvern blood, is very, very strong." Strong enough to heal a near-dead vampire. Strong enough to restore all the Born Master's powers. "My kind was hunted to near extinction in the 1500s because the vampires wanted our blood to enhance their powers."

Because his blood was twenty times more powerful than a human's.

"So if you're a vampire who was nearly staked and beheaded and you'd spent the last five years in the ground with the worms and the ants, the surefire way to get you back to normal would be—"

"To drain the blood of a dragon."

"But a big guy like you—you'd put up a fight." She turned away, began to pace the room in fast strides. "If the vamps were lucky enough to stumble onto a child of your kind . . ." She gave a hollow laugh. "They'd think they hit the motherlode."

Pretty much his thoughts.

She stopped, freezing near the foot of the bed. "That's why the woman's arm was burned. Not from the candles. *From little Cammie.*"

If the girl had been older, nothing would have been left of the woman, but he nodded.

"Got her uncle's temper, does she?"

Perhaps. For her sake, he hoped not.

"What—was her mom or her dad like you?"

"Her father."

She grunted. "You told me he was dead. Did the vampires get him, too? Jeez, no wonder you're not overly fond of my kind."

His head snapped up at that. "They're *not* your kind." They were nothing like her. "You aren't one of them."

"Uh, hate to break this to you, but as you've pointed out, I've got the fangs, the claws, the blood hunger. I am most definitely one of them."

Why did her words sound like a warning?

He swallowed back the angry words that rose to his lips. "Her father—killed himself after her mother died."

He expected her sympathy. Instead, he got—

"What the hell? You mean the guy just kissed his life goodbye and left the kid on her own?" She didn't wait for his answer. Just started pacing again, muttering about selfish bastards under her breath.

Anger began to boil in his gut. Jon had loved Ada. Loved her with every fiber of his being.

Loved her so much he'd chosen death.

And left his infant daughter behind.

"You don't know what you're talking about, Maya." She had no idea.

"Yeah, I do." Her fists clenched at her sides. "I know it's damn *selfish* and *weak* to take the easy way out and leave someone who can't even protect herself all alone in this shit-hole of a world."

Selfish and weak.

"You've never loved, have you?"

A short laugh. "No, Slick, I've never loved anyone enough to kill myself for 'em." Her gaze was hard. "And I never will. Dying is too easy. I know—been there, done that. It's the living, the making it every day when you see the pain all around you—that's the hard part. And if I'd had a child,"—a flash of pain lit her now black eyes—"then I'd sure as hell fight with everything in me to protect her as long as I could. I wouldn't just leave her alone in the dark."

As she'd been left?

Selfish and weak.

He lowered his head. Hadn't he secretly thought the same of Jon? When he'd taken Cammie into his arms, seen her crying and not been able to comfort her?

"You don't understand, brother. Centuries alone. Then she was there. My light. My Ada. I cannot, will not, be without her."

His brother's last words to him.

But what of his brother's child? Had abandoning her been so easy?

And would he have made the same choice?

No.

An uncomfortable truth. Perhaps he and Maya were more alike than he'd originally thought.

Maya huffed out a hard breath. "Look, your brother— that's none of my damn business."

That didn't seem right. Adam opened his mouth to reply.

But Maya continued, talking fast, "The girl, *she's* my business. We've lost two days here. And I really hate to tell you this, but you know that little whispering voice in my head? Well, let's just say that Nassor is starting to turn up his volume."

Fuck. "How soon until he rises?"

"Don't know, but *soon.*"

If they didn't find Cammie—

"Something else you need to know." Her lips tightened. "He's close. *Very* close to us. The vamps wouldn't have taken Cammie far from Vegas, because *the bastard is in the ground here.*"

Not enough time.

"What do we do?" He asked, feeling, for the third time in his life, absolutely helpless.

Maya's shoulders straightened. Her chin tipped into the air. "Why, we hunt, of course."

Of course. But where, how?

A very loud *thunk* sounded from the bathroom, followed immediately by the sound of rushing water.

What the hell? Adam tensed. An intruder. Someone had managed to get into their room.

The dragon started to growl.

Maya cursed. "Damn idiot. I told him not to be screwing around in there." She marched toward the bathroom, shoved open the door.

Adam followed right on her heels.

"You just don't listen, do you?" She snapped.

And Adam blinked, stunned to see a tall, muscled male standing, soaking wet in the shower. One gleaming handcuff was locked around his left wrist, the other looped around the now slanted and streaming showerhead.

"Uh, Maya?" He should have heard the guy sooner. How had he missed picking up on his heartbeats? His breaths. Unless—

One of the guy's eyes slowly rotated to stare at him.

Chameleon.

She glanced at him, shrugging. "Guess there was one other thing that I needed to tell you."

No shit.

Chapter 9

"Glad you two finished fucking around!" The man shouted, yanking on the handcuffs as the water streamed over him. "Now get me the hell out of here!"

You have to be quiet. You can't make a sound.

Now Maya's words made sense. Too late.

Not that he really gave a damn if this guy had heard him taking Maya. He'd never been the shy type and Maya sure as—

"You broke the pipe, you idiot!" Maya stalked closer to the chameleon, shaking her head. "Now, Max, didn't I tell you not to jerk around in here?"

Max?

"You handcuffed me in the shower and left me while you fucked!" The veins on the guy's neck stuck out.

Maya shrugged. "At least I haven't killed you, *yet*."

Max's mouth opened and closed like a fish. Rather fitting, considering the amount of water surrounding him.

"Maya . . ."

She didn't glance back at him as she said, "You were pretty out of it when we left Blood Rock, so you probably don't remember our little friend taking a drive with us."

"You knocked me out! Dragged me here—"

Her hand shoved against his chest, sending him slamming back against the tiled wall. Water soaked her arm and fingers. "Do you remember what happened the last time you pissed me off? 'Cause you wouldn't shut the hell up?"

The chameleon gulped and then a gleam lit his eyes. A gleam of hunger. "You bit me." Said on a sigh. He licked his lips.

Every muscle in Adam's body tightened. He remembered the heady rush he'd felt as Maya's teeth pierced his neck. The hot pleasure.

He knew by looking into the chameleon's eyes that the bastard had felt the same way.

Adam was across the room before he knew it, jerking Maya away and glaring at the chameleon as he snapped, "Tell me why I should let you live." He spared a brief glance for Maya. He'd deal with her later.

Tasting another, while he was near. Hell, no, that wasn't the way things were going to work.

A hot ball of fire lodged in his chest and as he tasted the ashes on his tongue, Adam recognized the fury for exactly what it was.

Jealousy.

He didn't want Maya near another male, much less drinking from him.

She was his. It was time she realized that fact.

"I'll tell you why," Maya said as the chameleon gaped at him. "Because he's gonna lead us to Cammie."

The chameleon shook his head, those strange eyes of his bulging. "No! I told you, I-I don't know where they took the girl."

"Ah, but there's a lot you *do* know," she murmured. "And you're going to tell us exactly what we need to hear." Maya was pressed close against Adam's side. There was anger in her voice. Steel.

She'd tasted the bastard. Adam's hand lifted to the chameleon's throat. There. He could feel the small pinpricks on the skin.

Her mouth. On him.

A haze began to cover his eyes.

"I was weak," she whispered the words in his ear. "So were you. I couldn't risk taking from you—not then."

So she'd taken from another.

Her fingers stroked his shoulder, as if—as if she were trying to soothe him.

Damn if it didn't work. The fingers he'd clenched around Max's thin throat began to relax.

The man drew in deep, shuddering breaths.

Adam stepped back. The water continued to stream down. Max's hand dangled from the cuff. "I gave you my blood. It helped you—healed you."

Why had Maya needed healing?

"Your hands—I saw what happened, how they changed." He licked his lips. "If—if you transform me, I'll tell you everything."

Because everybody wanted to be immortal.

Maya sighed. "What makes you actually think you're in the position to bargain?" Before he could answer, she said, "I'm not like those sadistic freaks you were working for. I'm not going to dangle forever in front of you in return for getting what I want."

What *they* wanted, Adam thought.

"There are two ways to do this," Maya said, raising her voice again. "Either we bite and claw the truth out of you—"

For the first time since he'd met her, Adam let his claws out. Long, gleaming. Several inches longer and a hell of a lot sharper than hers.

She grunted in approval. "Or we can all be civilized and you might get to keep breathing." From the corner of his eye, Adam saw Maya bare her fangs. "Your choice."

Max shook his head, over and over. "No. If they find out I told, they'll kill me!"

She laughed at that. "If you don't tell me what I need to know in the next five seconds, I'll make you wish you were dead."

That stopped the frantic head motions. Both eyes gazed at Maya, as if testing the truth of her words.

Adam didn't doubt for a moment that she meant exactly what she'd said.

Apparently, the chameleon came to the same conclusion.

He gulped, then whispered, "Torrence has a feeding room near the Strip. He goes there every night."

"And Torrence would be?" Adam asked, his voice mild as he fought the anger that still coursed through his veins. This bastard had been there, he'd known that the vampires had Cammie—and he'd done nothing to help the child.

Too busy serving the parasites. Trying to trade his life for the prize of immortality.

Fool.

"Torrence Zane. He's pretty much the alpha vampire while the Born Master's still in the ground."

Torrence. "Would this alpha happen to be about six foot two, with blond hair and a pretty-boy face?" One that he'd like to smash in.

The chameleon nodded shakily.

Adam smiled. Payback was going to be a real bitch for the pretty boy.

"I need an exact location," Maya said.

"I-I don't have one."

"Oh, that's just not what I need to hear right now." She made a faint humming sound. "Not at all."

He swallowed.

Enough playing.

Adam reached up and grabbed the center of the handcuffs. With one hard yank, he snapped the cuffs in half. Then he grabbed the showerhead and bulging pipe and twisted, hard.

The water immediately stopped.

The wet chameleon lifted the cuff that still circled his wrist, then looked at Adam with eyes that had widened even more. "What are you?"

"Damn," Maya said. "That was sexy."

Adam glanced at her in surprise. Found her staring at him with bright eyes and a small smile curving her lips.

"You've been holding out on me for too long." There was real desire in her eyes.

Oh, hell, if that impressed her, he had a dozen more tricks up his sleeve.

Later.

Business first. He grabbed the chameleon, yanking Max out of the tub and lifting him high into the air. "The lady asked you a question."

Max's entire body shook. "I-I told her—off the Strip."

"Off the Strip—where?" She sounded annoyed now. Maya ran a claw down his chest and the man shuddered.

That had so better have been a shudder of fear, Adam thought. Or he would hurt the asshole.

"Do you know," she continued in a light, soft voice, "just how many feeding rooms are in Sin City? Off the Strip?"

Max shook his head. His feet dangled off the ground.

"Too fucking many." Not soft anymore. Razor sharp. "Now tell me where to find this Torrence, *exactly* where, or I'm gonna start slicing." Her claws pressed lightly into the fabric of his shirt, right over his heart.

She should really be letting him do that. The sun was out, and transforming her fingernails into claws, though a small act, had to be draining on her.

But the lady seemed to be having a good time, and she sure as hell looked like she knew what she was doing.

He'd just make certain he gave her a nice, long drink to replenish her energy.

A drop of dark red blood appeared on Max's white shirt. "I-I don't know!" A frantic edge broke his voice. "It's off the Strip—a place with cages for human dancers and—and they always put blond women outside, Lures, you know, women in short skirts with tight tops—fuck, I swear, that's all I know!"

"Can you show us this place?"

"I've never been there." Max trembled. "Didn't want to go, didn't want to see—"

"Everyone get eaten?" she asked silkily. "But I thought that was what you wanted, Max. I thought you were serving the vamps so that they'd gift you with the change. And once you changed, *you'd* be the one in that bar, killing the humans one by one."

He blanched. "N-no. Wouldn't be like that." He jerked in Adam's hold, but there was no escape for the chameleon. Max sucked in a sharp breath. "My kind—we die young, too young. Hazard of the genetics in our body. I just—"

"What?" Adam pushed.

"I just didn't want to die!"

"But you didn't care if others did," Adam said. "You didn't care if Cammie died."

"I'm sorry about the kid," he whispered. "But there was nothing I could do."

"Yeah, well, there's plenty *we* can do." Maya's claws retracted. She sent Adam a hard smile. "I think I know where that bastard Torrence likes to party."

"What are we going to do about him?" Adam asked, jerking his thumb toward the chameleon, who sat, looking absolutely terrified, on the sagging couch.

"I'll take care of him," she said and damn if Max didn't look like he might faint.

Jeez. The idiot worked for vamps. What, did he think he could just wander off in the world, and live all happily ever after now?

Maya had found him trying to slink away from Blood Rock, running with his body tight to the ground. She'd hit him, hard and fast, and hauled his sorry ass back to the SUV.

A get-well present for Adam.

The guy had been an inch from death and he'd still managed to utter his niece's name. For some reason, that pain-filled whisper had jerked at her heart—the heart she'd long since forgotten existed. She'd found herself running back to the canyon, trying to think of any way to help Adam and Cammie.

And she'd stumbled, almost literally, into one of the chameleons.

Sometimes, she rather thought fate was just a twisted bitch.

A dull headache pounded behind her eyes and a sweeping lethargy weighed down her body. She needed sleep. A hell of a lot more than she was going to get in the next few hours.

Actually, she needed sleep *and* blood.

But she had to take care of good old Max first.

Maya grabbed one of the cell phones from her bag. Kept her gaze on Max as she punched in the numbers. She didn't identify herself when the male voice answered, just said, "Skye, I have a pickup for you. Desert Inn, Room 204."

Silence hummed on the line, followed by a soft click.

"Maya?"

She glanced to the left. Found Adam staring at her with narrowed eyes.

A dragon. A fucking dragon.

And she'd been the one trying to protect him.

No wonder the guy had walked into the feeding room that first night as if he didn't have a single fear in his heart. She doubted the L10 would have lasted even thirty seconds against him.

Hell, the vamp—Torrence—had needed to blow up the canyon to take him out, and even then, Adam hadn't stayed down long at all.

He probably hadn't even needed her to dig him out.

But she'd had to do it.

I couldn't leave him there. Not in the dark.

A fucking dragon. She didn't know exactly how strong the guy was, but she suspected he could kick her ass in a fight. And probably the asses of a dozen or so vamps—all at the same time.

Dragons were huge. Ferocious. Those scales of his—they'd sliced her fingertips right open. She'd be willing to bet that the Wyvern was a hell of a lot harder to kill than a level-ten demon.

Shit. She'd tried to transform him.

When shifters or demons or any other damn supernatural being became vamps, they lost all their powers—and gained only the strengths and accompanying weaknesses of a vampire.

Not an overly good trade. But, if you were a low-level demon looking to live forever or a shifter headed for a real short future, sometimes the tradeoff didn't seem half bad.

For Adam, it must have seemed like a real piss-poor proposition.

Now she understood why he'd jerked away from her.

"Maya?" He took a step toward her.

Ah, hell, she'd been staring at him like some kid with a crush.

So the man was a dragon. Yeah, she'd always kind of had a thing for dragons. They were big. They were strong. They could breathe fire and kill anything that got in their way.

She'd seen a picture of a dragon once. In this stupid fairy-tale book at her elementary school's library. The dragon—a big green beast with smoke coming from its nostrils—had been curled around the gates of a castle. A princess had been in the tower, peering down at him.

The teacher had told her class that the dangerous dragon was attacking the princess's castle and that only the little fairy tale star's true love would save her.

Bullshit. One look, and Maya had known that dragon was keeping the princess safe. Keeping everything bad away from her.

When she'd gone back home, found her mom passed out drunk on the couch, she'd wished, as only a kid can, that she had her own dragon.

She just hadn't exactly been expecting to eventually find said dragon in the form of Adam Brody.

Yeah, fate was twisted.

And getting more so by the second.

The tattoo on the base of her back seemed to burn.

Maya exhaled. "The guy on the phone—he'll be here soon." Then they could kiss their chameleon good-bye.

For a price.

Damn. This was going to make her even weaker.

Not the best situation considering the night ahead.

"Was telling him our location smart?"

His tone implied that it damn well hadn't been.

She lifted one shoulder. Let it fall in a careless shrug. "Skye won't sell us out to the vamps—he generally hates my brethren, thinks we're all a bunch of parasites."

Adam glanced away.

Huh. Her chin lifted. "For the right fee, he'll take care of our little problem. No questions asked."

Max whimpered.

"You sure you trust this Skye?"

Of course she didn't. But she could predict his actions, and that mattered more than trust. "Relax, Adam. I know what I'm doing."

Maya just hated that she'd have to bleed for Skye.

The warlock always required blood as his payment for services rendered.

While she waited for Skye's arrival, Maya slipped back into the bathroom, taking the cell phone with her. She had another call to make, one that required a bit more privacy.

She quickly dialed the number for Memorial Grove Hospital. Pressed the extension for Sean's room.

He should be awake by now. Maybe not completely coherent, but awake enough to—

"Hello."

The sound of his voice, slightly slurred, but definitely aware, hit her like a punch in the stomach. "S-Sean?"

"Maya? I—is that you?"

Her knees were shaking. Shit. She was a mess. "Yeah, it's me." He was all right, but he wouldn't stay that way, not if he kept hanging around with her. "Sean, I, ah, had to leave town and—"

"And you left me a panther shifter for a babysitter," he finished, his voice seeming to fade at the end.

"Triond isn't a babysitter," she muttered, wincing. "He's just there to . . . keep you safe." While she was too far away to do the job herself.

"Huh. Right." A sigh. "When are you coming back? I really, *really* want to see you soon."

And she wanted to see him. The guy was the best friend she'd ever had, the brother she'd *never* had. "I-I don't know yet." He was also the one person she wouldn't lie to. "I've got some business to deal with here first, then I'll be coming home."

Home. Funny. She didn't really have a real place to call home. Never had. Those foster houses she'd stayed in hadn't been home. The cheap motel she'd lived in with her mother—off and on—during the first ten years of her life hadn't been home.

"Maya? You there?" Worry filled Sean's voice.

Guilt immediately rushed through her. The guy should be resting, not worrying about her. "Sorry."

"For you to cut out of town like this, well, you must be working on something . . . really important."

Trying to save a girl's life. Yeah, it was important. To her.

"Where are you, Maya? Where'd you go racing off to?"

She hesitated a moment, staring at the back of the bathroom door. The wood was chipping. "The city of Sin, Sean. The city of Sin." She wanted to keep talking to him, but knew there just wasn't time. Skye would be there soon—he was always fast—and the man didn't like to wait.

She exhaled. "I've got to go, Sean. Take care of yourself, you hear me? Try to keep out of fights with creatures that you know can kick your ass."

He laughed at that. A strangled, rough gurgle. "I don't think it's gonna be that easy."

"Sure it will. Just do what Triond says, get better, and I'll be back before you know it." She hoped.

Triond was a good bodyguard. One of the best in L.A. She'd barely had time to contact him before she'd left with Adam, but knowing that the panther was there, watching Sean's back, made her feel better.

"Sean? I, uh, just wanted to—to thank you." When she'd seen him in the hospital, she'd realized—*too late*—that she'd never told the guy how she felt.

"You don't need to thank me." For a second, she could have sworn he sounded angry.

"Yeah, I do." She closed her eyes, shutting out the sight of the door and remembering the night she'd first met him.

The darkness.

The scream of sirens.

The tempting beat of his heart, thumping faster with fear as he'd realized the woman in the body bag wasn't dead.

Not entirely.

Shit. When she'd woken, she'd been scared to death, hungry as hell, and so damn angry.

And Sean had been staring at her, eyes huge behind the lenses of his glasses.

She'd expected him to run from her. Or to faint, as Monica had done.

Monica. She and Sean had really surprised Maya. After the initial shock, they'd helped her. Driven her away from the crime scene, given her bags of blood for her gnawing hunger, and then they'd stuck around.

Become friends, of a sort.

A call had been made to her Chief. She'd said one word to him, whispered, "Vampire," and he'd understood. Chief Bronson had been in L.A. all his life, patrolling the streets, day and night. The guy knew the score. Her "death" had been covered up and Maya Black had officially resigned from the police force.

To begin a new life as a monster.

Monica had finally broken last year. The demons, the death—it had all just become too much for her. She'd gone back to Kansas, back to a place, she'd tearfully told Maya, "Where I don't see devils every time I turn around."

But Sean had stayed by her side. Until she'd found him bleeding out on the street.

"You were there for me when I was at my worst," she told him finally, opening her eyes. "I won't forget that."

Silence. "Well, don't forget that you've saved my ass more times than I can count over the last five years."

Her lip curled. "That's 'cause you don't know how to stay out of trouble." Damn, but she missed that man.

"Are you staying out of trouble, Maya?" A slight warning edge sharpened the words.

Hell, she'd never been able to stay out of trouble. "Nah. You know me, I get bored if there isn't enough action going on." Her nails tapped against the wood. "I've got to go."

"*Maya . . .*"

Tension. Fear.

"What is it, Sean?"

The hum of silence. Then—

A heartbeat. Pounding, racing far too fast.

As if the phone had been lowered, placed over his throat. Over his pulse.

What the hell?

Fear.

Then the drumming faded and Sean's voice murmured, "Watch your back 'cause I won't be able to do it this time."

The call ended with a click.

But the sound of his racing heart echoed in her ears.

Sean Donnelley slowly placed the phone on the nearby hospital tray. His eyes met Triond's golden stare, then dropped to the claws that circled the panther's throat.

The pack of wolves were nearly motionless in the room. Three surrounded Triond. One stood at the door, and the leader, the ugly bastard with the torn ear, waited near the side of his bed.

"That wasn't so hard, now was it?" Lucas Simone murmured, and when he smiled, Sean caught a glimpse of his too-sharp teeth.

Selling out his best friend. Fuck, yeah, it had been hard.

But he hadn't been given any options.

"You heard everything?"

Lucas nodded. Damn shifter hearing.

"Then get the hell out of here." Damn, he was weak. Too weak to fight. Too weak to help Triond.

To help Maya.

The wolf shifter laughed. "Don't worry, human. I promise, I won't hurt the vampire bitch, at least not too badly."

Sean flinched. *I'm sorry, Maya.*

One of the wolves slammed his fist into the side of Triond's head and the panther went down, hard, his face smashing into the glistening floor.

Lucas stepped over the body. Headed for the door. His pack fell in line behind him.

They left his room without saying another word and went to hunt Maya.

Fuck. Sean's hands shook as he grabbed the phone. He tried to call her back, tried using that damn caller return system, but the line just beeped.

He didn't believe Lucas. Not for a minute. He'd seen the bloodlust in the guy's eyes. He'd hurt Maya, and he'd enjoy every minute of her pain.

"*Fuck!*" Sean threw the phone across the room.

He'd just killed his best friend.

Chapter 10

Her headache was getting worse. Maya slanted a quick glance over at the chameleon and thought about taking a little bite. Just to take the edge off and to replenish some of her much-needed energy.

Just a bite.

She stepped toward him, eyes on his throat. He didn't taste as good as Adam. Didn't taste of life and passion.

No, Max was more of a sweet peppermint.

She'd never had a particular candy fetish, but—

"No." Adam's voice. Growling from right behind her. His breath stirred the hair near her ear as he said, "You want to drink, then you drink from me."

Oh, she wanted to. Maya turned slowly, licking her lips. A taste of Adam would be heaven.

But she wouldn't be able to stop with just a taste. Not anymore. She wouldn't stop until she had him inside her, thrusting fast and hard and driving them both to release.

The bloodlust and the physical hunger she felt for him were intertwined now. She'd barely been able to hold back earlier. If she touched him again, she'd drink and fuck. And she wouldn't really care if a chameleon watched their every move.

Adam's green eyes heated, and she knew he understood. His nostrils flared as he took in her scent.

Her panties were already wet. "Adam, I—"

A knock at the door. Hard. Sharp. Skye.

Her breath blew out in a rush. Well, at least the problem of the chameleon would be solved.

Then they could get back to the matter at hand.

Sex and blood. And lots of it.

Maya paced across the room and pressed her eye against the small peephole.

Skye stared back at her, features slightly distorted, but definitely the warlock.

She opened the door.

He didn't enter immediately. His gaze swept over her. Then looked beyond her shoulder into the small motel room.

As far as she knew, Skye didn't have a last name. The guy was the quiet type—quiet and deadly.

Skye was as tall as Adam, but thinner. His skin was a light gold, and his dark eyes held a slight exotic narrowing at the corners, hinting at his Asian ancestry. His hair was short, blacker than coal.

He wore a black T-shirt that left his tattooed arms bare. A battered backpack was slung over his left shoulder. Torn jeans and scuffed boots completed his look.

He brushed by her and she caught the faint scent of incense.

Skye spared a look at Adam, then at Max. "I take it I'm here for the chameleon?"

"Yeah."

He nodded. Pulled off his backpack and rummaged inside. "You want him dead?" Spoken casually.

The chameleon whimpered. He seemed to do that a lot.

"I just want him out of town." She watched as Skye pulled a long, sharp knife from his pack. "And I want him to forget all about the little talk we had."

"Easy enough."

She'd thought it would be, for him.

Skye pulled out two large vials. Uncapped them and stood, knife in hand. "But I want my payment first."

What the man did with vampire blood, she had no idea.

He couldn't use it for a transformation. The transformation only worked if a vamp drank from the victim and then gave up her blood to him.

Maya held out her hand, wrist up. "Just hurry." Because this was only going to make her weaker.

He smiled, a smile that didn't reach his eyes and the knife slashed across her exposed flesh.

"You sonofabitch!" Adam was on him in less than a second, slamming Skye against the wall. The knife clattered to the floor.

Her blood began to drip onto the carpet. She glanced around, looking for the vials. No point wasting—

A deep, inhuman growl of rage stopped her. Glancing up slowly, she saw that Adam's fingers were digging deep into Skye's arms and that the dark tattoos lining Skye's body were starting to shimmer.

Not a good sign.

"Adam!" She grabbed his arms, tried to pry them off the other man. "Let him go!"

Adam's head jerked toward her and he gave her a look that clearly questioned her sanity. "He attacked you."

"No," she told him, wincing. "He was just getting his payment." A payment that was wasting as it slowly dripped onto the floor.

Adam's brow furrowed. He slanted a hard look at Skye. "You work for blood?"

"For her blood, yes." Skye didn't look scared. Or even mildly nervous. His lips quirked the faintest bit. "Perhaps for yours, too."

"*Skye.*" Maya put a warning edge in her voice. She didn't have time for them to get in a pissing match.

He only smiled wider.

She touched Adam's arm again, felt the muscle tighten beneath her fingertips. "Look, I like this whole kick-ass thing you've got going on, but now really, *really* isn't the time."

A muscle flexed along his jaw. His gaze held Skye's. "Come at her with a knife again, and you're a dead man."

Skye blinked at that. "What makes you think I'm not already?"

Ah, screw this. Maya marched away from them, found the vials, and held the first one under her bleeding arm. The knife had cut pretty deep and the blood flowed quickly. She capped the first vial and reached for the second.

When she looked up, she saw Max watching her with a kind of helpless fascination on his face.

I'm too tired for this crap now.

She shoved the vials back into Skye's pack. "Done." Maya jerked her thumb toward Max. "Now it's your turn."

Adam's hold slowly loosened. Skye stepped around him, slung the backpack over his right shoulder, and bowed slightly to Maya. "You are a woman of your word."

Not really.

Skye walked toward the chameleon. Frowned. "Would have been easier if you'd had him unconscious for me."

She'd just bled for the guy. Did she have to do everything? Her temples pounded in a fierce rhythm of pain. The fingers of her right hand gripped the wound, trying to halt the flow of blood. "I figured you might be in the mood for a challenge."

He laughed at that. A rusty, quick laugh. Skye knelt in front of the now cringing chameleon. "This isn't a challenge." He lifted his fist to his mouth and blew. A stream of dust shot straight into Max's face.

The chameleon slumped forward, completely unconscious.

"Huh. Neat trick." One she'd like to learn.

Skye hefted the chameleon over his shoulder. Didn't even so much as grunt at the weight. When he headed for the door, Adam was at his side, keeping his body between her and Skye.

At the door, Skye paused, glanced back at Maya. "You know, I said it was the right tattoo for you."

Yeah, he had. Right before he'd picked up his needles and gone to work on her.

"Thanks for the blood. I'll be seeing you, lady vampire."

Then he was gone, hauling the sleeping chameleon from the motel and leaving them in silence.

A silence that only lasted mere moments. Adam slammed the door shut, threw the lock, and turned on her, his eyes hot with anger. "Where the hell did you meet him?"

That was an easy one. "Tattoo parlor. During the day, Skye's the best tattoo artist I've ever seen." And one willing to work on the undead. It took special skills, not to mention some damn magical ink, to mark one of her kind.

"And during the night?"

Not so easy, mostly because she wasn't entirely sure. "Let's just say that at night, he's much, much more."

Adam swore, then crossed to her in long, quick strides. He grabbed her arm, holding up the slash, his fingers warm and strong around her. "The asshole cut you too deep."

Yeah, she knew that. She was still bleeding and getting weaker every second. She needed—

He caught her by the nape of her neck. Pushed her head against his throat so that she could feel the rapid pulse beating beneath her lips. Tempting her.

"Go ahead," he muttered. "Bite me."

It was all the invitation she needed.

Her fangs sank into his throat, and lust exploded in her blood.

Chapter 11

When her lips touched him, his cock swelled, hardening with instant arousal and thrusting against the zipper of his jeans.

And when her teeth pierced his flesh, when she began to suck on his neck and draw his blood into her mouth, he thought he'd come right then.

Adam clenched his teeth, biting back the groan that rumbled to his lips. Damn, but he hadn't expected to feel this way. Not from her bite.

Not with her.

His hands snaked between their bodies, fumbled with the clasp of her jeans. The need to touch her tight, hot sex screamed through him. He wanted to brush past those soft curls and feel her cream coating his fingertips. His cock.

He shoved the jeans down, ripped the panties in his haste. Then he was touching her, finally smoothing his fingers over the silken folds of her sex.

She moaned against his neck. Sucked harder.

Hell, yes.

His fingers stroked over her clit. A tremble shook her body, and his.

Adam's heart thundered in his ears. Her scent surrounded him, warm, wet woman.

Claim. Take.

His fingers parted her. Drove deep. Found her as hot and tight as she'd been before.

So good.

But not good enough. Not yet. Not until he was balls-deep inside her, plunging hard and fast and she was clenching around him, squeezing him tight with that creamy sex.

He lifted her up, heard her kick off the jeans that dangled around her legs. Her mouth never left his neck and the pleasure of her bite just pushed him ever closer to the edge.

He lowered her onto the side of the bed. Jerked open his jeans, and pushed the head of his cock right between her spread legs. Just where he needed to be.

Her tongue licked over his throat, soothing the faint wound.

His fingers dug into her hips.

He shoved deep inside her in one fast thrust.

His balls tightened. His spine tingled and he began to move, plunging into her hot core again and again.

She lifted her mouth from his throat. Met his gaze with eyes gone midnight black. Her lips were red, parted just enough to show him the edge of her fangs.

Adam growled and plunged harder. Her legs wrapped around his hips, clung tight, pulling him against her.

Feel me. He hadn't used their link before. Hadn't thought he'd ever be tempted. But the hunger was too much this time.

He wanted everything from her. Every thought. Every desire.

He wanted her body. Her mind. Her soul.

He opened his thoughts, letting his hunger pour forward and surround her. The lust. The greedy possession. The release that was building in a blinding swirl.

Maya gasped, and those fangs flashed even more. Then, it was as if a wall had fallen, and suddenly he was *inside* her mind. Feeling her desire. The tension that tightened every muscle in her body.

Closer.

Harder.

Deeper.

More.

Her thoughts, his, it didn't matter. The desire was one and the same. So he gave her what she wanted, what he needed, and drove deep into her creaming sex, loving the way her delicate muscles closed over his shaft and squeezed his cock from tip to root.

Then he felt the blast of pleasure slam through her. A white-hot ball of flame that burned her from the inside, taking her breath and leaving her shaking with the force of her release.

He felt it. Every single second. The tremors that rocked her, the ripples of her sex—milking him with her silken sheath.

Then he was falling—surging over the edge and climaxing deep and long in the cradle of her body. He came hard, pumping into her and holding her tight, marking her skin with the force of his passion.

More.

The whisper was in his mind. In hers. So he kept thrusting after his release. Driving deep, feeling his cock swell once again and thicken in the tight clasp of her sex.

Maya was moaning. Panting. And thrusting her hips back against him with desperate force.

He grabbed the hem of her shirt. Jerked it up so that he could find one ripe breast. He pushed the lace of her bra out of his way, and caught her breast with his mouth, sucking strongly on the nipple—

Even as his cock surged inside her in ever demanding thrusts.

She tasted good. Sweet. Not like a human. And sure as hell not like one of those undead vampires he'd killed in the past.

His tongue swirled over her nipple. Sucked the engorged tip.

Her fingers dug into his shirt, her claws pressing through the fabric and into the skin. Oh, damn, but he liked that. Liked the idea that she was marking him.

Even if the marks would fade all too soon.

His turn.

Adam bit her breast lightly. Not enough to break the skin. Not enough to hurt. Just enough to—

"Adam!" Maya shuddered, those black eyes hot with lust. "Not too much, my blood—"

Probably wouldn't change him. A victim had to be drained nearly dry before an exchange in order for a transformation to work. "Don't worry, baby, I won't make you bleed." *Just scream with pleasure.*

His fingers pushed between their bodies. Found her sensitive clit. Adam squeezed it lightly with two fingers and sucked deeply on her breast.

She came, her body jerking beneath his. "*Adam!*"

He slammed into her. Again. Again. Then stiffened as a second release shot through his body. He emptied into her, pouring every bit of his semen into her tight depths. When the climax finally ended, he felt hollowed out and so satisfied he never wanted to move again.

Beneath him, Maya stirred faintly. She blinked up at him, eyes slowing shifting back to brilliant blue. She licked her lips, and he realized he hadn't kissed her.

The passion had been too hard. Too fast.

He lowered his head. Pressed his lips against hers. Tasted the copper of his blood. And the sweetness of her mouth.

Maya broke the kiss, turning her head slightly and swallowing.

Her mind was closed to him again. As his was to her.

The way it should be.

But it just felt so cold.

His cock was still cradled in her sex. He didn't want to move, but he knew she was exhausted. The night ahead would be dangerous and she'd need all the strength she could get.

While she slept, his blood would recharge her, giving her added energy and power.

Then they'd face the vampires who waited for them.

And he'd get his revenge on the bastard who'd left him to die.

Slowly, he withdrew from her body, enjoying the way her muscles clamped over his shaft—as if she didn't want to release him.

They shifted in the bed, actually managed to make it to the pillows.

Maya turned away from him. Curled in on herself.

He stared at her back a moment. Came to a sudden decision.

Hell, no.

She'd taken his blood and his seed. She'd damn well sleep in his arms. He grabbed her, pulling her toward him and tucking her flush against him.

"No! What are you—"

"Shh." He stoked her cheek, and she blinked up at him as if she were completely confused. As if no one had ever held her before. "Just sleep, Maya."

"But, I—"

"Sleep." And he'd hold her. Protect her. As she'd protected him.

At first, she lay stiffly against him, her muscles too tight. Her lips thinned. But he stroked her back, smoothing his hands over her soft skin until she gradually began to relax.

It took twenty minutes before her breathing changed and she softened against him.

Adam smiled and pulled her closer.

Her hand rested on his chest. Small fingers, pale and smooth. He stared down at that hand, then frowned, his eyes narrowing.

There was blood beneath her nails.

Her fingers had dug into his hips when they'd made love—but not deep enough to cut.

He lifted her hand, brought it close to his nose, and inhaled.

The blood was old and it was hers.

The chameleon's words whispered through his mind. "*I*

gave you my blood. It helped you—healed you." Because she'd been hurt. "*Your hands—I saw what happened, how they changed.*"

He'd been buried under a mountain of rocks. Maya had dug him out—with her hands and claws.

He hadn't realized what the chameleon meant until that moment.

Why hadn't she just left him? Why had she risked so much to save him?

More rocks could have fallen down on her. She could have been trapped. The vampire who'd attacked him could have come back and killed her.

Why had she stayed in the darkness and saved him?

"Maya." The whisper fell from his lips.

She frowned in her sleep but didn't awaken.

Adam realized his questions would have to wait.

But not for long.

She hated it when blood was on her hands. Of course, that was a situation that happened all too often for her.

Maya showered as fast as she could, trying to rinse the scent of blood and sex off her body. The water barely trickled out, thanks to Max and Adam, but there wasn't much of a choice for her.

When she left the bathroom, she found Adam sitting on the edge of the bed. His eyes narrowed when he caught sight of her body. For a moment, she was tempted to go to him, to climb on those strong thighs and straddle him.

Then it would be her turn to ride.

But the sun was setting. Power and energy hummed through her veins—and she knew they couldn't delay the hunt.

Cammie needed them.

And the vampires who'd taken the girl, well, they needed to die.

The sex would have to wait.

Maya stalked to her bag, began to dress.

A warm, strong hand settled on her lower back. Right over her black tattoo. "Why the dragon?"

Because after her change, she'd realized that she didn't need anyone to protect her anymore. *She* was the fierce creature that threatened others.

She forced a shrug. "Impulse." Maya stepped away from him. She liked his touch too much and didn't trust her own self-control.

"Huh." The guy didn't sound particularly convinced by her answer. "Skye—you said he was the one who gave it to you?"

Maya tucked her gun into the back of her jeans. Slid a knife into her boot. "Yeah."

"So this isn't your first trip to Vegas?"

She smiled at that. "No." Good thing, too, or they would've had one hell of a time finding the feeding room.

But she remembered the place. Had even gone there once, only to leave when the stench of death began to choke her.

Skye had told her that place wasn't for her. "For the others," he'd said. But not for her.

Should have listened to him.

Should have listened—the story of my life.

Too late to change things now. She dug a second gun out of her bag, and gave it, handle first, to Adam.

His brows lifted. "You know I don't really need that."

"Yeah, well, I'm sure you can probably huff and puff and blow the whole place down—"

A muscle ticced along his jaw.

"—but if you did that, well, that wouldn't exactly be keeping a low profile, now would it?"

"And a gunshot is quiet?"

"Nah. Just not as messy as a four-alarm fire." Her gaze scanned the room. The weapons were ready. The sun was barely flickering through the blinds.

It was time. "Come on, Slick. Let's go find us some vampires."

* * *

It was the blood that drew her. The heady scent that floated on the wind and teased her nostrils, sending her heart racing and making her palms sweat.

She drove past the glittering lights and flashing signs of the main Strip. Went past the casinos with their elaborate promises of wealth. Drove past the pawnshops that offered more money for the next hand of cards.

The crowds were just as thick off the Strip. The bright lights still flashed.

She kept driving.

And the scent of blood grew stronger.

There. Maya pulled the SUV to the curb. A good fifty feet away from the feeding room.

Temptation. That was the name of the bar. She could see the scantily clad blond women strolling on the sidewalk near the entrance. Lures.

Not that they had to work too hard to reel in the prey. It was barely nine o'clock, far too early for the normal clubbing scene, yet already there was a line snaking around the building.

Fools.

How many would live to see the dawn?

Her gaze swept over them. Stopped on the two muscled guards near the entrance of Temptation. They both wore headsets. Small microphones were attached near their lips.

Well, well. Looked like the Vegas vamps were smarter than those in L.A.

If Hugh had been equipped with a unit like that, he might have been able to call out for help before that damn level ten had killed him.

But the extra security did mean she'd have to alter her plans a bit.

She had a feeling Adam wasn't going to be too wild about the strategy shift. But, well, there wasn't much choice.

They climbed out of the SUV. The gun pressed into her back as she walked. Adam's attention was on the feeding room, a frown pulling down his brows. "Can't they smell it?"

The blood. The death that hung in the air like perfume. Maya shook her head. "They're here for the thrill. They don't care about anything else." Too bad for them. Some thrills weren't worth the price.

She studied the building for a moment. Granite. With tall white columns and a wide entranceway. Not much had changed since her last visit.

Damn, but she'd been thirsty then. Thirsty enough to walk into this hell.

At least she knew her way around inside. That knowledge would make searching for the girl much easier.

Adam took a step forward. Maya's arm flew out in front of him, shoving back against his muscled chest. "Sorry, Slick. There's been a change of plans."

He blinked. "What?"

"You can't go in. I'm going to have to do this alone."

"The hell you are." His heart drummed furiously beneath her hand. "This isn't a solo game, Maya. You're not leaving me."

She jerked her thumb toward the guards. "See them? If I walk by, show some fang, flash a little hunter's black eye, they'll let me in, no questions asked." Her lips tightened. "But you—no scent, rage pouring from you—they'll notify the vamps inside about you before you can even say 'Screwed.'" Which they most definitely would be if he didn't listen to her.

"You're not going in alone." The words were bitten off.

Yeah, she was. "If you want to find Cammie, well, then I sure as hell will be." They were wasting precious time. "Look, there's a back entrance," she told him, pointing to the alley on the left. "If you stay in the shadows, no one will see you. I'll search the place, get the girl, and slip out to meet you." And if luck was on her side—doubtful, but maybe—at least this once, "Then we'll get the hell out of there without any of the vamps knowing what's happened."

"I want Torrence." Flames burned in his eyes.

"I know you do." But they had to prioritize, dammit. The guy couldn't just go on a revenge spree. "But what do you want more, him or your niece?"

His hands fisted. "Cammie."

She exhaled. "Good answer, Slick." Payback would have to wait. "Now go, and I'll meet you as soon as I find her." If she was inside.

She'd damn well better be.

They didn't have much longer to search for her. The whisper in Maya's head, that soft call, was growing more insistent.

Nassor would rise soon.

And call to those taken of his blood.

She turned away from Adam, began walking fast.

"Maya!"

His shout stopped her. There was something in his voice. A hesitation. A fear?

She glanced over her shoulder. Found him watching her with a face that looked hard and cold under the streetlights.

"Why'd you do it?" His voice was soft, but easily reached her ears.

"Do what?"

"Dig me out of those rocks." His gaze bored into her. "Why didn't you just me leave me—"

To die.

"Leaving you wasn't an option." She'd never even thought about it.

"Why?" Stark.

She didn't know. She just . . . hadn't been able to walk away. She couldn't leave, not when she knew he was down there, trapped under those rocks. Maya forced a shrug. "Hey, I'm sure you would have done the same for me, right?"

She turned away, not wanting to see his expression and Adam didn't reply, didn't speak again.

His silence followed her to Temptation.

*   *   *

"Hey, I'm sure you would have done the same for me, right?" Her words seemed to echo in Adam's ears.

But would he have done the same?

He watched her stalk away from him, back perfectly straight, shoulders thrown back. Her hips swayed slightly, a sexy roll that caught his eye—and the eyes of others.

Maya.

She marched past the crowd. Flashed the guards the promised smile and slipped inside. He could hear the doors slide closed behind her, a soft *whoosh* that seemed far too final.

Alone. Damn. He didn't want her in there without him.

Sure, the lady knew how to handle herself, but there was only so much that she could do against a gang of vampires.

Be safe, Maya. And get the hell out of there, fast.

He sighed and turned toward the alley. He'd wait for her, as she'd ordered, but if he caught even the faintest whiff of trouble, he'd knock down the bar's doors and go in after her.

"Hey, I'm sure you would have done the same for me, right?"

It was just as she remembered. Gold cages lined the walls. Scantily clad men and women undulated inside them, dancing in a slow, teasing rhythm to match the beat of the band.

A woman was lying across the bar as a vampire fed from her neck. She moaned in ecstasy, her hips rocking against the smooth surface.

Couples were dancing. Humans, vamps. Blood was flowing.

You come to fuck or to feed? That had been the question gruffly asked by the guard at the door.

She'd replied, as most vamps did. "Both."

Maya knew she wasn't going to find the kid in any of the main rooms. Not the bar, not the VIP lounge, not the sex rooms in the back. If Cammie was there—and since it was Torrence's little home away from home, it figured that the girl would be—then he'd have hidden her well.

Her gaze darted to the gray door marked "Private." It led below. She knew, she'd caught a glimpse of stairs when the door had opened before.

What waited below? *Who* waited?

The hair on her nape began to rise. Slowly, she let her stare drift around the crowded bar.

So many vampires.

Sex and blood. The scent filled her nostrils.

Her eyes locked on the tall figure of a man. A man with blond hair, a perfect face, and fangs that were just inches away from a woman's throat.

Torrence?

She couldn't be sure. He fit the description, but that wasn't saying much.

Just to be safe, she used the crowd as a cover and carefully made her way to the gray door. She'd search below first. If there was no sign of the girl, then she'd work her way back up until she covered every inch of Temptation.

Her hands were against the door when a shiver of awareness worked its way over her body. She glanced back.

And found the blond vampire smiling at her. Kind of like a cat who'd just caught a fat mouse and was now getting ready to have a really, really good dinner.

Fuck it. Maya shoved open the door and took the steps three at a time.

Chapter 12

The night was too quiet. Adam stood near the back entrance of Temptation, a steel door that was locked tight, and wondered why the night seemed so quiet.

Maya had been inside for ten minutes now.

Not enough time to search the bar.

Enough time to die?

He swallowed back his fear. He'd give her a little longer. She'd been right to leave him behind, he knew that. If he went inside, saw that bastard Torrence, the rage would overwhelm him and everything would go to shit.

And the feeding room would go up in flames.

Not a good plan.

Cammie came first.

Revenge would be a sweet second.

Hurry, Maya.

A lone wolf's howl ripped through the night.

Adam stiffened. *Aw, hell.*

Harold "Harry" Thomas knew that Temptation wasn't a normal bar. Each time the door opened, he'd caught the scent of blood. He'd seen the marks on the men and women when they came out—if they came out.

But he knew not to ask too many questions. If he did his job, he got paid and he got to keep living.

Seemed like a good enough arrangement to him.

Besides, the way Harry figured it, he wasn't really doing anything wrong. Those fools who went inside, they were looking for trouble. Not his fault if they found it.

Vampires. Shit. Who would have thought they were real? And sometimes, they looked so harmless. So normal.

Like that last woman who'd gone inside. Pretty little thing—silky black hair, body so small, and a sweet ol' face on her.

Then she'd smiled at him, shown him her fangs, and met his stare with eyes gone pitch-black.

You just never knew about those vamps—they were everywhere and could be anyone.

Static crackled in his headphones. "Send in more girls."

Harry motioned to the two leather-clad redheads at the front of the line. They'd been waiting for an hour. It was their turn.

They giggled as they hurried past him, their eyes a little too bright.

Maybe the drugs would make it easier for them.

Harry went back to his post. His partner Mac stood silently beside him.

It was gonna be another long night.

Harry's gaze swept the street.

The piercing cry of a wolf's howl split the night.

What the hell?

He stepped forward and saw them. Big, dark shapes moving fluidly in the night. Running. Snarling. Coming closer, *closer.*

The men and women in line began to scream, to run.

But the wolves just kept coming closer.

"Trouble! Shit!" He screamed into the microphone, stumbling back against the white column. "We've got—"

A man stepped from the middle of the snarling pack of wolves. A tall man, with black hair, eyes colder than hell, and a twisted smile on his lips.

The wolves, big, ugly bastards whose tongues and teeth dripped with saliva, snarled and backed Harry and Mac even farther against the hard columns.

The man stopped inches away from him. Lifted his hand to Harry's chest. "What you've got, my friend," he murmured, and Harry noticed his ear then. It looked as if it had been partially bitten off. "Is more than trouble. You've got hell at your door." His fingers lengthened into claws.

Harry tasted fear on his tongue. A voice in his ear was screaming, demanding to know what was happening, but Harry couldn't speak.

"You've got something I want inside," The man—no, he wasn't a man—*the monster* snarled. "And *I'm going to fucking rip this place apart!*"

Harry knew he was looking into the face of the devil.

Company was waiting for Maya at the bottom of the stairs—company in the form of three of the biggest, ugliest vampires she'd ever seen in her life.

She literally stumbled off the stairs and landed in front of them. She hadn't caught their scent—the scents of vamps were everywhere. Too hard to distinguish amid all the blood.

Hell. She'd always had piss-poor luck.

But a pretty passable ability to act. She flashed a smile. "Hi, guys, wanna party?"

The guy in the middle—probably the ugliest—stepped forward and the dim overhead lighting winked off the piercings that began at both earlobes and looped to the tip of his ears. He was bald, with a shining scalp and a face that looked like it had been beaten in more than once during his mortal life. His fangs flashed—and they were sharp.

Maya didn't step back. Just kept smiling.

His gaze raked over her. A growl rumbled in his throat.

There was a door just behind him. A thick, steel door.

These guys were in the basement for a reason—guarding that special door. So what waited on the other side? She couldn't wait to find out.

But first, she'd have to get rid of her company.

The vampire in front of her reached out a hand and trailed

his thick fingers over her arm. "A horny little vampiress wants to party, huh?"

Not likely.

The two vamps in the background stepped closer, eyes beginning to shift black.

"I wanna go first," the guy on the right said, his tongue snaking out to lick his lips. "I haven't drunk from a vamp bitch in years."

And it would be years before he did again.

The bald leader snarled at the other vamp's words and hit him with a barrel-like fist to the face.

Oh, nice.

The guy slammed back against the wall.

One down, and she hadn't even worked up a sweat.

The clang of a metal door slammed from above her. *Shit.* No more time for games or partying.

Maya stepped closer to the pierced vamp. Stood on her toes and whispered in his ear, "This is gonna hurt." Then she grabbed his head and pushed him back, slamming his skull straight into the steel door. He fell with a whimper.

She had her gun drawn and aimed at the third vamp's heart before he could even move. "Open the door." The other two weren't dead. Just stunned. And someone had entered the stairwell. Two flights separated them. *"Now."*

His lip lifted in a sneer. "Bullets won't kill me—"

"These will." Her finger tightened on the trigger. "Wanna find out?"

His black gaze dropped to the barrel of the gun.

"Tick-tock, asshole," she snapped. No time for this.

A scream tore from upstairs. Another. Roars. Growls.

What the hell?

The vamp bent down, fumbling inside Baldy's pocket. Maya heard the jingle of keys. The guy lifted up the key ring, holding out one silver key—

Maya rammed the butt of the gun against the side of his head.

Three down.

Footsteps thudded on the stairs. Whoever had been up there had decided to join the game.

The muffled sound of screams still teased her ears.

Focus.

All hell seemed to be breaking loose above her, but she had to finish her mission.

Find the girl.

Maya pushed the key into the lock, shoved open the door—

A low, rumbling growl came from the dark depths of the room.

Shit.

Her eyes adjusted to the dim lighting instantly.

A wolf was chained to the far wall. A snarling, spitting, furious, black beast that stared at her with pure hate in its glowing eyes.

Maya stepped forward.

The wolf lunged for her, only to be jerked back by the chain. The beast howled in fury.

The scent of blood was heavy in the room and her eyes caught sight of the glistening red drops matted in the wolf's fur. He'd been fighting the chain until he bled.

A thick metal collar circled the wolf's throat. Blood stained the edges of the metal.

Maya judged that the length of chain was about fifteen feet. If she moved two steps closer, she'd be savaged.

She pointed her gun—

"Help!" A child's voice. A girl's. A hollow thud followed the cry, as if the child had banged her fist against—

The wall.

Another door was behind the wolf. A second steel door.

"Please, get me out! It's dark." Muffled sobs. "I'm s-scared. I don't wanna be alone."

Cammie.

"It's all right, sweetheart!" She pitched her voice high, trying to cut across the rapid growls. "I'm going to get you out of there." Once she got past the guard dog.

Her fingers were locked tight around the butt of the gun. The wolf was snarling, pacing in quick lines in front of the second door. "Nice dog," she whispered, stepping forward. She didn't want to hurt him unless she had to. The beast obviously hadn't chosen to be locked in the basement and chained up by the vamps.

His lips peeled back, exposing teeth far, far sharper than her own.

No, she didn't want to hurt him, but she *would* get that girl out.

The wolf stopped pacing and planted its body solidly before the door.

The girl wasn't talking anymore. She was still crying, Maya could hear the faint whimpers, but the pleas had stopped.

A whisper of breath behind Maya, she turned—

Too late.

The tall, blond vampire stared down at her. Too damn close. The wolf's growls and snarls had enabled him to clear the stairs and sneak up on her.

Hell, this was really not turning out to be her night. Maya's gaze swept over him. "Tell me, your name wouldn't by any chance be Torrence, now would it?"

He smiled.

"A friend of mine is looking for you," she murmured. "If I were you, I'd probably try to get the hell out of Sin City before you get burned."

"Don't worry about me, bitch. Worry about yourself."

Okay. Adam had wanted to take down the vamp leader, but beggars couldn't be choosers. Maya aimed her gun and felt a smile curl her own lips.

Torrence pulled a small black remote from his pocket. Pushed a button. A soft *swish* sounded behind her.

Fuck.

Please, don't let that be—

Razor-sharp teeth tore into her right ankle.

Maya went down, hard, as the wolf attacked her. Torrence

smirked at her even as he hurriedly backed away. "See how long you can last with him, bi—"

She fired. Screw aiming. She hated being called a bitch, especially by a murdering butcher.

Th wolf jerked her, dragging her body back three feet.

The bullet ripped across the skin of Torrence's arm. There was a solid *thunk* as it lodged in the wall behind him. Dammit!

Then he was gone.

The steel door slammed shut and the snapping of the lock echoed in the room, sounding even over the wolf's snarls and growls.

Locked in. Trapped with a now-free wolf. A wolf who was currently trying to bite her foot off.

We attack the legs first, that way the prey can't run.

She'd heard a wolf shifter say that once. At the time, she'd thought it was a particularly vicious attack method.

She still thought that.

And damn, but it hurt!

She twisted around. Shoved her body upright and slammed the butt of the gun against the wolf's head. "Let go!" She hit him again, harder, harder.

He howled and jerked back, freeing her. The thick collar still encircled the beast's throat, but the heavy chain had fallen away, courtesy, no doubt, of the vamp's little toy.

Maya didn't look at her ankle. She really didn't want to see it right then. She scrambled back like a crab. Okay, so much for not hurting him. She'd shoot the beast right between his golden eyes.

Maya fired at the same moment the wolf lunged. The shot went wide, and the wolf's powerful paws landed on her chest. His weight knocked her back and her head banged against the floor with a thud.

The heat of his breath burned her skin, then his teeth locked on her throat.

Hell, no.

Maya caught his head in her hands, digging her fingers deep

into his fur. "Get off me, dog," she snarled. He'd pierced her flesh, just barely, and she could feel the blood dripping down her throat.

She held him back, no easy task even with the enhanced power she'd gotten from Adam's blood. The wolf was pissed, *enraged,* and riding a hard bloodlust.

Maya drew a deep breath. She was in trouble and she knew it. She had no idea where her gun was. Her knife was still in her left boot, but it wasn't doing her much good there and it wasn't like she had a free hand to grab it.

The wolf's claws dug into her chest, gouging deep.

"Fuck!"

She used the pain, pulled it close, then heaved the wolf back with all of her strength.

The second he cleared her body, she lurched to her feet and yanked out her knife. Her right ankle buckled immediately. *Shit.* Crouching—because it was the best she could do—Maya held up the blade and caught sight of her gun.

Almost close enough to grab.

The wolf shot toward her. Maya hurled the knife. It flew, end over end, then landed hilt-deep in the wolf's front leg. Maya sprang forward and grabbed the gun.

Golden eyes glared at her. Anger. Pain. Fear.

The wolf padded slowly around her, circling until it stood before the door that trapped Cammie.

"I don't want to kill you," Maya whispered, "but I will if I have to. I'm getting that girl."

Its nostrils flared. Its eyes narrowed.

She saw the wolf's muscles bunch as he prepared for another attack.

One.

Two.

He growled and jumped into the air.

Maya fired. *Not gonna miss this time, asshole.*

The wolf howled in fury, a long, terrible howl that sounded like a scream.

No, wait, that *was* a scream. The girl was screaming behind the door.

And the wolf was on the floor, shaking. Her bullet had found its mark.

Maya closed her eyes for just a moment. Her whole body hurt.

Get the girl. "I-it's all right," she managed. "I'm going to get you out of there."

The screams stopped.

Maya glanced around the bloodstained room. Crawled and found the keys she didn't even remember dropping.

She pushed to her feet, holding the wall for support. The wolf had done a serious number on her ankle. Limping, losing way too much blood, she stepped over the wolf and reached for the lock. The third key she tried fit.

Finally.

Maya turned the key, pushed open the door, and caught the faint scent of smoke in the air.

The room was dark, pitch-black actually, but she could see the girl easily. Huddled in the corner, hair tangled and hanging down her back. "Cammie?"

The little girl flinched.

"I-it's all right, I'm not here to hurt you." She crept forward.

The girl let out a scream and spun around to face her. "Stay away from me!"

Maya froze. "It's okay," she said, trying to make her voice soothing. "I'm here to help."

But Cammie shook her head. "You're one of them," she whispered.

True. The girl obviously had her uncle's sharpened senses. "I'm working with your uncle Adam. He sent me to find you."

Maya watched the child's lips tremble. "U-uncle A-Adam?" Desperate hope filled her voice.

She tried taking another tentative step forward. A couple

more feet and she'd just grab the girl and make a run for it. "He's waiting outside for us. But we have to hurry, Cammie." She didn't know what was happening upstairs, didn't really want to find out, and she was afraid if they stayed there much longer, more "company" would arrive.

She just wasn't in the shape to win another fight.

Maya inched forward.

The child's hands pressed into the wall behind her. "You're lying." Said with absolute certainty. "H-he wouldn't have sent someone like you."

Sure he would have. To hunt monsters, you use one of their own. A sudden idea struck her. "Cammie, come with me into the light. I'll prove that he's waiting." Taking a gamble, Maya stepped back. Fire shot through her ankle as she moved. Slow steps. Nonthreatening.

Cammie began to follow her.

Yes.

Maya eased over the wolf's body. He was still alive, his breathing heavy and ragged, but he was losing a lot of blood and he wasn't in any shape to fight her anymore.

Cammie inched forward. One step. Another.

She gasped when she saw the wolf and tears poured from her brown eyes, leaving white tracks on her dirt-stained cheeks.

Hell. "Look at me, Cammie," Maya ordered. Then she turned her back partially to the child and lifted the edge of her shirt.

Silence.

Maya glanced at the girl. Her eyes were wide, and the tears still fell in a steady stream.

"Adam wanted me to show you the tattoo," Maya said, lying without a second's hesitation, "to prove that I'm on your side." Now that part was true. The lie was one that a child would believe. Almost like a secret message.

Maya held out her hand. "Now, sweetheart, I need you to trust me because we don't have much time. We need to get to your uncle and get out of here." *Fast.* Because if they were attacked, she feared she'd be too weak to protect the girl.

Cammie stared at her offered hand, then glanced back at the wolf. Her fingers lifted, stroked the bloody fur on his side.

"Cammie . . ." Screw it, she'd just grab her and run.

The girl placed her hand in Maya's.

Maya's breath expelled in a relieved rush. "Good girl. Now, I want you to stay with me, no matter what you see or what happens—*you stay with me.* And I promise, I'll get you to your uncle."

A slow nod.

"Then let's go."

Death. Blood. Screams. Howls.

As she'd thought, all hell had, indeed, broken loose in Temptation. Maya crouched in the stairwell. She'd opened the door a bare slit, just enough to see what was happening.

And, well, it definitely wasn't good.

Full-on shifted wolves were destroying the bar. Big, muscled beasts were breaking furniture and attacking the vampires, one after the other.

The humans screamed and ran for the exits.

The vamps fought back, trying to take down the wolves with claws and teeth.

The fact that the werewolves had *even bigger* claws and teeth made it one damn bloody fight.

Cammie's fingers tightened around hers. "I'm scared," the little girl whispered.

Maya raised her gun and prepared to enter the battle. But first, she cast a quick look back at the kid. Forced a smile. "Don't be, baby. I'm going keep you safe—I promised, remember?"

Cammie swallowed. Her lips lifted in a ghost of a matching smile.

Maya's heart pounded like crazy in her chest. She wouldn't be able to move fast enough, not with that damn ankle, so she'd probably have to take a few of the bastards down.

Unless they were smart enough to stay the hell out of her way.

Adam kicked in the back door, fear pumping through his blood as the screams filled his ears.

Cammie.

Maya.

He ran through the kitchen, past the men and women crouched on the floor and whimpering. He followed the howls, the scent of death.

He shouldn't have let her go in alone. He should never have let Maya—

"You're supposed to be fucking dead," a furious voice snarled and a bloody, blond vampire jumped in his path.

Torrence.

Fire shot through him and the dragon began to roar. "Sorry to disappoint you." Wolves raced around the room, vampires fought them, blood flowed.

"This time, I *will* kill you," Torrence promised.

Not damn likely.

"Just like I killed your vampire bitch!" Torrence leapt forward.

Maya.

The heat of the change swept through him. Adam lunged for the vamp. He'd rip the bastard apart, drink his blood, burn his flesh straight from his bones, and—

A shot rang out. Torrence jerked, black eyes flaring wide. Smoke rose in a slow, curling plume from the wound in his back.

The vampire fell, shrieking.

Adam came face-to-face with Maya.

"Idiot didn't kill me," she muttered, but looked very much like she was in jeopardy of falling down, too. "He just pissed me off."

The vampire was still alive. Adam reached for him. Time to finish—

"U-uncle Adam?"

The voice he heard in his dreams. He glanced back up, saw a pair of tear-filled brown eyes peering around Maya.

Cammie.

He jumped over the vampire. Grabbed his niece and held her as tight as he could.

He felt her heart racing against his. Felt her small arms curl around his neck. "Sweetheart, I've missed you."

She cried into his shirtfront.

"Uh, I'm all happy about the reunion," Maya said, "but you need to get her the hell out of here, *now.*"

Adam looked up. Noticed that Maya looked too pale—too weak. *Just like I killed your vampire bitch.* "What'd he do to you?" He demanded.

A shrug. "Sicced his dog on me."

What?

Her lips firmed. "Get her out of here, Adam. Take her back to the motel and I'll meet you—"

Adam kept a stranglehold on Cammie but reached for Maya with his right hand. "Screw that. We're all leaving—"

She shook her head. "I-I can't. There's someone I—" A vampire grabbed her from behind, and Maya spun around, slashing with her claws.

The vamp backed away, shrieking.

More dead and wounded littered the floor.

Maya froze, her gaze trained across the room. "Hell."

Adam followed her stare and saw the fierce black wolf standing on the table, fangs bared. A wolf with half a right ear and eyes blazing with fury—eyes that were locked on Maya.

"Get her out of here," she ordered, lifting her gun and taking a stumbling step forward. "I'm not finished here yet."

"Maya, no!"

But she was hurrying into the fighting crowd, shoving and pushing her way through the throng of bodies.

Cammie trembled against him.

Get her out of here. Her words slammed through his mind, following their blood link.

Adam turned away, clutched Cammie tight.

And left Maya in the swirl of hell.

The words she's said less than an hour before played through his mind, lashing against his heart. *You'd have done the same for me, right?*

Fuck.

Chapter 13

Maya stumbled down the stairs. Shoved open the steel door—

And found a nude, dark-haired boy on the floor of the basement. A metal collar circled his throat.

He lifted his head at her approach, stared at her with pain-filled eyes.

He was a kid. Barely looked sixteen. Soft face. Desperate gaze.

Torrence and his vamps had trapped him there, held him captive.

The kid didn't deserve to die in that pit.

She took a step forward.

He lifted his right hand, claws ready.

A fighter to the end. "Take it easy. I'm not gonna hurt you." Any more than she already had. She moved toward him slowly, hands up. Her gun pressed against the base of her spine.

The bullet had caught the kid in the gut, and from the look of things, the silver bullet was still in him, slowly poisoning his body.

"You've got to let me take the bullet out," she said. "Then we have to get the hell out of here." Her fingers lifted toward him.

He flinched away from her, moaning.

"I have to take it out, do you understand?" She wasn't

sure he did. Silver poisoning—it could really screw with a wolf shifter's head. Drive him crazy. Slowly kill him.

The bullet *had* to come out.

"I'm going to reach for my knife, okay?" Not much cleaner than her claws, but it was sharper and should work easier. "I'm not pulling it as a weapon, got that? I'm gonna use it to dig that bullet out of you." She just hoped it wasn't too late for him.

The kid had tried so hard to protect Cammie.

Golden eyes locked on her hand. Followed her inch by inch as she reached for the knife.

Maya pulled in a slow breath. "I have to dig the bullet out. It's going to hurt"—more than the kid could imagine—"but otherwise, the poison will kill you."

He just stared at her.

"Do you understand?" she asked, desperate. "Do you even know what I'm saying?"

His head moved. A slight nod. Or had she imagined it?

"Don't attack me, kid. I'll fight back, and I'll hurt you even more." Not her game plan.

Her fingers tightened around the knife.

The boy stiffened.

She brought her left hand down on his shoulder. Pushed him back, stared at the deep wound.

The smell of his blood teased her nostrils. She was weak and the scent was so sweet.

No.

She brought the blade of the knife down, pressed against his skin. "Scream if you want," she murmured, "'cause this is gonna hurt like a bitch."

The knife dug into his flesh.

And he screamed.

The wrenching sound echoed, shattering her nerves as she worked, cutting into him and feeling his blood coat her fingertips. The bullet was lodged in deep. After a few minutes, the tip of the knife finally hit the silver, then her fingers slipped inside the wound, claws ready, and she latched on to the bullet.

Not clean. Not safe. And I sure as hell hope I'm not leaving any shards inside.

A shifter would be able to heal from any infection and the bullet wound itself would mend at his next changing. The silver, that was the killer for his kind.

She slowly pulled the bullet out. The screams ended—the kid had passed out. Good for him. Not so much for her.

Maya tossed the bullet onto the floor. Wiped her knife on the side of her jeans and then tucked it back into her boot.

The kid was small. Skinny as a rail. Surely he couldn't weigh more than 130 pounds. On a good night, that weight would be nothing to her.

This wasn't a good night.

She lurched back to her feet. Her ankle still bled like a bitch. Not a good sign. When she put her weight on it, pain shot through her leg.

She could deal with pain. She'd done it enough in the past. The question was . . . how long would her body hold out?

Her gaze fell on the boy. *You don't know him*, a soft voice whispered in her mind. *You can leave him here. You took the bullet out.*

Cops didn't leave victims behind, and this kid—even though he'd attacked her—he *was* a victim.

But she wasn't a cop anymore.

She wasn't.

Maya turned away from him. Took one unsteady step toward the door.

The kid really was small. Maybe not even 120 pounds.

"H-help . . ." His voice. Whispering. Maya glanced back. The kid's eerie eyes were closed.

Shit.

She stalked to him, grabbed him by the arm, and jerked him up. Slung him over her shoulders in a fireman's carry.

She'd been a damn good cop.

Some instincts just wouldn't die.

Maya wasn't exactly sure how she got so lucky, but she made it out of Temptation with the kid. Her body trembled with every step she took, but they'd escaped.

The boy was still unconscious—and still bleeding. If she could just make it back to the motel, then they'd be safe. Adam had probably taken the SUV and gotten the girl to safety. Since it was damn unlikely that a cabbie would stop for a woman who looked like death and happened to be carrying a bloody, naked teen, she would have to stick to the shadows as best she could and—

Footsteps pounded on the pavement, thundering in the night. Close, too close. Goose bumps rose on her arms.

Hunted.

Someone was out there, stalking her in the darkness. Vampires? Wolves?

Maya glanced around quickly. Found an alley. Saw garbage cans. Dumpsters. The stench of rotten food and mold filled her nostrils. She could hide the kid there. Hope the alley's smell covered his own scent.

She'd conceal the kid, then run like crazy in the opposite direction to throw off the hunter. *Hunters*

Maya hurried into the alley. Oh, she didn't like that place. Too narrow with tall buildings on the left and right. Trapping her in.

This hadn't been the best idea, but there was no choice.

She looked around once more, tightened her hold on the kid and—

"*Bitch!*" Maya was hit, hard and fast. She slammed onto the pavement, dragging the boy down with her.

"You've got his fucking blood all over you—now I'll make *you* bleed, vampire!"

A man's voice. Screaming with fury. Maya eased her hold on the kid, tried to cover him with her body.

Claws raked across the top of her back. Dug deep into her flesh. She clenched her teeth, refusing to cry out from the pain.

Take the pain, let it make you stronger. She'd done that as a kid. Taken every hit. Used it to make herself stronger.

A wolf shifter was attacking her. The bastard from L.A. She knew his scent.

She'd let him live before. Her mistake.

Maya liked to believe she never made the same mistake twice.

Wolf shifters often attacked each other, so she wasn't sure if the kid would be safe if the asshole succeeded in killing her.

So she'd better make sure he didn't succeed.

"Don't move," she whispered to the kid and his eyelids flickered, just a bit.

Snarls filled the air behind her and the weight on her back grew heavier as the claws shifted and pressed deeper.

The bastard was changing, shifting from man to beast. To better make his kill.

Not tonight.

A scream of fury ripped past her lips and Maya spun around. The claws raked over her back, shredding her shirt and her skin. She kicked out at the shifter, knowing he was weakest during the brief moments of change. Her foot caught him in the jaw, wrenched his head to the right, and made him stumble back.

Her turn to play rough.

Maya bared her fangs and reached for the gun. Screw using claws and fangs, a bullet would work a hell of a lot better.

Howls split the night. Too many to count and the thud of padding feet shook the ground.

No, no!

Wolves, dozens of them, black, white, silver, all ran into the alley, snarling, mouths dripping saliva and blood.

Too many.

Her gun stayed trained on the alpha, the one who'd attacked her first. The man was barely visible now. The beast was taking complete control.

She could fire at him. Kill the bastard. The sweet temptation called to her. But the others would take her down before the bullet found its mark.

Too many.

How many bullets did she have left? How many wolves could she take down before they killed her?

The wolves circled her now. Nostrils flared. Bodies vibrated with tension.

Adam. At least he was safe. And the kid. They'd be all right. She'd done her job.

And for a few moments with Adam, she'd been able to feel like a woman again. To feel passion, need. To feel alive.

Pity. It looked like she'd be dying, for good this time, very soon.

A sharp growl snapped her attention back to the alpha. No sign of a man. Only the beast remained.

Her death was in his eyes.

So this was the way it was gonna end for her.

Another fucking alley.

Her finger tightened on the trigger.

She wasn't going out without a fight.

Maya fired and the pack closed in.

He caught her scent on the wind. Roses. Woman.

Blood.

Death.

Adam slammed on the brakes, bringing the SUV to a jarring halt.

Maya. He called to her, using their blood link.

Silence. A silence too heavy, too unnatural.

Fear iced his veins.

He shouldn't have left her. She'd risked so much for him, and he'd *fucking left her.*

Adam's fingers tightened around the steering wheel. The open window drew in her scent.

And the stench of the wolves.

"U-uncle A-Adam?" Cammie, too small, too scared, sat huddled beside him, her body shaking.

Maya had saved his niece, and in return, he'd left Maya to die.

Adam jerked the gearshift into reverse. "Hold on, baby."

He followed her scent, followed the snarls and the howls that screamed in the night.

Found a pack of wolves circling her still body.

Fire burned in his gut.

Not dead. Not yet.

Not his Maya.

His.

Adam turned off the SUV. Killed the lights. The wolves hadn't noticed him yet; they were too intent on their killing frenzy.

The bastards had no idea what a true frenzy was, but he'd show them.

"Lock the doors, Cammie. Then close your eyes and keep 'em closed until I get back." She wouldn't need to see what he'd do. The kid shouldn't have that memory.

He kissed her, a quick, hard kiss on her forehead. Then he climbed out of the vehicle.

He watched Cammie lock the doors. Tears filled her eyes. He stared at her, waiting.

Her lashes lowered.

Good.

Adam turned away from the SUV, stalked toward the wolves, and let the fire rage inside.

Time to free the beast.

Her gun was empty. She'd managed to take five of the bastards down. But her gun was empty.

Her knife had lodged in the back of one of the wolves. Her claws had ripped open another.

She swallowed, tasted blood, and stared up at the circle of teeth and muzzles around her. Pain had almost numbed her body now. A good thing, really, because she wouldn't feel it as much when they ripped into her.

"N-no." A faint whisper. A plea. Not hers. She would never beg. *Never.*

The kid's voice. Barely audible over the pack's rumbles.

"H-hel . . . ped m-me . . . S-save . . . h-her . . ."

Nice try, kid. But no way were those guys going to listen to him.

Maya looked up at the alpha and forced her nearly numb lips to raise into a fuck-you smile. Then she sent one final message to the man she'd never see again.

Good-bye, Adam.

Good-bye, Adam.

Her voice, only in his mind. Weak. Final.

Hell, no.

He ran into the alley. "Get away from her!" He roared. His teeth were sharpening and he could taste fire rising in his throat.

The wolves jerked. Glanced back at him with fury in their glowing eyes.

But they didn't move from their positions, and the leader—he knew the bastard with the torn ear was the leader—lowered his head and brushed his mouth over Maya's face.

"*Get away from her!*" The alley shook this time from the force of his rage.

Two of the wolves stumbled back. The others turned to him now, the growls quieting in their throats.

The alpha took a step toward him, a snarl on his lips.

Adam raised his arms. Let the change begin to sweep over him. "I'm going to burn you," he promised as the scales began to form over his flesh. His fingers lengthened, became deadly talons. "Burn the flesh off your bones and *make you scream!*"

Whimpers. More wolves backed away. White-hot power burst through him. He felt the wings rip from his back, shredding his clothes and growing, stretching—

The alpha held his ground.

The others huddled against the alley's walls.

Maya lay on the ground. Not moving, but still breathing. Still living.

He wouldn't be able to say the same thing about the wolves in a few moments.

A smile twisted his lips, revealing the teeth that were growing ever longer, stronger.

The alpha lunged for him.

Still in half-human form, Adam caught the wolf around the neck with one hand and threw him back ten feet.

"You don't know who you're fucking with," he said, his voice deeper, rougher as the fire worked its way up his throat.

A boy crawled forward from the darkness. Some kid covered in grime and blood with eyes that looked too big. He crouched over Maya.

The alpha climbed to his feet.

"L-Lucas." The kid's voice. Weak. "H-help . . . h-her . . ."

The wolf's head cocked toward her. His body tensed. Then he leapt—

Placing his body between Maya and Adam.

"Give her to me," Adam ordered, fighting to stay human for just a few more moments. When the change took him fully, hell would come. Fire. Death. The rage he felt was too strong. Too hot.

The wolves would all burn.

Everything would burn.

Monster. Devil.

Maya had thought she was the evil one—she had no idea just how damn evil he could be.

The alpha growled.

"Give her to me or I'll burn your pack to ashes!" He was ready. Smoke drifted from his nose.

Hold on, stay human until she's safe. Don't hurt her.

The wolf's head lowered toward the ground.

Submission.

Adam ran forward. His wings flapped in the air in powerful bursts behind him. Not fully formed, not yet.

Soon.

He grabbed Maya, slicing her arms with his talons and scales as he picked her up and pressed her to his chest.

Her heart stuttered against him.

No!

"Let me help you."

Adam's head jerked up.

A man stood where the wolf had been. Naked. Muscled. Head still bowed in submission. "Let me help you both, Wyvern."

"Don't so much as move!" Adam snapped. The dragon was too close to the surface.

The woman in his arms was his only link to control. If she died, that link would shatter.

Using a talon, he slashed a line across his chest. Forced her mouth to him. She had to drink. If she took his blood, if he could just get her to *drink*—then she'd be all right.

Don't leave me, Maya. I need you.

More than he'd realized.

Her lips were still against him. Soft lips.

Cold.

"Drink!" His snarl screamed into the night. *Drink.* The plea whispered through his mind, hers.

Her body trembled and her lips parted. The blood trickled into her mouth. She moaned, shifted her head, and her teeth sank into his chest.

Adam groaned and held her tight.

His gaze met the wolf shifter's.

Her mouth suckled him, drawing his blood from right above his heart and taking it with her tongue and lips.

The lust he felt each time she drank from him exploded through his body.

The wolf kept watching him.

The pack stayed in the shadows.

Adam shuddered. *Her mouth.*

Maya's lashes fluttered. He didn't want her to see him as he was—some horrible mix of man and dragon. Face changed, teeth deadly, wings, talons, scales.

Her eyes opened.

No fear.

Hunger. Need.

No fear.

Her tongue licked across the wound. Then her mouth lifted, lips red and glistening. Her lips trembled, curved. "I . . . was . . . hoping to see you . . . again, S-Slick."

Her words were for the man, not the beast. His arms tightened around her.

Maya's smile slowly faded and her lashes closed.

Chapter 14

She felt like she'd been hit by a truck. Or maybe by a dozen very pissed-off level-ten demons.

Maya groaned, feeling pain in every cell of her body. Her mouth was bone dry and her lashes felt like weights were holding them down.

"It's all right." Adam's voice. Close. A hand, *his hand,* smoothed over her cheek. "You're safe."

Safe. She liked that word.

But she hadn't been safe before. She'd been in the alley, surrounded by the pack. Snarls. Growls. Pain.

Then he'd been there. Adam. Her dragon. Roaring with fury. Fire on his breath and wings on his back.

Maya forced her lashes to lift. She needed to see him.

Bright light flooded her eyes, making black spots dance in the air around her head. She blinked them away, found him.

Sitting beside the bed. Shirtless. Streaks of blood on his chest. Worry on his face.

She lifted her hand, wanting to touch him.

He caught her fingers in a grip of steel. His gaze held hers. So intense. Emotions swirled in his stare. Anger. Fear. Lust.

"You're a liar, Maya Black." He said the words softly.

Not exactly the impassioned words she'd been hoping to hear. "Y-yeah, w-well—" Damn, her throat hurt. She needed a drink, bad. "Y-you're a w-winged dragon."

He blinked at that, then leaned forward, closing the space

between them and keeping his gaze on her. "You told me you didn't help people." His lips thinned. "Then you risked your life not just for Cammie, but for that boy."

The young shifter. Her heart lurched in her chest. "I-is he all . . . right?" Her voice was getting stronger. She swallowed a few times, trying to ease the ache at the back of her throat.

A muscle flexed along his jaw. "You should worry about yourself."

Well, the pain she felt meant that she was alive. What more was there to worry about? "H-how . . . is he?" That boy, with the tortured eyes—had he survived the wounds *she'd* inflicted on him?

"He's healing." His fingers tightened around hers. "What the hell were you thinking?"

She'd been thinking the boy was just a kid. Tortured. Held prisoner, and, thanks to her, poisoned with silver. "C-couldn't . . . leave him."

"Like you couldn't leave me?"

No, that had been different.

"And what about that prostitute on Quentin Street?"

What?

"You fought that demon when you saw him attacking her. You couldn't just leave them alone, either, could you? You had to *help*."

He made the word sound like a curse.

Beneath the pain, her own anger begin to stir. "I do . . . w-what I want." She didn't need some thousand-year-old dragon telling her how to run her life. "I-if I hadn't gone back, the . . . boy would be dead." Of course, until Adam had told her that the kid was healing, she'd thought he *had* died.

"You almost died saving him."

Maya shook her head. "S-saving him was . . . the easy part." She sighed. "Damn p-pack . . . they nearly . . . k-killed me."

"And I nearly killed them." Stark.

A frown pulled down her brows as she stared at him. "Adam . . ."

He brought her hand to his lips. Kissed the palm and she felt heat tingle across her skin. "I nearly killed them all," he whispered again. "I wanted to burn them to dust."

She swallowed. "What stopped you?"

His breath blew against her hand. "You did."

Oh. She didn't exactly remember stopping him. Maya just remembered opening her eyes and being damn grateful to see him.

Because for a few minutes there, she hadn't thought that she'd ever look into his eyes again. "Adam—"

"You need to drink."

Her eyes immediately fell to his throat.

"You fed in the alley, but it wasn't enough. You need to take more blood."

She licked her lips. His blood would soothe her terrible thirst and help her fight the weakness that weighed down her limbs.

He eased into the bed with her. Brought her hand to his chest. Such a warm, strong chest.

His fingers tangled in her hair, urged her head close to his neck. "Take all that you need," he said, his voice rumbling against her ear.

Her tongue smoothed over his flesh. Felt the vibration of his pulse. Fast and hard.

"Take, Maya. Take from me."

Her teeth pierced his skin and the rich taste of his blood filled her mouth.

More.

Her lips tightened greedily around him and she drank, loving the flavor of his essence. So much power, so much strength. She could literally feel it pouring into her.

Her fingers trailed down his chest. Dug into his skin. And she kept tasting him, drinking him in and strengthening the bond between them.

He shuddered against her and shifted his body, pressing the swollen length of his arousal against her leg. She could feel the thick shaft, through the thin sheet, through the bloodstained jeans he still wore.

Maya was aware of an emptiness inside. A hollow ache. She wanted him to fill her, to thrust deep and sure into her sex and stop the yearning.

Her tongue swept over his neck, catching the drops of blood that trickled over his skin. She moaned, the tightness in her body changing swiftly from pain to taut need.

"Easy," Adam said, and his hands caught her shoulders and pushed her back against the pillows. "Your body needs more time to recover."

His blood would heal her. Her body would mend. She needed him. Her breasts were tight, the nipples hard and eager for his mouth.

She saw the slight flare of his nostrils, knew that he could smell the cream spreading between her legs. Yet his hold on her didn't ease and she didn't have the strength to fight him. "*Adam.*" A whispered demand.

He stared at her with eyes a stormy emerald. His pupils were expanding, his lust rising to match her own.

"I need you." Maya held his gaze, needing him to understand. It wasn't just his blood, *it was him.*

His head lowered. His lips swept over hers. Too light. Too fast. A protest rose in her throat, but Adam just shook his head.

She tried to break free of his hold, to grab him and force him back—but his strength was greater than hers.

"Relax, baby. I'll take care of you." His words were said against her neck. His breath tickled her skin. His lips feathered over her, and then she felt the wet lick of his tongue right over her pulse point.

Her hips arched. *Yes.* That was good, that was—

His teeth closed over her flesh. Bit down. A bolt of sexual heat spiraled straight from her neck to her sex as a choked moan eased past her lips.

"You're not the only one who likes to bite," he grated and then he was moving down her body. Kissing her flesh. Licking her. All the while keeping her hands pinned on either side of her head.

His breath fanned over her breast, making the sensitive nipple tighten even more. His lips closed over the pink tip. His tongue lashed her, then he bit her flesh.

"Adam!"

Not too hard, not hard enough to pierce the skin. The bite was just fierce enough to send pleasure ripping through her.

And to make the hunger burn even more.

His mouth widened and he took her breast into his mouth. Sucking strongly, pulling at the nipple with tongue and teeth.

Maya's head pushed back against the pillow. Her legs shifted restlessly against the bed. She could smell her own arousal, could feel the quiver of her sex.

He turned his attention to the other breast. Laved the nipple. Drew it deep into his mouth. She arched into him, clenching her thighs tight in a vain effort to ease the throbbing need.

"I love the way you taste," he muttered against her breast. "Sweet. Hot. *Like you're mine.*"

His head slid down. His teeth grazed her stomach. His tongue swirled over her belly button.

Then her hands were free.

He touched her, spreading her thighs wide and lowering his head between them. "The taste is even better here," he said, the words full of a dark lust.

His fingers parted her folds, spread the cream over her flesh. Then he drove two fingers into her, thrusting them knuckles-deep into her straining opening.

His mouth pressed against her clit. Kissed. His lips parted, closed over the bud, and sucked, hard, *harder*.

His fingers pulled back, only to plunge inside again. Maya's breath caught in her throat. Her fingers dug into the mattress, claws scratching, cutting.

Adam withdrew his fingers. Licked her clit, pressed the edge of his teeth against her—

"*Yes!*" She hissed out the word, feeling the promise of pleasure tighten her body.

His tongue pushed against the opening of her body. Then thrust inside. Warm. Wet.

Tasting her.

Devouring her.

Maya came on a long, hard wave of release. Her hips bucked against him, but Adam grabbed her, chaining her in place with an iron-hard grip.

And he tasted. He drove his tongue into her again and again and lapped up her cream as she shuddered and moaned beneath him.

When the climax ended, she went limp, every muscle loosening as she lay sprawled beneath him.

Adam's hands slowly eased their fierce hold. His head lifted and his mouth glistened from her sensual moisture.

Maya lifted her hands, reaching for the snap of his jeans.

"No." He caught her fingers, held them tight. "That was for you."

She shook her head. She'd never been the type to take her pleasure while another needed.

Adam *needed.* She could see the desire on his face. Feel it in the long bulge pressing against her.

But he was pulling away from her. Rising from the bed. Clenching his hands and gazing at her with eyes that held secrets.

She didn't like secrets.

If she weren't suddenly feeling so damn tired, she'd find out just what was happening behind those spooky eyes of his.

"Rest, Maya." His lips quirked the faintest bit. "When your strength is back, I'll have my turn."

His turn. She liked the sound of that.

A knock rapped at the door. A male voice called, "The girl's awake."

The girl. Cammie.

Adam drew the sheets over her. Pressed a kiss to her lips. "Rest." He stalked to the door.

Maya closed her eyes.

"You . . . worried me."

Her eyes squinted open at that.

"I thought you were going to die, before I could get those bastards off you." A muscle flexed along his jaw. "And I thought that I was going to fucking kill them all."

She didn't know what to say.

His gaze held hers. "Don't risk yourself like that again." An order.

Then he was gone—

Leaving her with the memory of a selfless pleasure and with the strength of his blood spreading through her body.

The second time she awoke, Maya's senses were sharp and focused—and she realized that she wasn't in their dump of a motel.

The room was big. With white walls and windows covered by thick shutters. She was lying in a brass bed, and a leather chair sat to her right.

Where the hell was she?

Her clothes were at the foot of the bed. Not the clothes she'd worn earlier, because those babies were probably ripped to shreds, but clothes she'd left in her bag, *back at the motel.*

She rose slowly. There was no sign of Adam. Probably with the girl. She'd better go find them, make certain Cammie was all right—and figure out exactly where she was.

Maya pulled on the cotton panties and the plain white bra. Jerked on her jeans—

And caught the scent of a wolf.

She spun around.

He pushed open the door.

Dark hair, blue eyes. She didn't even need to glance at his ear to recognize the asshole who'd tried to kill her.

"What the fuck are you doing here?" she snarled, raising her hands, claws at the ready.

His gaze met hers. One black brow lifted. "I'm not here to hurt you, vampire."

"Yeah, well, I can't make you the same promise." She remembered the jerk's claws raking across her back. "You didn't answer my question."

What could have been a smile curved his lips. "This is my house. One of them, anyway."

She was in the wolf's house? Why hadn't Adam thought to mention that important little fact to her? Maya yanked up the zipper of her jeans, snapped the button closed, and reached for her T-shirt.

"Don't dress on my account," he murmured and his gaze dipped down to her chest. "I find the view rather enjoyable."

Oh, she just bet he did. Maya wrenched the shirt over her head—then slammed him back against the wall. "Tell me why I shouldn't kill you right now." She didn't have any warm, fuzzy memories of this guy. No, he was just a pain in the ass.

One that sorely needed to be eliminated.

"I shouldn't have attacked you," the wolf said. "I'm sorry."

Maya blinked, caught completely off guard. "Er, what?" No way he'd just apologized.

"Uh, you're cutting into my flesh." Spoken calmly, with not a hint of pain in the words.

Glancing down, she saw that her claws were, indeed, buried in his chest. "Oh, my bad." But she didn't feel particularly bad about the slip.

She hadn't dug nearly as deep as he had.

But still—she stepped back.

He exhaled.

"Who are you?" she asked him softly, keeping her body tense, ready. Just in case this was all an act and she had to attack.

"My name is Lucas Simone. I'm the leader of my pack."

Yeah, she'd guessed he was the boss.

"Why have you been hunting me?" she pressed him, eyes narrowing.

"He wasn't." A softer voice. Male, but younger. Not as hard.

Maya slowly turned her head. She'd caught the other wolf's scent just seconds before he spoke, but since she didn't particularly view the kid as a threat, she hadn't reacted.

The teen looked cautiously at Lucas, then glanced back at her. "He was following me."

Her gaze darted between them. Same dark hair. Chin. Nose. Hell, subtract about twenty years from the alpha and he and the kid would almost be twins. "So what's the deal?" she asked. "You his son?"

"Jordan is my brother."

Ah.

"I thought you'd attacked him, tried to kill him, and I—"

"I did," she said. *Hell, no sense lying over that one.*

Lucas stiffened.

"But she also came back for me and carried me out of that hellhole," Jordan whispered.

Yeah, but she *had* shot him.

She didn't look at the alpha, just kept her eyes on Jordan as she said, "I didn't want to hurt you." Damn, those words sure seemed hollow and he looked so young. He was pale, but his injuries, like her own, seemed to have healed. "I had to rescue the girl and it was obvious you weren't going to let me pass unless I'd either killed you or incapacitated the hell out of you." A touch of admiration filled her tone.

The kid was a fighter.

She liked that.

"I thought you were gonna hurt her. Thought you were just another vamp come to make her scream." He swallowed. Glanced down at the floor. "They were always coming to make us scream."

Bastards.

"Well, I've got to say, you sure managed to hold your own against me." She tapped her right foot. The ankle was fine now. "You were about five seconds away from taking my foot off."

"Kill or be killed," Jordan said, the words cracking slightly. "I was ready to die."

To protect Cammie.

The kid was gonna grow up into one fine man.

"I think we're even," she murmured, then pointed a claw at him. "But don't ever so much as think about coming at me in wolf form with those teeth again."

His lips hitched into a half-smile. "I-I won't."

"Good." Now she looked back at Lucas. So he'd been tracking his brother. Good cause. But she still didn't trust the asshole. "The first night, at Marie's place, you should've just told me you were looking for the kid."

"You didn't give me a chance."

Because the pack had been coming for her, fangs bared, talking and playing nice hadn't exactly been on her mind.

He rubbed his shoulder. "But you sure as hell gave me something to remember you by."

"I don't like to be forgettable."

"You aren't."

The floor squeaked just beyond the door. Hell, someone else? The room was getting too crowded as it was. She inhaled, expecting another wolf, but she caught the scent of—

Nothing.

No one.

The floor squeaked again and Adam strode inside. His eyes narrowed when he caught sight of the wolves.

"I-I should go," Jordan muttered, ducking his head and then brushing quickly by Adam.

Lucas sighed. "You scare him," he said to Adam.

"Smart kid."

Adam's eyes darted to Maya's bare feet. Then back to the wolf. "Am I interrupting something?" A hard edge sharpened the words. A hint of anger.

She shrugged. "Just trying to figure out why wolfie here has been trying to kill me."

"Um." Adam was still staring at Lucas. "Damn good thing he didn't succeed."

Lucas held his gaze. "I told *you* what happened. I came here to clear things up with her."

He'd been trying to find his brother. By tracking her. "What made you think I'd even know where your brother was?"

It was Adam who answered. "Because he heard you were working with me."

Lucas nodded. "I knew the same vamps who'd taken his niece had also taken Jordan."

Her breath expelled in a rush. "Shit. They were planning some kind of special feast for Nassor, weren't they?" Two shifters. So much power.

They would have been drained dry.

What a great Welcome-Back-to-the-Undead-Life gift for Nassor.

"Once you started helping Brody, I figured you had to be blood linked to that bastard Nassor."

Yeah, like she could help that.

"I knew you could lead me straight to him." One brow lifted. "Then that fool demon sent me chasing shadows."

Ah, Tim. She'd known to count on him to sell her out. "But then you smarted up, didn't you? You went to the hospital, threatened Sean, and found out exactly where I'd gone."

Adam's head jerked toward her. "What?"

Maya pursed her lips at the surprise on the wolf shifter's face. "What? Damn, give me some credit, would you? I knew you were there when I called him."

"How?" Lucas looked pissed. Poor wolf. He'd probably thought he'd been so smart.

Not smart enough.

"Sean warned me."

"No—I was there, I heard everything."

"*I* heard his heart, beating too fast." A deliberate tip, a method they'd used in the past. "I told him where I was, knowing that you'd come." She'd just hoped to have a little more time—enough time to free Cammie and disappear. "You got here faster than I thought." And her grand plan had gone to hell.

But at least she'd gotten the girl out.

The fact that Maya had nearly gotten herself killed, well, that had definitely not been in the master scheme.

"You should have told me," Adam snapped, taking a step closer to her.

She winced. Yeah, she'd known he wouldn't be too pleased about her keeping that fact secret. "We had to move, Adam. The fact that the pack was coming—it didn't matter. We had to get into that feeding room."

If the clock turned back and she had to do it all again, knowing she'd wind up in that alley—*shit, did it always have to be an alley?*—she'd do it.

"For the record," she said, "I don't appreciate it when my friends are threatened." She smiled, showing her fangs. "I don't appreciate it one damn bit."

Lucas nodded. "Message understood."

"When I get back to L.A., I expect to find Sean unharmed. He'd better be."

"He is."

She grunted. "Don't ever threaten him again, wolf. Got it? Ever." She didn't trust the wolf. Not as far as she could throw his furry ass. And that would be about ten feet. She still wasn't sure how she'd wound up *in his house* and as soon as he got his butt out of the room, she planned to grill Adam.

A vampire hiding with a pack of wolves. That just had bad news written all over it.

But, then again, any of Nassor's goons who happened to be searching for her and Adam sure wouldn't expect to find them rooming with the wolves.

"So I guess we have a truce, vampire," Lucas said, voice soft. "For now."

Maya's head tilted back. "I guess we do." Weak truce though it was.

She watched him stalk to the door. "Lucas."

He glanced back at her.

"Tell me, when you were having a grand old time destroying Temptation, did you happen to kill a tall, too-pretty vampire with blond hair? He would have been hurt already, shot in the back." She'd missed his heart, dammit. But there hadn't been a choice when she'd fired.

The asshole had been between her and escape.

"Torrence." Lucas spit out the name. Ah, so he knew about the vamp leader. "Bastard got away."

Hell.

"I'll find him," the wolf shifter said. "He's the one who took Jordan. I'll find him—and I'll peel the skin from his bones."

Nice visual. Maya knew the guy meant every dark word. No empty threat from the wolf.

"Easy, wolf. That bastard is mine," Adam said. "Keep your claws to yourself."

Lucas just shook his head, then left the room with his shoulders tense and his back tight with tension.

Uh, oh. A pissing match for death rights.

She'd put her odds on the dragon.

Maya faced Adam fully and found him staring at her with narrowed eyes. "What?"

"He wants you."

A choked laugh slipped past her lips. Damn. That had been the absolute last thing she'd expected him to say. "Uh, I think he wants to kill me."

"No." Definite. Angry. "I could smell his lust. *He wants you.*"

She hadn't smelled a hint of arousal from the other guy, but—

Adam's senses were sharper than hers.

She rubbed her temples, aware of a steady, dull throbbing. "Well, I doubt it was anything personal. I mean, show a guy a pair of breasts and he usually gets horny."

"*What?*"

She looked at him then, really looked at him. The hard set of his jaw. The tight lips. The narrowed eyes. "Slick, are you jealous?" *Of a hairy wolf?*

He didn't answer, just stared at her with glittering eyes.

Well, well. First worry, now jealousy. Wasn't the dragon just full of surprises?

A smile began to tilt her lips.

Adam moved in a flash, his fingers clamping around her arms. "Don't play with me, Maya. You don't want to rouse the beast."

Maybe she did. A heady excitement swept through her. Adam had been at the edge of his control with her before. What would it be like to see that power completely unleashed? To push him over the edge?

Oh, but she wanted to find out.

Maya lifted her hand, trailed a sharp nail down his cheek, and watched his eyes flare with arousal. "You didn't finish what you started earlier," she murmured.

His fingers tightened around her. "Maya . . ."

She liked the way he said her name. Liked the hunger she heard in his voice.

It was a pity that she'd have to leave him soon.

But maybe, just maybe, she could have one last, wild ride with her dragon.

She parted her lips, wanting to feel his mouth on hers, to taste his breath on her tongue.

He stepped back. Drew in a deep gulp of air. "There's—I came in here—because Cammie wants to see you."

"Cammie?" She felt like she'd just been doused by icy water. "Why does she want to see me?" As a rule, she wasn't exactly good with the kiddies.

She'd saved the girl. Gotten her back with her uncle. End of story.

"She won't talk to me," Adam said, running a hand over his face. "She gets quiet every time I go near her." His lips twisted. "She just talks to that boy, and she keeps asking about you."

"Uh, what about me?" She'd probably scarred the kid for life. Dragging the girl through that hellhole, shooting a vampire in front of her—oh, yeah, not exactly scrapbook moments.

He shrugged and looked a bit helpless. "I-I don't know. She just wants you." His voice hardened. "So I told her I'd get you."

Ah. Now this was the Adam she knew so well. The hardass. The do-what-I-say dragon.

Lucky for him, she was curious about the kid. Maya found her boots. Finished dressing. Her gaze scanned the room. "Where's my gun? My knife?" She'd sure feel better if she were armed in this den of wolves.

"The wolves didn't feel too safe leaving the gun and the silver bullets around you."

Smart of them.

Adam bent down, drew her knife from his boot. "But I kept this for you."

The blade had been cleaned. It glinted, beautiful and deadly. Her fingers closed around the hilt. "Thanks." Who said the way to a girl's heart was candy and flowers? She'd take weapons any day.

She tucked the knife away, already feeling better. Claws, teeth, and a blade. Yeah, she was getting back to her old self.

Which meant that, pretty soon, it would be time to hunt.

And time to leave the dragon behind.

Damn. Why did that thought make her ache?

Chapter 15

Adam watched Maya creep into Cammie's room. His vampire looked nervous as hell and she kept glancing to the left and the right—like she expected to be attacked.

By a nine-year old.

Cammie sat on the bed, dressed in a pair of pale blue pajamas. When his guards had arrived—they'd flown in the minute he had Cammie safe—they'd brought Cammie's clothes with them. And for an instant, the girl had smiled. *An instant.*

Cammie looked up at Maya's approach and her eyes widened.

"Uh, hi, kid." Maya rubbed her palms over the front of her jeans.

Cammie stared at her, swallowed, then cast a quick glance over at Adam.

"Hey, beautiful," he said, forcing a smile. Cammie talked to him, but only when she absolutely had to do so. He was worried about the tension he sensed in her, the fear that bubbled below the surface.

Adam eased back, moving to stand next to the wall. He tried to keep his body as still as possible, wanting to watch and see just why his niece seemed so fascinated by Maya.

Hell, maybe it was just a family addiction.

Because the vampire most definitely fascinated him.

The fucking wolf had better stay away from her.

Adam clenched his teeth, fought the burn of jealousy in his heart, and waited.

Maya eased onto the edge of the bed.

Cammie's head cocked to the side. "Can I see your teeth?"

"Uh, sure." Maya smiled, baring her fangs.

His niece jerked back.

"Hey, wow—it's okay. I didn't mean to scare you." Maya rubbed her temples. "Look, your teeth get pretty sharp, too, right? I mean, I've seen your uncle's—"

"I hurt someone." Whispered words.

He saw Maya's spine straighten. "You did? Well, if it makes you feel better, I've hurt lots of someones."

He had to close his eyes a moment at that one. Not exactly what he'd been hoping she'd tell his young niece.

"I . . . b-burned her. She wanted t-to b-bite me . . . so I burned her." Cammie's chin jerked up. "I-I didn't mean t-to, I just—"

"It's all right, kid." Maya's hand reached across the bedding. Touched the tips of Cammie's fingers. "You did what you had to do in order to protect yourself."

She shook her head. "I hurt her, b-bad."

"And she would have hurt you." Maya obviously wasn't trying to sugarcoat things. He wasn't sure if that was a good idea or not, but now that Cammie was talking, he wasn't about to interrupt.

"You did the right thing," Maya continued, her voice firm. "Don't let it eat you up inside. You saved yourself, that's all that matters."

"I see her wh-when I close my eyes. *I see her.*"

"You'll probably keep seeing her," Maya said matter-of-factly. "And you'll hurt and you'll cry and then you'll realize that you're alive, and you're strong. Then one day, those images you see—they'll just stop."

"When?"

"When you're not scared anymore."

"Do you . . . ever s-see things that scare you?"

Not likely, Adam thought.

"Sometimes," Maya said slowly.

"Like what?"

What would scare a fierce vampire who'd killed demons and shifters?

"Spiders." Maya gave a quick shudder. "I hate those hairy eight-legged freaks."

Cammie giggled. *Giggled.* But as fast as her lip had curved into a smile, the brief hint of humor faded and sadness flashed across her face.

"What about you, Cammie? What else scares you?"

Adam watched the little girl's hands tremble. "Vampires."

Maya didn't so much as flinch. "Yeah, we can be pretty scary." She lowered her head toward Cammie. "And you sure were introduced to the worst of our lot."

A tear tracked down Cammie's cheek. "Yes."

"Those vamps—they'll never hurt you again. You'll never even so much as see them for the rest of your life." The words sounded like a vow.

"P-promise?"

No hesitation. "I promise."

The little girl's breath pushed out in a rush. "You don't—you don't look like them. I mean, besides the teeth, you don't."

Adam inched forward, just enough to catch Maya's smile. "What do I look like, then?"

"An angel." A flush stained his niece's cheeks.

His gaze shifted back to Maya.

She laughed, a quick deep laugh that filled the room—and hit him in the heart. "Oh, kid, trust me on this, I'm no angel."

"I think you are." Hushed. Cammie's eyes were on her hands. On the fingers that Maya held. "You saved me. Took me away from th-those m-monsters."

Silence. Maya stared at the girl's bent head.

"I would have died without you," Cammie whispered.

"Your uncle never would have let that happen."

Damn right he wouldn't.

A tear fell onto the bedspread. "My mom's dead."

Cammie was sure opening up to Maya. Adam couldn't remember the last time the girl had talked so much. Even before the kidnapping, she'd never—

"Yeah, so is mine." A pause. "Hard, isn't it?"

A nod. Then. "M-my dad, he's gone, too." Cammie's blond head tilted back as she gazed at Maya.

Adam rubbed his palm against the ache in his chest.

"Your uncle told me that," Maya said, still not looking at him.

"I-is your dad gone? Or is he—"

"I never knew my dad. It was just me and my mom. Then when she passed, well, it was just me." She finally glanced back at Adam. "But you're not alone like I was. You've got your uncle."

Cammie turned her bright stare toward him, blinking away tears.

"You know what he did, Cammie?"

The girl shook her head.

"He came all the way to Los Angeles to find me—because he knew that I could find *you.*"

"He did?"

"Um. He was attacked by wolves, and vampires, but he just kept fighting—kept looking for you."

The tears fell faster.

"You know why he did all that?" Maya squeezed Cammie's hand.

The small blond head shook in a quick "no."

"Because he loves you." Maya motioned Adam toward the bed. "When you've got somebody like your uncle who loves you, you don't ever need to worry about being alone or being scared—because he'll always take care of you."

As long as he had breath in his body.

Cammie's lips trembled. She jumped out of the bed, ran to him, and threw her arms around his stomach.

Maya swallowed. Smiled faintly.

Then she stood and walked out of the room.

Adam held Cammie as tight as he could.

Thank you, Maya.

* * *

Shit. She was crying. Maya hurried past the guards at Cammie's door—human guards that Adam had told her that he'd brought in for the kid's protection—and nearly ran for the balcony doors at the end of the long hallway.

Crying. Her. She swiped away the tears and pushed open the glass door. All because a kid reminded her of—

A life long ago. A life she'd forgotten. *Tried to forget.*

Her temples pounded viciously now. A steady, aching drumbeat of pain.

She'd been like Cammie once. Scared to death. Terrified of being alone.

But she hadn't been lucky like the kid. There'd been no Uncle Adam in her life.

What if there had been?

Maybe things would have been different.

Maybe she wouldn't be a vampire.

Maybe she'd be living a normal life. With a husband, a kid of her own.

Or hell, maybe she wouldn't. Maybe fate just had a plan for everyone, and the plan for her had been—

To become one of the monsters that little girls feared.

The terrible throbbing in her head stabbed at her, and Maya winced. Damn, what was happening? Why was—

Come.

Her fingers reached out, grasped the wrought-iron railing and clenched. No, not yet. She wasn't ready.

Come.

The whisper in her mind—not a whisper any longer. A hard demand. A call that cut straight to her soul.

Come.

She stared into the night, knowing without any doubt that the Born Master had risen.

And he was calling his family home.

Come.

The words she'd spoken to Cammie played through her mind, battling that insistent call.

Those vamps—they'll never hurt you again. You'll never even so much as see them for the rest of your life.

P-promise?

I promise.

The wrought iron began to bend beneath her fingers.

Come.

A promise had been given.

Cammie didn't need to live in fear.

Maya tilted her head back, gazed up at the bloodred moon. A killing moon. Fitting for Nassor.

Maybe fate had planned this night for him. And for her.

"I'm coming, you bastard. I just hope you're ready for me." Because she'd bring hell to his door.

Adam held Cammie while she cried, cradling her against his heart and silently vowing that she'd never know fear again.

He'd protect her and make damn certain the vampires who'd taken her didn't see another sunset.

He lifted her into his arms and carried her back to the bed. Her cries were muffled now, but her hold was still as fierce and desperate as before.

He lowered her carefully onto the mattress, then arranged the pillows beneath her head.

She sniffled and caught his hand. "I love you, Uncle Adam."

"I know, baby." He pressed a kiss to her brow. It was a nighttime ritual they'd practiced the last five years. "I love you."

"Always?"

"Always."

She smiled at his usual response and some of the fear finally faded from her gaze. He stayed with her, sitting by the bed until her lashes lowered and her breathing eased into the natural pattern of sleep.

Cammie had been the bright spot in his life from the first moment he'd seen her.

He'd never understood how his brother could give her up. So much joy—so much life—in such a little body.

He pushed back a strand of her hair. Hoped that her dreams would be good and that the nightmares wouldn't slip inside.

When he was certain she was settled for the night, he eased slowly from her room.

He stopped to speak to the guards at her door. Guards who'd flown in that afternoon from Maine to protect Cammie. "You stay with her," he ordered, "every second, until I return."

The men nodded.

Adam exhaled. Things weren't finished with the vampires, not yet.

But they damn well would be—very soon.

He followed Maya's scent down the hallway, stopped at the glass balcony doors, and stared out at her.

Maya's back was to him. Her head tilted back as she gazed up at the dark sky. In the distance, he could just make out the glittering lights of the Vegas Strip, shining like a beacon across the desert.

"Do you always mark what's yours?" Lucas's voice rasped from right behind him.

He'd known he was there, of course. He'd caught the wolf's smell the minute Lucas climbed the stairs.

His gaze drifted down Maya's back. Her jeans hung low on her slender hips, and the T-shirt she wore had ridden up, exposing the pale flesh of her lower back and the black etchings of her tattoo.

Not his mark, but it could have been.

Might as well have been.

The light on the balcony was dim, but with his enhanced vision, he saw the dragon tattoo easily, and he knew that Lucas could see it, too.

"You need to stay away from her," he told the wolf, not bothering to turn his head. He enjoyed his current view too much.

The wolf stepped beside him. Pressed a hand against the glass. "Think that'd be up the vampire, don't you?"

Adam tramped down on the anger that began to rage in him. He turned his head, just a fraction, and saw Lucas watching Maya. "No, it's up to me." His voice roughened as he growled the words. The guy needed to learn his place—and that place was nowhere near Maya.

He hadn't marked her, but he sure as hell wished he had.

She was his.

He wasn't about to give her up to some furry asshole—an asshole who'd tried to kill her.

"She's strong." The wolf didn't sound particularly intimidated. Fool. Lucas continued, "She's a hell of a fighter—and she'd make a passionate mate."

Adam grabbed him, slapping his hand around the wolf's throat and hauling him away from the door and away from Maya. He forced him back against the wall, held Lucas there with the strength of one hand. "I think you're forgetting just who I am." Maybe it was time for a reminder.

"I haven't forgotten a damn thing!" Lucas's eyes began to shine with the power of the wolf. "A woman like her—she might just be worth any fight I have to—"

"She's not for you." His fingers tightened. The wolf's face reddened.

"Is . . . she . . . f-for . . . y-you?" He was huffing out the words.

"Only for me." He lifted Lucas and then slammed him back against the wall. He could still see Maya's body, sprawled on the ground in that filthy alley. If he hadn't gotten there, this jerk would have killed her. *And now he wanted to screw her.*

Not going to happen. Ever.

"I don't care if the woman strolls in front of you naked," which his lady vampire was prone to do, "you so much as touch her and I'll make you wish you'd never walked on this earth." His breath blew across the wolf's face and a cloud of smoke rose around them. Adam smiled, letting his sharp teeth and the smoky air carry his threat. "You understand?"

The wolf tried to nod.

"Good." Adam dropped him.

But Lucas didn't leave. He raised a hand to his throat. "Wh-what . . . makes you think . . . she'd w-want to stay . . . with you?"

Adam glanced back at Maya's figure. At her tattoo. "'Cause the woman has a thing for dragons."

He turned away from Lucas. The urge to rip the wolf in two was strong, but the desire to go to Maya, to touch her, was so much stronger.

Adam shoved open the door and stepped into the night.

"You two finish up?" Maya asked, her back to him.

"Yeah." For now, but if the wolf tried to make a move on Maya, he'd find hell raining down on him.

She glanced over her shoulder, eyes reflecting the stars and moonlight. "You don't have to worry, you know. I don't usually decide to sleep with men after they try to kill me."

He exhaled and took a step toward her. "Good to know."

Her lips curved, just the faintest bit. Her shoulders were stiff, and there was a strange tenseness to her face. "Maya?"

She looked back at the moon. "I didn't thank you."

He stalked closer. "For what?"

"Getting me out of that alley. Saving my ass." She shook her head and the silky mane of her hair drifted around her face. "I died in an alley like that once—or at least, my human self did. I sure as hell didn't want it to happen again."

He reached out his hand. Curled his fingers over hers. "Hey, you would have done the same for me, right?" He tossed the words back to her, expecting a smile, preferably a full one, or a laugh.

Instead, she said, very softly, "Yeah, I would have." She swallowed, opened her mouth, then hesitated.

"Maya?" Something was going on, something he didn't understand.

"When she was fifteen," her fingers were steel tight beneath his, "my mom gave birth to me in an alley like that. I was born in the dirt and the trash."

He stilled, his heart thundering. This was important. She was trusting him with her past.

He knew Maya Black didn't trust many people.

"I was in foster homes at first, then she got me back—don't really know how. She was always drinking and whoring herself out—there were so many men. Men who liked to hurt her."

There was more she wasn't saying, he knew it. "Did they like to hurt you?"

A nod.

Bastards. What he wouldn't give to find them all and to—

"She died when she was twenty-four. God, no one should die that young." The wrought iron groaned beneath her fingers. "There was so much blood. I stepped in it, trying to get to her. Her eyes were open, staring straight up. She'd always been pretty, even when she was drinking and high, but—he made her ugly. In death, *she was so ugly*. Face smashed in. Lips cracked and dripping blood . . ." She broke off, shaking her head. "I couldn't help her. I wanted to, so badly. But there was nothing I could do."

That's why she'd become a cop, he realized. To atone for a life that hadn't even been hers to save. "It wasn't your fault, Maya."

"No, but she didn't deserve to die like that." Her sigh drifted on the wind. "She tried to be good to me—sometimes she'd take me to the park or buy me some crayons, but she was sick, you know? The drugs—they had her too messed up inside."

There was an ache in her voice, one that made him hurt.

"I went back to the homes after she died. Bounced around for years. Didn't let anyone get too close."

She still didn't, he thought, and wished things were different.

"Cammie said she closed her eyes and saw the vampires. For most of my life, I'd close my eyes and see my mother." She shook her head. "I don't want the same thing to happen to the kid. I don't want her to live with fear. To stare into hell."

"She won't." He'd make certain of it.

Maya's hold finally eased on the railing. "No, she won't." Said with absolute assurance. She shook her head, as if shaking off the past, and turned toward him. "She'll live a long, good life, won't she, Slick?"

If he had anything to say about it, yeah, she would. He nodded.

"Good." One of her hands was still beneath his. Her fingers turned, curled around his. "You're a pretty solid guy, you know that? For a, you know, thousand-year-old, fire-breathing dragon." The words were light, but there were lines of tension near her mouth.

She was still holding something back from him.

"And you're something damn special, Maya Black, for a vampire with a serious attitude problem." *She was special,* and so very important to him. Becoming more so each moment.

Her lips curled into one of those real smiles that he liked.

Her fingers broke free of his and rose to stroke his chest through the shirt he wore. "I've been thinking about you," she said, and her voice was tinged with the faintest huskiness.

At her touch, his cock immediately began to swell. "Oh?" He'd wanted her since she first woke and he'd gotten to taste her sweet flesh. He'd tamped down the hunger, wanting to play the gentleman and to show her that *he* had control, not the beast that lusted within him.

But she was looking at him now, with a fierce need in her eyes, and her lips—so red and wet—were just inches from his.

"After the way you touched me, I couldn't stop thinking about you." Her index finger traced over his left nipple. "I think it's time we finished what you started."

He wanted to, with every cell in his body, but . . . "Maya, the wolves are patrolling, they'll see us." He didn't want anyone seeing her body but him.

Her smile stretched, but didn't reach her hungry gaze.

"Relax, Slick." She pushed him back, forcing him deeper into the darkness alongside the house. "No one can see us from here."

He wasn't so sure about that. His back was to the wall. The glass doors were about five feet away, and Maya—

She was undoing his jeans.

"Maya—"

"Relax." His zipper slid down with a loud hiss. "Isn't that what you said to me?"

His cock sprang into her waiting hands. At her light touch, his erection tautened, arousal building hot and fast.

She made a faint *hum* in the back of her throat and her fingers tightened around him.

Adam clenched his back teeth.

Her hand began to move on him, slow, steady strokes from root to tip. Again and again.

"Do you like this?" She asked, her voice husky.

"Yes . . ."

She kneeled before him, lowering her mouth just over his straining erection. "What about this?" Her lips closed over the tip of his cock, sucking lightly.

"*Yes!*"

Her tongue licked him, a long, winding caress that covered the head of his shaft. Then her mouth was moving on him, sucking strong and hard and she took more of him into the wet warmth of her mouth. More, *more*.

Adam thrust against her, unable to stop the desperate movement of his hips. *Her mouth—so damn good.*

She took him in deep, caressing every inch of his cock with her skilled tongue and lips.

His balls were tight, his muscles locked, and he knew that if he didn't stop her soon, he'd come in her mouth, *in the next thirty seconds.*

"Maya." Her name was a warning, one gritted from between his teeth.

She didn't stop.

"*Maya.*" A shudder worked over him. So close.

Her mouth tightened around him.

He grabbed her head, forcing her to stop the delicious motions. She looked up at him, eyes wide and full of dark desire.

The man struggled to hold on to his control as he stared at her, on her knees before him. The beast raged in a maelstrom of greedy lust and need.

Then Maya scraped the edge of her teeth over his shaft. Pleasure ripped through him.

The man's control shattered as the beast took over.

He growled, a deep rumble that filled the night, and jerked Maya to her feet. Their hands fought, struggled as they both tried to strip her clothes away.

She kicked out of her jeans. He ripped her underwear. Lifted her into his arms. "Wrap your legs around me." Because he was going to take her there. Screw any audience who might be watching.

He'd take his woman right there.

His shaft pushed at the entrance of her body. In the past, he'd waited, wanting her to be ready for the hard length of his cock.

Now, he couldn't wait.

He had to take.

His hands clamped tight over her hips. Her legs clamped around him. Her gaze, black as the night, held his.

Adam thrust inside her, burying his shaft in her creamy warmth.

Her mouth opened on a gasp and the tips of her fangs peeked out at him.

Need thundered through him. "Bite me," he snarled, pumping his hips against her, driving as hard and deep as he could go.

Her teeth closed over his throat, pierced the skin.

Fuck, yes.

His cock swelled even more inside her and her delicate muscles clamped around every inch of his erection.

So. Damn. Good.

She took his blood, sucking, licking—and he took her,

thrusting harder, harder, as the beast inside screamed for release.

Her hips jerked against him, rising and falling in a frantic rhythm. She ripped her mouth from his neck, blood on her lips—

She came, squeezing him with her climax and soaking his cock with her cream.

The dragon broke free of his reins.

His claws lengthened. The scent of smoke rose in the air around them. *Claim. Mate.*

In a swift move, he spun around and shoved her against the hard bricks of the house.

He pulled his cock out, keeping only the tip in her quivering sex. He stared down at the flesh glinting with the cover of her cream—then plunged in as deep as he could go.

Maya moaned and her claws dug into his shoulders, ripping past the fabric of his shirt.

Fire built in him, a ravenous blaze of lust and need, greed and possession.

Mine.

A thrust that shook her body.

Mine.

He yanked up her shirt, shoved her bra out of his way, and clamped his mouth over one tight nipple.

Mine.

He'd never thought to have a woman of his own, not after Isabella. He'd taken his pleasure over the centuries, more times than he could remember, but Maya, she was different.

Mine.

The base of his spine began to prickle. His balls were drawn up tight, and—

Maya came again, shuddering, and the shields around her mind fell away and the blood link clicked into place.

Hunger.

Need.

Mine. His thoughts, hers. It didn't matter.

Adam thrust deep into her, faster, faster, his control gone, only aware now of the animal need to take.

The soft thud of their flesh filled his ears, the scent of sex blended with the smoke in the air.

"Maya." Never had he wanted like this, not with any other woman, not in all the centuries he'd lived.

He knew he'd never feel this way again.

Her mouth locked on his throat again. Drinking, sucking so strongly.

Adam sank into her as far as he could go.

His climax exploded through him in a blinding wave of passion. His cock jerked, semen flooding inside her as he came, calling her name and holding her tight.

His shout echoed in the night and he didn't give a damn who heard him call—

Her name.

The release shook him, sending a burst of euphoria to every nerve in his body and lasting—*lasting*—

Adam shuddered. *Fucking perfect.*

When the orgasm finally ended, the soft vibrations of Maya's sex, aftershocks of pleasure, swept over the sensitive head of his cock.

Her tongue swiped slowly across his neck. Her head lifted. Black eyes met his.

Her heart raced in a rhythm far too fast.

Just like his.

They stared at each other in silence. He tried to reach out to her mind, but found she'd put a shield in place, effectively blocking their link.

Her heart slowed and her eyes lightened. After a moment, her legs lowered and she pushed against his shoulders.

He didn't want to move. He wanted to take her again.

"Adam . . ."

His jaw clenched and he withdrew, hating the loss of her creamy warmth.

After the whisper of his name, she didn't speak again while

she dressed. Her movements were fast, too quick, and her shoulders were stiffening on him again.

He adjusted his jeans while he watched her. Adam was uncomfortably aware that while he'd just taken Maya's body, her mind and her heart were closed to him.

"You—you're something else, you know that, Slick?" She didn't look at him as she tossed out the words.

He wasn't sure how to take that. *Slick.* He was growing to hate that nickname. He liked it when Maya called him Adam, her voice flowing softly over the name.

She took three steps away from him.

"Maya." He needed her to look at him. Was she angry about the sex? He'd thought she wanted him, but maybe he'd been too rough. Maya might be a vampire, but she was so much smaller than he was. He could have hurt her and not known and—

Her gaze met his. So many secrets were in her eyes.

"Did I—" Aw, hell, this was one damn awkward conversation. "I didn't hurt you, did I? I-I know I lost control and I—"

She smiled at him. One of her real smiles. "Slick, you gave me just what I needed—exactly what I'd been hoping for."

He blinked. There was a ring of truth to her words that he couldn't deny.

Her smile dimmed. "Good-bye, Adam. Tell Cammie that I'll keep my promise." Then she walked away, opening the glass doors and slipping inside.

What the hell?

He stared after her. *Good-bye.* Not "good night." *Good-bye.*

She did the job you hired her for. She got Cammie back. Of course, she's going to leave now.

No, no, he couldn't let her just leave.

She's going back to her old life.

But he didn't want to go back to his life, not without her.

He took a step forward, stopped. Something else was happening. Something that nagged at the back of his mind.

Good-bye, Adam. Tell Cammie that I'll keep my promise.

All the puzzle pieces clicked into place and a hot, blinding rage burst through his veins.

Hell, no.

A good-bye fuck. That's what she'd given him, then she'd walked away.

She'd known all along what she was doing. She'd told Cammie, *"Those vamps—they'll never hurt you again. You'll never even so much as see them for the rest of your life."*

How could she keep a promise like that—unless she meant to go after the vampires?

Fuck.

Adam ran to the edge of the balcony. Maya was below him, stalking toward the line of parked cars, and there was a gun in her hands.

A good-bye fuck, then off to monster slay. *On her own.*

No damn way.

Maya Black had a lesson to learn.

She couldn't walk away from him. If she wanted to fight vampires or demons or any other monsters that waited in the night—well, she'd damn well do it with him watching her back.

Adam grabbed the railing, swung his body over the wrought iron, and dropped to the ground two stories below.

Chapter 16

Maya tucked her gun into the back of her jeans. It was fully loaded with her silver/holy water bullets. After she'd left Adam, it had taken her all of thirty seconds to find Lucas and force the wolf to return her weapon.

It felt good to have her baby back. Now, if she could just get some transportation—and stop thinking about Adam—she'd be good to—

Ah. Three motorcycles were lined up just past the row of black cars and SUVs. Perfect, gleaming Harleys.

"Come to mama," she whispered, her hands already curling in anticipation of feeling the handlebars beneath her fingers.

The air rustled behind her. Maya spun around, and came face to face with a very pissed-off-looking Adam.

"Going hunting?" A velvety voice chaining fury.

Her chin lifted. She'd tried to play this nice and easy with him. No big scenes. Just a good memory for them both to carry through the future.

Well, a good memory for her, anyway. She wasn't sure how Adam felt about what had happened on the balcony, but the pleasure had been the best she'd ever had.

Adam had been the best she ever had.

"You didn't really think I'd take the good-bye fuck and let you just walk away, now, did you?"

Good-bye fuck. Her shoulders tensed. It had been more than that, at least to her. A hell of a lot more. "I did my job," she said. "It's time for me to go." He didn't need to make this any harder on her.

Come.

It was already more than damn hard enough.

Hell, when had she started to care for the dragon? Back in L.A.? In Vegas, when she'd pulled him out of that cave-in? Before that—when he'd stood so silent and steady by her side when she'd confronted that abusive bastard Chuck?

It didn't really matter when she'd started to care, Maya realized. The problem, well, the problem was that she *did* care. Maybe too much.

The time had come for her to face the devil in her own past—and to make absolutely certain that devil never hurt Cammie or her uncle again.

In Adam's arms, the desperate voice in her mind had quieted, if only for a few precious moments. But the call was back now, and she had to leave him.

There was no choice for her.

There never had been.

"Where are you going? Back to L.A.?" he asked, taking an aggressive step toward her. "Or maybe somewhere else? Maybe some place where a Born Master is resting?"

Smart bastard, she'd give him that.

Another long step forward. He was closing in on her. "Come on, tell me. Don't just say good-bye and walk away. *You tell me exactly what you're planning to do.*" He was on her now. Jaw clenched, eyes blazing.

Maya held her ground. "You know what I'm planning."

He shook his head. "You think you can kill them all? Torrence? Nassor? The rest of the vamps in their sick little family?"

Sick little family. A family she was part of, whether she liked it or not.

Bound by blood. *Taken.* Linked for all time.

Unless the Born Master died.

Could she kill him? Kill the others? Maya shrugged. "I'm gonna try."

He grabbed her arm and jerked her close. "Not without me, you aren't."

That wasn't the plan. "No, you have to stay with Cammie. She needs you, she—"

"You nearly died the last time you went out on your own." She could see flecks of gold in the depths of his green eyes. Flickering, like tiny flames. "I listened to you then, and look what happened."

"I saved Cammie, *that's* what happened."

"You almost died."

"Almost doesn't really count, now does it?"

His fingers bit into her flesh and he lifted her up onto her tip toes. "You're not going after them alone."

"*Adam.*" She was getting tired of this arrogant asshole routine. She'd been trying to protect the guy, to keep him away from the vamps who'd like nothing more than to drain a dragon's blood and steal his power.

Without Cammie and Jordan, Nassor wouldn't regain his strength. Another "gift" would be needed—and she didn't want the vamps to turn their attention to Adam.

"You don't get it, do you?" He eased his hold and the soles of her boots touched the ground. "The rules of the game have changed, Maya. You're not flying solo anymore."

What?

Come.

She winced at the scream in her mind.

Dammit, she didn't have time to argue with Adam. The bastard Nassor was splitting her head wide open.

His resting place was close. Closer than she'd realized.

"We're doing this together," Adam said. "You're not going to ditch me and take them on your own. You can't."

Can't. She wasn't too sure about that. She figured that she had about a 40 percent chance of getting to Nassor and killing the bastard.

And giving Torrence the death he was begging for.

"If you try to leave," Adam said, his voice hard and cold, "I'll follow you. I might not be able to track Nassor like you can, but I can track *you*. Anywhere. I've got your scent, Maya. You're not getting away from me."

Shit.

Gravel crunched beneath a boot. To the left.

Maya jerked her head around. Saw Lucas standing less than ten feet away. "He's not the only one who can track your scent."

Her eyes slit. The air around this place was thick with the stench of wolf, so she hadn't smelled the alpha's approach. Just how long had he been listening?

"Torrence took my brother." Lucas's hands balled into powerful fists. "No way that vamp is getting away from me."

Pack justice. Do unto others as they've done to you. Everyone knew their rule.

"*Torrence is my kill.*" Adam glared at the wolf. "That fucking bastard took my niece and left me to die."

Lucas smiled at him, flashing his sharp canines. "Then I guess whoever finds the asshole first gets the pleasure of ripping him apart."

Maya exhaled heavily. She didn't have time for this.

Besides, Torrence had tried to kill her, too. The men could rage all they wanted, but she planned on being the one to send the blond vamp straight to hell.

She pulled away from Adam. Climbed on the bike. Lucas tossed her a set of keys. She caught them with her left hand. In seconds, the motorcycle revved to life beneath her legs.

Oh, yeah. She'd missed this.

Adam and Lucas crowded around her.

She didn't want to take them with her, but she understood their need for vengeance.

And backup, well, maybe it wouldn't be such a terrible idea. Because she didn't know how many members of her little "family" would be waiting to greet her.

"So here's the deal," she said, raising her voice over the growl of the bike. "Adam and I are going in first. You wait until we're clear—then you bring your pack in," she told Lucas. "You wait, got that? If they catch your scent too soon,

war's gonna break out and we'll all be lucky to get out alive."
Much less succeed in killing Torrence and Nassor.

"You." She pointed to Adam. "You ride with me, and do
exactly as I say." Maya had a feeling Adam wasn't going to
like the plan spinning through her mind, but if they both
wanted to get close to Nassor, well, she figured there was
only one way to do it.

The Born Master needed a dragon's blood to regain his
strength.

Maybe she'd just give him one.

"Are we gonna catch the bastard while he's sleeping?"
Lucas asked, his smile curving another inch.

"No." She pushed back the kickstand. "The Master's up
and waiting." *Calling.*

His smile disappeared. "Shit."

Adam climbed onto the bike behind her. Locked his arms
around her waist. "How long?"

A shrug. "About an hour." So he was still weak. Even if
Torrence had a nice food supply lined up for the Master, his
strength wouldn't be at peak level.

Now was the time to attack.

You had to cut off the head of the snake in order to kill the
beast. Once Nassor was dead, the vampires would flee. The
call would stop.

Her fingers tightened around the handlebars. *This was it.*

She looked across the desert. He was waiting.

Come.

The bike shot forward with a howl of fury. Spun with a
shriek and headed away from the blazing lights of the Strip.

Headed deep into the desert.

It was a beautiful night for death.

Maya lost track of time as she drove the motorcycle. The
vibrations from the bike traveled up her legs, pushed against
her sex. Adam didn't speak. Just kept his arms around her.
Tight and strong.

With every mile that passed, the call in her mind grew louder.

No wonder Torrence had been keeping Cammie and Jordan at Blood Rock. He'd wanted the Master to have easy access.

They rose over a hill and Maya brought the bike to a shuddering halt.

There. A massive house, with a thick security wall surrounding it on all sides. Guards. Dozens of them. Patrolling with weapons, and with fangs and claws. *Vampires.*

Lights blazed from the house—not really a house, Maya thought. Too big. Made of heavy stone, the place looked more like some kind of fortress, rising from the desert.

She counted at least three stories. Knew there had to be a basement. With vampires, there was always a basement.

Four floors. Maybe more.

So where would she find Torrence? Nassor?

Her foot pressed against the hard earth as she stared at the Master's lair.

"What's the plan?" Adam's breath blew against her ear. "How are you planning to get past the guards?"

Ah, that was the tricky part. Odds were good that Torrence wouldn't be one of the low-level goons patrolling the gates. So, getting in shouldn't be a problem, not with the gift she was bringing.

Maya glanced back at him. "Do you trust me?"

They were so close that barely an inch separated their faces. She could see straight into his eyes.

"Yes."

Absolutely certain.

Maya swallowed to ease the lump in her throat. The damn bad thing was that she trusted him, too. With every bit of her soul, she trusted the dragon. "Th-that's good, Slick. Real good." She revved the engine. "Remember that, okay?" She shot down the hill, forcing the bike to go as fast as it could.

The guards saw them coming. The vamps ran for them, shouting and drawing their guns.

Bullets rained into the ground on either side of her. One slammed into the front of the motorcycle.

Maya whipped the bike to the right, brought it to a stop in a cloud of fumes and burning rubber. "I've come for the Master!" Her voice rang out, cutting past the shouts and the bullets. She barred her teeth and said, "I'm answering his call."

The vamps closed in, suspicion heavy on their pale faces. Black eyes drifted past her to study Adam. The tension that swept over the crowd had Maya leaping from the motorcycle and jerking Adam behind her.

"He's got no scent." This came from a short, bald vamp who stepped forward with his gun raised and his lips peeled back into a snarl. *Ah, the one in charge. The boss always liked to speak first.*

Maya's gaze dropped to the gun. Probably just regular bullets, in case any curious humans happened by. The shots would hurt like hell, of course, but it wouldn't be anything fatal to her.

But she couldn't afford to be slowed down.

Maya lifted her hands, moving them in a fast blur, and locked her claws around Adam's throat. "Don't even think about hurting my gift," she warned, voice deadly.

The vamps hesitated.

"What is he?" This came from the leader, who eyed them both with deep suspicion.

Maya smiled at him and deliberately pressed her claws into Adam's flesh. A trickle of blood flowed down his neck.

He didn't flinch. His body was rock-hard beside her.

"He's a dragon," she said, and brought her mouth to his throat, licking away the blood. "He's going to make Nassor very, very happy."

A rumble swept through the crowd. Most of the vamps began to inch back.

But the guy in front just curled back his lip. "Bullshit."

"Adam." A little demonstration would be in order. "Why don't you show these guys just what you can become?"

He held up his arm.

The skin slowly began to shift colors, getting darker. The flesh become harder. Scaled.

"That's enough," she said, not wanting to push him too far, yet.

Adam's arm transformed back to a man's.

"Are you crazy?" The vampire shrieked, raising his gun. "That bastard can kill us all!"

Well, at least he believed her now.

"No, he can't." *Sorry, Adam.* "He's linked with my blood, and he'll do whatever I want." She turned slightly, looked up into his eyes. *Sleep.*

He blinked.

She'd never wanted to force her power onto him, but there wasn't an option now. If the vamps thought he was any kind of threat, they'd never let him inside.

Sleep.

His eyelids flickered. "Y-you . . ."

She forced the compulsion on him, hard and deep.

Then she stepped back as his body began to fall.

Adam hit the ground with a thud.

She forced a shrug. Glanced back at the leader. "Problem solved."

The vampires rushed forward, hands reaching for Adam's body with greedy lust.

"No!" She stepped in front of them. "This one's for the Master, and *only* the Master."

The guy who'd been screaming at her minutes before now spit onto the ground and snapped, "Fine, but when he's done, we get what's left over."

Maya laughed at that. *Idiot.* "There's not gonna be anything left."

She grabbed Adam, hoisted him over her shoulder. Barely felt his weight. "Now are we gonna stand out here, screwing around all night, or do I get to see Nassor?"

"What's happening?" The whisper from Daniel, his second in command, drifted on a breath of sound.

Lucas tightened his hold around the binoculars. "They're going inside." Although not the way he'd anticipated.

What game was the vampire playing?

He'd thought she wanted him to wait in the shadows and then attack to cause a distraction for her and the dragon.

But what if Maya had a different plan in mind? What if she had been playing him? What if she was inside, even now, telling the others about his pack?

He could be walking straight into a trap.

Lucas was willing to bet the dragon sure as hell hadn't counted on being carried into the vamp's lair, unconscious. Vulnerable.

Could he trust her?

"What's our move?" Daniel asked.

Lucas drew in a deep breath. He'd never trusted a vampire before.

Maya had gone back into Temptation to save Jordan. He couldn't overlook that fact.

Of course, she'd also been the one to nearly kill his brother.

"Lucas?"

"For now, we wait."

If the vampire betrayed him, he'd make absolutely certain it was the last thing she ever did.

Maya was taken through the entrance gates, led across a courtyard, and escorted up to the main entrance of the fortress. As she walked across the cobbled courtyard, she could feel eyes on her, dozens of them, watching her every move.

When she stepped inside the main building, the stench of death flooded her nostrils.

Humans had died here. The stench was old, as if the bodies had long since decayed and turned to dust. But she also caught the smell of fresh kills. Sweet blood.

"We'll put him with the others," the vampire in front of her said, glancing over his slightly stooped shoulder.

The others. Yeah, she'd expected that Nassor had a back-up power supply. "No. He doesn't leave my sight." Like she'd trust any of the hungry bastards around a dragon's blood.

The vampire's face tightened. "He goes with the others."

They were in a long hallway now. One lit with faint, fluorescent lighting.

Where was Nassor?

She heard the moans then, the whimpers.

Prey.

The Born Master had to be close.

Maya kept her gaze on the vamp leading her. "*He* is a very special gift. One I'm taking straight to the Master." She didn't know how much time they'd have before the wolves attacked. The closer she could get to Nassor, the better.

The vampire grunted. "You don't wanna be facing him yet."

Ah, but he was exactly the one she wanted to face.

Slick, time to rise and shine.

She felt the sudden alertness of his body.

This was gonna hurt. Not her so much, but—

"Shit! Something's wrong, the bastard's awake!" She threw Adam against the heavy stone wall.

The vampire spun around, terror on his face and in his black eyes. "What? No, he—"

Maya already had her gun ready. She grabbed the vamp and pressed the barrel right against his heart. "Don't so much as breathe hard," she said, "or you'll see what it feels like to be burned from the inside out."

He stilled instantly. "Y-you're bluffing."

"I don't bluff." She smiled, a hard barring of her teeth. "Holy water bullets. The kind just right for cooking vamps."

He swallowed hard.

From the corner of her eye, she saw Adam rise to his feet. "You all right?"

A muscle flexed along his jaw. "A warning would have been appreciated."

Yeah, but a warning would have tipped off the vampire.

She glanced around the hall. She'd tried to time her attack for the moment when they had maximum cover. She didn't think anyone had seen them, but just in case, it was time to cut to the chase.

"Look, asshole, either take me to Nassor, or I'll kill you." Simple. Straightforward.

"If I take you to him, I'm dead." His black eyes were beady, full of hate and fear.

The guy just didn't get it. "If you don't start moving your ass, you'll be dead in the next five seconds."

"At least you'll make it fast." The vampire shook his head. "Nassor won't."

"You—"

Adam grabbed the vamp, his fingers locking around the back of his neck and spinning him around. "I won't make your death easy," he said, his voice a hard rumble. "I'll slice your flesh away, then make you beg for my fire."

Maya's brows rose. Okay. She hadn't quite been expecting that.

The vampire began to shake. He hadn't thought she'd torture him, but obviously, he had no doubt that Adam would carry out *his* threat.

And neither did she.

"I-I'll sh-show you j-just—"

Maya caught the stench in the air then. Too-familiar. "Adam—"

A thunder of footsteps.

Adam swore, slammed the vamp against the wall, and lunged in front of her.

Too late.

The vamps surrounded them, a mass of claws and teeth that came from both sides, trapping them in the middle of the hallway.

So much for the sneak attack.

Laughter. Mocking male laughter that made the hair on her nape rise. She knew which asshole was having himself a good old time even before Torrence pushed his way through the army of vamps.

Adam leapt forward.

"No!"

The vampires grabbed him, six of them taking him down and pounding him into the floor.

Shit.

Maya swallowed back the fear that rose in her throat. Adam couldn't take the vamps in his human form. What the hell had he been thinking?

She forced her gaze to lift and to lock on Torrence's. "If they kill him, Nassor's going to be pissed."

Torrence lifted his right hand.

The attack on Adam immediately ceased. Torrence smiled at her. "Ah, come now, we both know a dragon can take a hell of a lot more punishment."

Yeah, but she didn't want to see him suffer.

Torrence's gaze shifted from her to Adam.

Maya's whole body tensed.

She could so do with a distraction about then. *Where were those damn wolves?*

"Dragons are wild, unpredictable beasts." His mouth frowned with distaste as he stared at Adam. "So hard to control."

"You're fucking dead!" Adam yelled, the words rumbling from within his chest. The air around them grew thick and a deep, menacing growl filled the hall.

Torrence stepped toward Maya.

She still had her gun in her hands. Ready to fire. No way could she take them all out, but she could hit Torrence straight in the heart.

But then the other vamps would rip her apart before she could get to Nassor.

What would happen to Adam? To Cammie?

"He was protecting you, wasn't he?" Torrence asked.

Maya didn't answer.

"I saw him. He put his body before yours—and *he* attacked." Torrence tilted his head to the side. "Got a pet, do you, bitch?"

She bared her teeth at him.

He lifted his hand, ignored her gun, and pressed the tip of his claws against her cheek.

Maya felt the warmth of blood on her face.

"Get away from her!" Adam wrestled free from two of the vamps, broke the neck of a third—not something that would kill the guy, but it would definitely take him out of commission for a bit.

Her eyes closed. *No, Adam, don't—*

The claws dropped to her throat. "Move and I'll cut her head off."

Her lashes lifted and she met Adam's desperate stare.

Dragons—so fierce. So emotional. Damn, but the guy made her heart ache.

Torrence circled behind her. "Drop the gun." He whispered the command into her ear.

The gun hit the floor with a clatter. Maya was hoping a bullet would shoot out at the impact and kill one of the goons. No such luck.

Adam wasn't moving. The vamps had him pinned to the ground. His head was tilted up, and he stared straight at her.

"You've got a weakness, don't you, dragon?" Torrence taunted. "And it's this bitch."

Adam didn't speak.

"Let me tell you what's going to happen." His claws dug into her neck. "You're going to do what I say, when I say it, or the woman's going to find herself without a head."

"Adam . . ." If he shifted into the dragon, he could take the vamps surrounding him, she knew he could.

But she also knew the shift wasn't fast. He'd need precious minutes to fully transform—and she'd be dead before the dragon could fight.

At least he'd survive.

"Don't worry about me," she said, her voice firm as she gazed down at him.

"Fuck that!" He made no move to fight his captors—or to transform.

"I've always known there was something special about a female vampire's pussy," Torrence murmured and she felt his tongue lick down her face, tasting the blood that fell from her cheek. "It's all that drinking and fucking—makes men into slaves."

The scent of smoke teased her nostrils.

The dragon was close.

Change, Adam. Change. Forget about me—you have to stop them so Cammie will be safe.

She didn't know if he heard her mental plea, but she drove the words as hard as she could through their blood bond.

"Get him up."

The vampires dragged Adam to his feet. His eyes never left Torrence's face.

"Nassor wants them—and we don't want to keep the Born Master waiting."

Where were those damn wolves?

The vampires yanked Adam down the hallway.

"You shot me, bitch." Torrence grabbed her hair, jerked her head back.

She ignored the pain and said, "And I'm going to kill you."

He laughed at that—right in her face. "When Nassor's done with you, we're going to play." His mouth pressed against her throat. Licked away the blood. "*If* there's anything left of you."

Then he shoved her down the long hallway, and the rest of the vampires swarmed in behind her.

"Lucas?" Daniel's voice was tense.

He put the binoculars down. Fifteen minutes. Maya and the dragon had been inside for fifteen minutes.

There was barely any activity outside the fortress.

Doubt nagged at him. Was it a trap?

Or could he trust her? Was there even a choice?

Fuck it.

Time to hunt.

He threw back his head and howled.

Chapter 17

Torrence took her downstairs. Not just to the basement, but down a good three levels. They entered a room lit with torches. A room with a dirt floor and a golden throne. A room with an opened sarcophagus that waited, half in the earth.

Blood stained the dirt. Human bodies—at least seven—littered the floor.

And the Born Master waited.

He turned at their approach, moved his body in a slow glide like a snake.

His skin was golden, his hair black and loose around his shoulders. His face wasn't handsome—it was absolutely perfect. Sensual lips, sculpted cheekbones, strong nose—the guy could have been some kind of cover model—

If he weren't the leader of the dead.

Time had frozen him young. He barely looked twenty years old, but his glittering black eyes reflected the centuries he'd lived—and the evil he'd wrought.

He smiled when he saw her, lips curving back to show his white fangs. "Ah, my little cop." His voice held no accent, but was a deep, echoing rumble. "I've been waiting for you, dreaming of you, for so many years."

She'd didn't want this guy so much as *thinking* about her. He lifted his hand to her cheek, touched her—not with claws but with soft fingers.

She expected to be repulsed by his touch. Instead, her heart began to race and a strange hunger swept through her.

What the hell?

Thrall. The answer whispered through her mind. Nassor was an ancient. He'd be able to control her, make her feel anything he wanted.

Oh, shit.

His nostrils flared as he stared down at her. Then his eyes lifted to Torrence. "You tasted her."

He sounded seriously pissed.

Torrence gave a jerky nod.

Nassor smiled. Maya let her gaze drift over him, helpless against the draw she felt for the Master. There was a red line circling his neck. Puckered skin. A scar—but vampires didn't scar.

Not usually.

The guy had almost gotten his head chopped off. The wound had nearly killed him, and, judging by that scar, he still hadn't fully healed.

Or the scar would be gone.

Nassor was dressed in a pair of dark, flowing pants. His chest was bare, completely hairless, and Maya saw the second scar that lined his chest. Right over his heart.

Because he'd been staked.

Staked and nearly beheaded—and he'd still lived.

Killing him was going to be damn hard.

"We have something for you," Torrence said, bowing his head slightly.

Nassor's lips locked in a snarl.

Oh, yeah, seriously pissed.

"Bring him in!" Torrence ordered, and she glanced back, watching as the vamps forced Adam into the room. "As you wanted, we've brought you a dragon."

Nassor's long tongue swirled out, licked across his lips—as if he were already tasting Adam. "A pure-blood?"

Torrence hesitated.

"*Is he a pure-blood?*"

"Yeah," Adam snarled, "I am. Now get the hell away from my woman!"

Nassor's teeth snapped together. His stare drifted back to Maya. "Yours?" He shook his head. "Sorry, my Wyvern, but the little cop has been mine for five years." He leaned in close to her, his nostrils widening as he caught her scent. "Picked just for me—and only me."

Her nipples tightened. He was creeping into her mind, planting images, fantasies. She tried to resist his sensual pull, hating the power of his thrall.

"I've handpicked every member of my family," he said. "Every. Single. One. All chosen because I wanted the strongest, the most powerful, and the deadliest for my clan."

A warning whispered through her mind. A foreboding. She didn't want to hear what he was—

"The minute I saw you, patrolling in that filthy park, then fighting with every breath in your being, I knew you were for me." He lifted her hand. Brought her palm to his lips. Kissed her.

Then sank his teeth into her flesh.

Adam snarled.

Maya stiffened her body, fighting the need snaking its way through her.

His head lifted. Her blood stained his lips. "I could feel the darkness in you. Just waiting to come out." He smiled at her. "A killer, waiting to be set free."

No.

"You're just like me," he whispered. "I know it. The darkness in us—we're the same."

Screw that.

"When your mother died—"

How the hell did he know about that?

"Weren't you happy? Didn't you enjoy the feel of her blood on you?"

Cold water iced her veins. She fought his thrall, tried to gather her strength. She wasn't like this sick bastard. Not one bit.

"I loved the taste of my mother's blood," he told her. "I cut her throat when I was a boy and I laughed as she bled."

Maya swallowed.

He turned away from her and began to pace alongside the torches that lined the far wall. "I sent Tyrus to you. Ordered him to change you. So few females can survive the change— their bodies are too fragile—but I knew you'd make it." He paused, glanced back at her with admiration on his face. "You killed him, even as you drew your first new breath of life."

Her hands tightened into fists. Fragile, her ass. *Weapon.* Where was—

"I know you've been quite the bad girl while I've been away." He shook his head and glanced toward Torrence. "Killing more of your own kind. Your own family."

Her family—her mother—was dead. This SOB was not part of her family.

"I'm going to give you a choice, love."

She wasn't his love. She was the vampire who was going to make certain he went to hell.

"You can die. I'll let every vampire in this room drink you dry until only a shell remains of you."

Not the option she'd like. "Or?" Her voice came out husky.

"Or you can give me your allegiance. Join me, be the mate I've waited for, wanted all these years."

Yeah, and after he screwed her, Nassor would still probably kill her.

Choices, choices. Maya spared a quick glance for Adam. He was surrounded. If he had a hope of changing, she'd have to get those vampires away from him.

And she knew just what she had to do.

She wished she could risk sending him a mental call through their blood link, but Nassor was so strong, he might pick up on it and she couldn't risk tipping off the bastard. Maya stared into Adam's eyes. "Sorry, Slick. Guess it's the end of the road." She tried to keep shields up in her mind, not wanting Nassor to know what she planned.

His lips tightened.

"Pity I never got to see if you looked like my tat." It was all she could say, but she hoped he got her message.

She sauntered across the room. The torches blazed on either side of Nassor's perfect head.

She stopped in front of him, bared her neck. "I'll choose to live."

The Born Master had his hands on her.

Adam watched, fury burning through him as Nassor pulled Maya close and sank his teeth into her throat.

No!

The vamps around him loosened their hold as they watched Nassor feed. They were obviously anticipating a damn good show, and by the way Nassor's hands were caressing Maya's body, they'd get one.

The edge of her shirt rose as Nassor's fingers trailed up her back.

The dragon tattoo stared back at him.

Pity I never got to see if you looked like my tat.

Well, she was about to find out exactly what he looked like, *if* the vamps didn't kill him before he changed.

Nassor gulped down her blood, sucking strongly and swallowing thickly.

Adam's claws shot out and he wanted so badly to rip the bastard apart.

The Born Master lifted his head.

Maya swayed before him, putting her small hands on his chest for balance.

All eyes were on her.

Adam began to call the dragon.

Maya slid her body around Nassor's. Rubbing, teasing. Blood dripped down her neck.

She stood behind the master now. Her hands slid up his chest. Her claws scratched his skin.

She stood on her toes, staring at Adam over Nassor's shoulder. Her eyes were black but bright with the flames that surrounded her.

And her face was hard with anger—*rage*.

He knew her next move even before he saw her fingers rise.

Maya! The scream blasted in his mind.

Her hand closed over the nearest torch, jerked the metal post up, and slammed the fire into Nassor's back, then his head, his pants—

The Born Master screamed, shrieking in pain and fury as the flames burned his flesh.

The vampires lunged forward.

Maya grabbed another torch.

She wasn't going to have much time.

But he'd only need a few moments.

The smell of burnt flesh seared her nostrils. She hadn't killed Nassor, just hurt him like hell. A pain, unfortunately, that wouldn't last long enough.

The vampires swarmed him, some throwing their bodies onto his to stop the flames that were eating away at his pants.

When they finally stepped back, Nassor lay huddled on the floor.

Blisters covered his upper arms. His hair had been burned away. His pants hung in tattered clumps, exposing flesh scorched bright red.

He shifted and she saw his back—the burns that ravaged his skin.

He rose slowly to his feet.

Maya lifted her torch.

"That wasn't smart, bitch."

Ah, so she wasn't his "love" anymore, huh? Too damn bad. "What can I say?" She asked. "I've got a shitload of darkness in me and I just live to kill—kill—kill." Maya smiled. "And for the record, I choose option three, the one where I don't have to fuck you, but I do get to send you to hell."

He lifted his hand, pointed one blistered finger at her. "Bleed her dry."

A growl of hunger swept through the crowd. Fangs glistened.

"And bring me the dragon—I need to—"

A howl echoed from upstairs. Followed by another, another—

About time.

Her knees trembled as relief swept through her. Now if Lucas
would just hurry his ass up and get the pack down there—

"What the fuck is that?" Nassor snarled.

Her smile widened. "My backup plan." Her fingers were
locked tight around the base of the torch.

"Upstairs!" He screamed the order to Torrence. "Kill any
damn wolf you find."

Torrence jerked his hand up, and half the vampires ran
ahead of him, charging for the stairs.

Good little soldiers. They'd make great prey for the
wolves.

And suddenly, her odds were much better.

"You could have been a goddess," Nassor grated. "Now
you're going to die, begging."

"Ah, and here I thought you knew me so well." Maya
took a step forward. "I never, *ever* beg."

"You will," he breathed the words—then he shot forward
and the other vampires attacked.

Lucas stared up at Torrence, muscles quivering, fangs ready.
He could all but feel the vampire's neck between his teeth.

The blond vamp is mine. He sent the mental order through
his pack.

Growls answered him.

Then the pack charged.

And blood soon filled the hallways.

Her right arm was burned, scored with blisters and red
flesh. They had her pinned on the ground, and their hungry
breath battered her skin.

Nassor stood above her, a satisfied smile on his no-longer-
perfect face. "Ready to beg?"

One of the vampires bit her, his teeth tearing across her
wrist.

Pain lanced her. "N-no."

"Fool." He bent and his fingers wrapped around her throat. "You could have ruled at my side, now you'll die at my feet."

Her lips trembled. She tried to smile as another vampire sank his teeth into her shoulder. "B-behind . . . y-you . . . ass . . . hole . . ."

His eyes narrowed and it seemed to take a moment for her words to register, then he released her and spun around.

She craned her neck, still wrestling with the others, and fought to see—

The two vampires who'd had the sense to stay back and guard Adam lay on the ground, completely still, and Adam, he was—

Huge.

Dark green, with a body covered in thick scales. His claws— no, *talons*—were longer than her hands, and sharper than knives. His legs were as large as tree trunks. Hell, maybe bigger. Tall, thick spikes began at the back of his head and lined his backbone, ending at his swirling, powerful, and distinctly pointed, tail.

His wings—batlike, with piercing talons on the tips—had spread wide, touching the tall, cavernous ceiling and the dirt floor.

His head looked like a serpent's and his teeth seemed to explode from his mouth—just as sharp as those talons. His eyes blazed with green fire and his fist-sized nostrils flared, sending puffs of smoke billowing around him.

Oh, shit.

The vamps were gonna die.

Her smile rose fully. Her eyes stayed locked on his. "A-Adam . . ."

When his mouth opened in a roar, and the scent of brimstone filled the room, she knew the battle was over.

The vampires ran, fighting each other as they fled for the door.

He snarled. His tail slapped against them, the sharp tip piercing straight through two vamps and ripping out their hearts.

Fire scorched three more, a blaze that blasted from his mouth. Then his tongue, notched in two like a snake's, licked across his lips.

The room was hot now, as fire chased up the walls.

Sweat coated her skin. Maya tried to push to her feet. Adam could stand the heat, no question, but she couldn't say the same for herself.

Nassor grabbed her, jerking her against him and holding tight. His body shook against her and she could smell his fear, even over the flames and death.

"H-he won't hurt you," he said and his claws were around her neck, again.

Maya dug her own claws into his arm.

"Stay away from me!" Nassor shouted to the dragon.

She wasn't sure the beast understood. Was the man gone completely, and only the dragon remained? If so, then if she didn't get out of there, fast, she would join the dead vamps on the floor.

The dragon's wings flapped, sending the air whipping around them and making the flames dance higher.

"Back away. I'll kill her if you don't—"

The dragon's mouth opened, teeth dripping with saliva.

Wow. Maya's heart thudded furiously against her chest. Adam was sure as hell amazing in his dragon form. Not beautiful. More like damn scary, but she'd never realized the raw power and fury that the man held in check.

As the dragon's hot breath fanned over her, she fully understood just how much he'd been holding back from her.

The man had immense control.

Did the beast?

Nassor began to creep toward the door, using her body as a shield. The others fled, screaming as if they'd seen the devil.

Or a very pissed-off dragon.

And Nassor had thought he'd be able to control Adam. *Idiot.*

They'd almost made it to the door when the dragon lunged forward. Its powerful tail snaked behind them and blocked the exit. Then the dragon crouched over them, its wings curling forward.

"I-I'll kill her!" Nassor screamed.

Maya stared at the dragon, gazing as best she could into its glowing eyes.

The dragon's mouth opened.

She drew in a breath. Tasted fire.

Knew what was coming.

Nassor shrieked, jerking her in his fury and fear.

She closed her eyes, and trusted the beast as she trusted the man.

His fiery breath danced across her skin and a scream of pain and horror echoed in her mind.

When she opened her eyes, she was on the ground, her body covered in ash. Maya shook her head, rose slowly and swept her gaze around the room.

The fire crawled up the walls, bright, hungry orange flames that crackled and seemed to laugh as they destroyed everything in their path. Smoke billowed around her and the heat lanced her skin.

Skin that Adam's fire had never touched. The dragon had been in control. Just like the man. She and Nassor had fallen to the floor, and the flames, they'd gone straight to Nassor.

She spun around, looking for Nassor. Where was—

"He's gone." Adam's voice, sounding slightly hoarse.

She stilled, then gazed over her shoulder.

Man, not beast. Tall, muscled, *naked*, he stood in the middle of the fire, his tanned skin unmarred by the flames.

Maya ran to him, throwing her arms around him and holding on tight.

Adam was stiff within her grasp, his body too tense. Her head lifted, "Adam, wh-what's—"

Part of the ceiling fell down, the wood giving way with a shriek.

They jumped back, barely dodging the flames.

Maya coughed as the smoke filled her lungs. "We've . . . got . . . to . . . go." *Now.*

Adam took her hand and they ran for the door.

They raced up the stairs, toward the screams and howls that shook the fortress even as the fire greedily chased at their heels.

When they reached the first floor and shoved open the thick door, they walked into a war.

Wolves. Vampires. Clawing. Biting. Dying.

Adam grabbed the vampire in front of him, drove his claws into the guy's chest.

The fight was on.

The smoke drifted through the doorway, sneaking into the hall and through the fortress like a thief—and she knew the flames would soon follow.

Automatically, Maya fought the vampire that grabbed her from behind, raking him with her claws, pounding with her fists—and then she heard the humans.

Their screams were weaker. Broken.

Prey.

Still trapped, wherever Torrence had caged them. Helpless against the fire that would soon sweep over the entire fortress.

Maya grabbed a chair that had fallen onto the ground, a thin, spindly chair that looked like it was about two hundred years old.

She snapped the legs in two. Reaching for the broken wood, she bared her teeth at the vamp who lunged for her.

She staked him in midair, driving the wood into his heart and watching his eyes widen in an understanding that came too late.

Before he hit the ground, she was already searching through the fighters.

There.

The bastard who'd first led her into Nassor's lovely home. Trying to slink away.

Not gonna happen.

Casting one last glance toward Adam—he was more than

holding his own—she ran for the vampire she should have killed on first sight.

Adam fought to hold on to his control. Once unleashed, the dragon had been nearly impossible to cage.

The death around him, the screams and the blood, they called to the Wyvern.

Destroy.

Burn.

He shuddered and fought another asshole who grabbed him. The fire was spreading. He could hear the flames now, the hungry crackles coming ever closer.

The beautiful fire.

They needed to get out of the house. He looked over his shoulder, ready to grab Maya and—

She was gone.

Sonofabitch.

He shoved the vampire into the wall. Heard the thud of his head connecting and turned away.

"Maya?" Damn, his voice was hoarse. Like a frog's. Because of the flames that had burned up his throat.

Where was she? He knew she hadn't fled—she wouldn't leave him. He understood that fact with absolute certainty, so where—

He caught a glimpse of blond hair. Saw the side of a man's face, twisted with fury.

His hands clenched and the dragon roared.

Torrence.

He leapt forward, shoving aside wolves and vampires. He had only one intent—*kill*.

Another roar echoed his and the house trembled.

A huge black wolf lunged for the vampire, reaching him two seconds before Adam could.

The wolf knocked Torrence to the ground, locked his fangs around his throat.

And the vampire lifted a too-familiar gun.

Maya's weapon.

He aimed it at the wolf's head.

Adam kicked out, breaking bones and sending the gun flying into the air.

The wolf snarled and his fangs found their mark.

The vampire screamed, then his voice died to a gurgle. Blood spilled from his lips.

Adam watched, dispassionate.

When the wolf lifted his head, his teeth were stained red.

The vampire's head had been severed from his body.

"Get your pack out of here," Adam ordered, barely sparing a glance for the corpse. "The fire's going to destroy everything." Even now, the flames were eating the hallway. Licking against the ceiling.

The wolf nodded its massive head and howled, sending out an unmistakable order to the pack.

Adam searched through the chaos. *Where the hell is Maya?* His nostrils widened as he tried to catch her scent, but all he could smell was the fire.

Shit.

"*Maya!*" Not the yell he'd intended. A desperate croak of sound.

Where would she go? *Where?* And why?

His jaw locked and he stalked forward.

She'd gone back into Temptation to rescue the wolf. She'd pulled him out of Blood Rock. Maya didn't believe in leaving anyone behind.

He stopped, barely dodging a wolf who hurtled past him as the beast took down a vampire.

The prey.

The humans who were still alive. She wouldn't leave them for the fire. The cop in her wouldn't let the vampire just walk away.

Then he saw her. Leading a line of crying women and men, trying to fight off the vamps that leapt at her.

"Lucas!"

The black wolf turned, easily hearing the rough cry.

Adam ran even as he ordered, "Tell 'em to protect the humans!" Because Maya wouldn't be able to get them all out on her own.

The flames were too hungry now. The heat surrounded them. So hungry, and too close. He grabbed Maya's hand. *Not going to lose her.*

Nassor's fortress burned to the ground and the screams of the vampires trapped inside echoed the taunting whispers of the fire.

The humans were safe. Huddled in the darkness, staring with wide eyes that were glassy with confusion and fear.

Maya's gaze locked on the house. She'd tried to go back for the vampires inside, but they'd fought her, wild, maddened, and determined to die with their Born Master.

Dumb-asses. Hell was going to be a lot hotter than that fire.

Lucas paced toward her. She turned toward him. Found him naked, as were the other werewolves. "Torrence is dead."

She raised her brows at that. She'd wondered about him. She'd seen no sign of the bastard once she reached the main floor. "Your kill?"

He nodded.

"Then your pack has been avenged." Word would spread about his vengeance, because not all of the vampires had been stupid enough to choose the fire. Some had escaped, and they'd carry the tale of this night. Wolf attacks. A dragon's revenge.

Don't screw with the wolves, or the dragons. She could already hear the whispered warnings that would haunt the feeding rooms and bars.

Some would just be stupid enough to forget in the coming years.

Such was the way of the supernatural world.

"Your dragon saved my ass."

She blinked at that. Her gaze darted to the left for an instant. Adam stood next to the humans, talking softly to them. He wore a pair of jeans—too tight. She didn't know where he'd gotten them, probably taken them from one of the humans.

"Torrence was going to use one of your silver bullets on me, a head shot." Lucas grimaced. "The bloodlust was riding me so hard, I didn't realize what was happening until too late."

Adam had wanted the kill, but instead he'd saved the wolf. The Wyvern could still surprise her.

"I owe him a debt." He nodded his head toward Adam. "Tell him. If he wants to collect, he'll find me in L.A."

A blood debt owed by an alpha wolf. Not something that was offered every day. "I'll tell him."

Lucas stared at her with eyes that reflected the moonlight. "If you grow tired of the dragon, you know where you can find me."

She held that powerful stare. "Yeah, I know." But it wasn't really a matter of her growing tired of Adam. It was a matter of the job being done and of them having two separate lives, on two separate coasts.

"When the pack's clear, I'll call the cops. Make sure they know where to find the humans," he said.

She needed to leave the scene before the boys in blue arrived. As it was, she knew Adam was trying to convince the men and women that they'd just been at a party that got *way* out of control—too much alcohol, too many drugs.

The humans were dazed, frightened, and probably willing to latch on to any explanation.

Sometimes it was just easier to believe a lie than to accept the truth—especially a truth that would change a person's life.

"Good-bye, vampire." He lifted his hand to her.

Her fingers wrapped around his. She kept her gaze on his face, all too aware of the naked power of his body. "Good-bye, wolf."

He smiled at her then. "You weren't what I expected."

Yeah, she got that a lot.

"I'll be near, should you need me." Soft, almost tender words. So at odds with the hard jaw and the fierce gaze.

Before she could speak, the man disappeared. Shifted into a wolf with a snap of bones and a shudder. Fur exploded over his flesh. His nose elongated, a muzzle appeared, and powerful claws shot from his fingers.

The wolf tossed back his head, howled at the night.

Whimpers came from the humans.

She heard Adam swear.

The pack took off, running hard and fast across the desert.

Maya knew she hadn't seen the last of Lucas.

Not a friend. There was too much uncertainty between them for that. But perhaps, just perhaps, he was someone she could count on when her back was to the wall and hell broke lose in L.A.

Adam strode toward her.

She noticed a human male huddled behind him, clad only in a pair of dark boxers.

Ah, the mystery of the jeans had been solved.

"Where's the wolf?"

"Gone." It was time for her to go, too. She began to march toward the motorcycle, Adam at her side. "He wanted me to give you a message." She straddled the bike, looked back at the burning house. The flames were so bright.

"Yeah, what did he say?"

Her gaze turned to him. "He owes you. If you ever want to collect, come to L.A."

He nodded.

She started the motorcycle, felt the powerful vibration of the engine. "The cops will be here soon—we need to be gone by then."

He climbed on behind her. His arms squeezed her tight.

The humans were talking, murmuring softly. "Will they be all right?"

"They don't know what the hell happened to them, but they're alive, so, yeah, other than nightmares for the next year, I think they'll be fine." A pause. "What about you?"

She pulled the motorcycle into a long, lazy spin. Smoke filled the air behind them. "What about me?" She'd been bitten, no big deal. The wounds hurt like a bitch, but with blood and rest, she'd be fine.

Her wounds didn't matter. The only thing that mattered

was that Cammie was safe now. Nassor and Torrence would never bother her again.

Maya had kept her promise. Done her job.

Her work was finished.

"You . . . saw me. Not many have seen a dragon shift and lived to tell about it." There was a vulnerability in his voice. A fear.

The big, bad dragon was afraid because she'd seen him go all scaly? Maya laughed. "Ah, Slick, it's gonna take more than seeing you blow fire to get me scared."

He relaxed against her. The hard squeeze turned into more of a hug. "Good," he murmured, nuzzling her neck. "Because the last thing I wanted was for you to fear me."

The bike took off, flying across the terrain. "I don't fear you," she told him, her voice barely carrying over the roar of the motorcycle.

No, she didn't fear Adam. She wasn't afraid of the beast he carried.

Or of the man that he was.

But . . . she was afraid. Of herself. Because she cared about the dragon. More than she'd ever cared for anyone.

And caring would just lead to a world of hurt. It always did. The people she cared about, *they* got hurt. Her mother. Sean. She wouldn't add Adam to the list.

They rode in silence back to the wolf's safe house. Streaks of gold began to creep across the sky as the sun fought to rise against the night.

When they got to the house, the wolves were nowhere to be found. Gone. Probably already on their way back to L.A.

She'd be on her way soon, too. Though the thought of walking away from Adam made her feel like she'd taken a punch in the gut. But she had to leave him. There wasn't a choice.

She'd go once she finished her final piece of business.

Maya strode through the home. Adam followed behind her, his steps slower. She pushed by the guards at Cammie's door and crept inside the darkened room.

Drawing a deep breath, she moved close to the bed. If the girl was asleep, she'd wait and—

"Maya." Cammie whispered her name as she opened her eyes. "I was dreaming about you."

She sat on the edge of the bed. "Good dream, I hope." Her fingers lifted, smoothed back the girl's hair.

Cammie nodded. "You were saving me."

"Was I?"

"You and Uncle Adam."

Maya glanced over her shoulder. Adam wasn't there. She could hear the rumble of his voice as he talked to the guards outside.

Cammie yawned and her eyes began to drift closed.

"Cammie."

The girl's lashes fluttered.

"You're safe now, okay? I kept my promise, and *you're safe.*"

The girl's eyes closed, but her lips curved into a smile.

"Have good dreams, sweetheart," Maya said softly, staring down at her. "'Cause the monsters are dead. They won't get you ever again."

Yeah, her job was finished. The case was over.

Time to get back to her old life.

She was going to miss Adam. He'd gotten under her skin.

His life was with Cammie, though. And the kid—Cammie didn't need someone like Maya in her life. Someone already touched by the darkness.

"You're just like me." Nassor's words whispered through her head. *"I knew it. The darkness in us—we're the same."*

He'd been right. There was a darkness in her. She'd always known that. A hard core that blocked her heart and made her so good at killing the prey she hunted.

A kid like Cammie should never be around that darkness.

Maya stalked to her window. Gazed down at the motorcycle parked below. It had been a hell of a ride for her. Being with Adam, loving with him, fighting with him by her side— yeah, one hell of a ride.

But the ride was over now. She'd never been the type for those mushy good-byes.

She climbed through the window. Dropped to the ground twenty feet below and barely felt her knees buckle.

Her time with the dragon was up, but she'd remember him. For many, many of the long years that stretched before her, she'd remember him.

After all, Adam Brody was pretty damn unforgettable.

She started the motorcycle, refused to glance back, and drove away from the safe house, blinking eyes that were suddenly, inexplicably tearing.

Gone.

Adam gazed through Cammie's window, watching as Maya rode away from him.

The little vampire never even looked back.

His fingers clenched around the loose curtains."

No good-bye. No "see you around."

Nothing.

She'd just run, leaving him in a trail of dust and regret.

No. It wasn't going to end like this. There was too much he had to say to her, too much she didn't understand about him, *about them.*

"Uncle Adam?" Cammie's voice. Confused. Slurred with sleep.

With an effort, he managed to turn away from the vision of Maya leaving him. He crossed to Cammie's side. "It's all right, baby. You're safe."

She smiled up at him. "I know. Maya told me. Said I'd always be safe."

His heart tightened at her words. "You will be."

She settled back against the bed. "I like Maya, Uncle Adam. When I grow up"—a big yawn that showed all her teeth—"I wanna be like her."

Adam blinked. Two Mayas? He wasn't sure the world was ready.

"She's not . . . scared of anything," Cammie murmured, and even with his sensitive hearing, Adam had to strain to hear the whispered, half-asleep words. "Wanna be . . . like her . . . strong. Not . . . afraid."

His gaze drifted back to the window. Yeah, Maya was strong. No doubt about it. Strong. Brave. But—

Maybe there was something out there that Maya feared.

His lips thinned.

She'd run so fast.

Maybe, just maybe, Maya had lied to him.

Maybe she feared . . . him.

His hands clenched into fists.

I would never hurt her. Never.

Didn't she understand?

He stalked back to the window. Maya was barely a speck in the distance now. The sun was rising fast. He hoped she found shelter before it rose too high. And she was weak. She'd been bitten too many times.

If she'd stayed, he'd planned to feed her. To make love to her.

And ask her to spend the rest of her very long life with him.

If she'd stayed.

But she'd run.

"It's not going to end like this," he whispered the words, knowing she'd never hear him. "It can't."

Maya wasn't Isabella. She was strong enough to face him and the beast inside.

He wasn't just going to walk away.

Not without a hell of a fight—and he knew—his Maya loved a good fight.

"Run while you can," he said. "But then it will be my turn to hunt you, sweet vampire." As Maya would learn, a dragon was one hell of a hunter.

Run, but I'll find you.

Chapter 18

She'd managed to track the level-seven demon to the boarded-up warehouse in front of her. She could hear the squeak of rats from inside the building's shell, could smell garbage and the demon's own stench drifting in the air.

He'd attacked a cop last night. A rookie who'd had the bad luck to be assigned to the wrong neighborhood on the wrong night.

She knew the cop was still in the intensive care unit, his face and chest crisscrossed with deep stab wounds. The doctors had said there was no guarantee he'd make it.

But if he did, she'd be there. She had plans to go and check on the rookie. She'd try to help the guy understand just what the hell had happened to him.

Maya inched toward the building. There wasn't room in L.A. for an L7 who liked to screw with cops. Hell, the cops had enough trouble fighting the human criminals—they didn't need to tangle with demons, too.

Besides, that was really more her department.

She studied the building, looking for weaknesses, the best way to sneak in. Hmmm. Maybe she should just kick in the front door, forget being subtle and—

Maya stiffened, her nostrils widening as she caught a new scent of the wind. *Hell.* "You've got to stop following me," she muttered, turning around to glare at her stalker. "I told you already, Sean, you're out of this part of my life. No more night hunting, got it?"

Sean slunk out of the shadows, his glasses slightly askew on his nose. Other than looking a bit too pale and a little too thin, he was back to his old self.

His old, sometimes, *annoying* self.

He crossed his arms over his chest. "You knew I wasn't going to let you go out alone."

Her back teeth ground together. Jeez—was she not the powerful vampire? And wasn't he the weak human? "You've only been out of the hospital a few days, there's no way you're strong enough to—

"And you're off your game," he snapped, taking a few quick steps toward her. "Something's been different about you ever since you came back from Vegas."

Yeah, so? Couldn't she get a little tired? A little run-down?

Okay, maybe she hadn't been sleeping well. Every time she closed her eyes, she saw Adam. And when she *did* manage to catch a few minutes of rest, she woke up, reaching for him.

So she was "off her game". That didn't mean she couldn't still take care of the local assholes. She was more than strong enough to deal with the L7, without Sean.

"I'm not making you a target again," she told him, her voice fierce. "So walk your butt back down the street, get in your car, and *go home.*"

But he just shook his head. "No, you need backup, I can't let you hunt alone—"

"She has backup," a deep, rumbling male voice drawled.

Maya stiffened, feeling that voice reverberate through her entire body. She hadn't caught the man's scent, hadn't so much as heard his approach.

She turned, just a fraction, and her gaze met Adam's. Her palms started to sweat. "What are you doin' here?" He looked *so* good.

He stepped off the curb, strolled toward her with a confident, almost cocky walk. "Watching you."

The hair on her nape prickled. She'd had a sense, both last night and this evening when she'd left her safe house, that someone was out there. Watching.

Adam.

"Shouldn't you be back in Maine, taking care of Cammie?" What in the hell was he doing there? And did he have to look so dark and sexy as he stood there, staring at her with those eyes that saw far too much for her comfort?

"Cammie's safe—don't worry about her." He stopped less than a foot away.

"Oh." Not a great comeback. She just didn't really know what to say.

"Who the hell are you?" Sean demanded.

Ah, leave it to her best friend not to be at a loss for words.

Sean tried to step in front of her and Maya grabbed his arm, holding him back and barely managing to hold back an eye roll. *The guy just can't remember he's the weak one.*

Adam's gaze swept over him and his lip lifted just a bit at the left corner. "Good to see you on your feet, Sean."

"How do you know who I am?"

"He was with me when I checked up on you at the hospital." She couldn't seem to drag her eyes away from Adam. She'd missed him. *Really* missed him. More than she'd thought she would.

She'd felt kind of hollow inside when she got back to L.A., and when she closed her eyes at dawn, she didn't see her mother's corpse anymore.

She saw Adam.

Sean snapped his fingers. "You're the guy she helped in Vegas."

Adam nodded. Then said, "And I'm the guy who is going to be watching her back from now on."

Her spine straightened at that one. "I don't need someone trailing me." Not him, not Sean.

"Um." Those eyes were so deep. "You know," he mused softly, "I really never pegged you for a coward."

She took that hit straight on the chin.

Sean sucked in a sharp breath of air, then exploded, "Are you fucking crazy? Maya's not afraid of anything or anybody, she's—"

"It's all right, Sean." She touched his arm lightly.

He glared at Adam, but stopped snarling.

Maya licked her lips. So he wanted an explanation. He'd hunted her down, when she'd just hoped for a nice, quick break that didn't hurt either of them.

A mistake, of course, because she hurt like hell, but she wasn't going to tell Adam that fact. "I didn't run because I was afraid of you." She thought he'd realized that. "The dragon doesn't scare me and neither do you." Sure, he was strong, probably the strongest being she'd ever encountered. So what? He wasn't going to hurt her, she knew that. The guy would give his life to save her. She didn't doubt that fact for a minute.

Adam shook his head and the dark locks of his hair brushed across his shoulders. "I didn't say you were scared of me, sweetheart."

His words had her eyes narrowing. "Then just what is it you think I'm so scared of?"

"Yourself. The way you feel about me." He lifted his hand and ran his finger down her cheek. She steeled herself against the touch. "And you do feel something for me, don't you, Maya?"

Yes. Damn him, she did. "Look, I left Vegas, because the job was finished."

"But we aren't."

Sean watched the byplay between them, eyes wide. She growled, aware of a burn inside that could have been embarrassment. "Go back home, Sean. This is something I need to handle on my own."

He hesitated. "But the L7—"

"I told you," Adam interrupted, "I've got her back, from now on."

Sean still didn't look particularly convinced.

"It's okay, really," Maya told him. "I'll see you tomorrow."

"And you'll tell me what the hell's going on with this guy?" He jerked his thumb toward Adam.

"Yeah."

He shoved his hands in his pockets and marched away. He'd only taken about six steps when he stopped and glanced back at her. "You know, I realized something was different about you, I-I just didn't realize what it was." There was a sad slant to his mouth. "I don't think you're gonna be needing me anymore after all."

Then he was gone, heading fast into the shadows and leaving her on the dark street with Adam.

Maya sighed and cocked her head to the right as she studied him. "You had to make this hard, didn't you?"

He grabbed her arms, pulled her close. "Tell me you don't care about me."

Her lips thinned.

"Go ahead," he said, "lie to me. Try to make me believe that you don't feel this connection, this need that I do."

She wouldn't speak.

"Can't do it, can you?" He whispered, his lips too close to hers. *Too close.* "Because you want me, just as much as I want you."

His words had her temper spiking. "Wanting isn't everything!" It sure wasn't enough for her. She'd wanted her entire life. Wanted her mother's love. Wanted a normal home. Wanted a husband. A family.

Screw wanting—it got you nothing.

Taking, claiming—that was the way of the world.

"I could feel you, even when you were gone," he said and his lips pressed against hers in the briefest of caresses. "Smell you on my skin. Taste you on my tongue."

Maya swallowed as heat rose in her belly. Her sex began to moisten as the lust built with his softly spoken words.

"When I close my eyes, I see you," Adam told her, before pressing another kiss to her lips.

And she saw him.

"I've been alone a long time, Maya, too long. I didn't want to love another human—humans are too weak. They die too soon. There are too few of my own kind. I had no hope of finding a lover who'd shift like me, and then you—"

What the hell? Maya shoved away from him, rage wrestling with the lust her body felt. "So you wanna be with me because I'm a vamp and I can keep living as long as you do? It doesn't matter a shit *who* I am inside—you just want a long-term bed buddy and I'm available?" He was lucky she hadn't knocked him on his ass. And this was the guy she'd been mooning over?

A thin line bisected his brows. "What? No! Dammit, listen to me!"

"I was listening, you said—"

"What I was saying was that I don't want anyone else—not another Wyvern, not a human—no one!" His voice was a roar now, shaking the streets.

And, no doubt, alerting the L7.

"You're the only woman in my life who has looked at the dragon—*and still seen me.*"

She blinked. Well, of course she saw him. The man's soul and the dragon's, they were the same.

"Others in my life have feared me. Ran screaming when they saw my dragon form." He lifted his hand as if he'd touch her again, but his fingers stopped just inches from her arm. "But not you. You felt the breath of the dragon on your skin, and even then, you didn't fear me."

She'd never fear him.

A muscle ticced along his jaw. "You're rare, Maya. Damn rare. I could look this whole world over and never find a woman with your strength."

Ah, now he was just bullshitting her.

"You are so fucking strong, but you're running scared now."

"What?" She wasn't—okay, so maybe she *had* run from Vegas, but—

"Maybe it's because you're afraid of your feelings—and I *know* you have feelings for me—and that fear is trapping you. Stopping you from having the life you want. A life with me."

She looked over his shoulder, staring at the darkened factory. "Nassor was right about me, Slick. There are things inside me, a darkness that you just can't understand." That darkness was dangerous.

"Let me try." His fingers finally touched her arm, curled over the skin. "Give me a chance. I think you'd be surprised at the things I can understand."

Oh, damn, but his words tempted her. If she just had herself to consider, she'd be all over the guy already. "What about Cammie? The kid's been through enough, she doesn't need someone like me coming into her life and bringing demons and shifters and—"

"Cammie's asked about you every day that you've been gone." For a moment, humor glowed in the depths of his gaze. "She told me she wants to be like you when she grows up."

Poor delusional kid.

Maya rubbed her chest, where she could feel a dull, throbbing burn. "I'm not gonna change who I am. I-I can't. I'm gonna keep hunting, fighting—"

"I don't want you to change." His hand slid down her arm, curled around her wrist. "I'm crazy about you—vampire, demon slayer, wolf tamer—whatever. I'll take you, any way I can get you." He pressed a kiss to her palm. "Just don't walk away from me again." His voice was ragged. "Hell, I'd rather face Nassor and his vampires another time than to watch you walk away from me."

His words shocked a surprised laugh from her, and made her realize that walking away from him again, well, she didn't know if she could do it.

About Nassor. A stab of guilt had her stiffening her spine. "You know I had no choice about the compulsion, right? I had to put you to sleep, there wasn't any other way to get inside—"

His lips twisted into a faint smile. "Ah, Maya, you never put me under a compulsion."

"What?"

"I pretended to sleep and then pretended to wake when you needed me." A shrug.

Well, well. So the dragon still had a few secrets, after all. "You control the link, don't you?" It had never been her, even though she'd taken his blood.

"The Wyvern line is old, and very, very powerful."

Yeah, she got that picture, but she wasn't sure he was understanding *her.* "People who are around me, those who get close to me, they have a way of winding up either hurt"—like Sean—"or dead." Like her mother. She didn't want to risk him, too.

Adam just shook his head. "Don't you know yet that I'm one hard asshole to kill?"

She licked her lips. "Adam—"

"Our lives are about risk, Maya. That's who we are. *What* we are. Don't give me some bullshit line about me being in danger because I'm with you. Hell, I'm always in danger. That fact doesn't change anything for me."

There was a ring of truth to his words that she couldn't deny, and though she tried to fight it, a wild flaring of what could have been hope grew inside her. He knew the risks and still wanted to be with her. "So what is it that you're offering me, Slick?" She finally asked him, because she needed to know, needed to be sure.

"I'm offering you a partner. A lover. Someone who'll watch your back and hold you when you sleep."

Hold you when you sleep. Because Adam did hold her, keeping her wrapped in warm, strong arms. And, damn, but it felt right when he held her.

In the past, she'd always wanted to sleep alone after sex. She hadn't wanted a false closeness.

But with Adam, it wasn't false. The connection she felt, it was real. She'd missed him, missed his touch and his scent and his strength the last few nights.

She'd missed his arms, holding her.

"Maya . . ." The rumble of his voice made her swallow. She stared into his eyes, unable to look away as he said, "I'm offering you all the blood you need and all the sex you can handle," he continued, heat roughening his words.

Wow. No smart vampire would turn that down.

Silence, just for a beat of time, then, "I'm offering you forever with a man who'd do anything you wanted—just to make you smile."

Well, damn.

Maya parted her lips to speak, but found she didn't know what to say.

Forever. Such a long, long time. Especially for her. And for Adam.

"Nassor was right about the darkness in you," Adam said and Maya felt her heart lurch to a stop.

No, no—

"I've got that same darkness. I know what it's like to live with that kind of power inside." His gaze bored into hers. "I control that darkness, and so do you."

But what if she lost control? What if, one day, the beast inside took over?

His fingers tightened around hers. "You'll always leash the beast, baby, because the woman in you is a hell of a lot stronger than the darkness."

He lifted her hand, pressed a kiss against her palm. "What will it be, vampire? Do you choose to walk with me or do you choose to walk alone?"

She'd thought she'd chosen before. When she'd left him, she'd planned to fight on her own. To live on her own.

But Adam was offering her something now—something she'd barely ever dreamed she'd have.

A partner, a lover of her own. Someone to turn to when the nightmares rose and even when the laughter beckoned.

"What about Cammie?" It was the only thing holding her back—if she ever did anything to hurt the kid . . .

"It took me a week to get here because Cammie and I had to pack up the house in Maine. She wanted to come to you, and so did I." The briefest of smiles. "Don't you know, you're her hero now? The woman who saved her from the monsters."

Oh, but she wanted to take what he was offering. The chance for happiness. For a life not lived in the shadows.

"I . . . love you, Maya. More than I think you'll ever know."

Shit. Her knees almost buckled on that one. *He loved her?* Her pulse raced now, far too fast. Her hands were soaked with sweat and a wild, raw pleasure filled her heart.

He loved her.

"I know you—you don't love me, not yet, but, dammit, we've got a hell of a lot of years ahead of us, and if you'll just give me a chance—" Adam broke off, drawing a deep breath. "One day, one night at a time, Maya. That's all I'm asking."

One night at a time. She could handle that, but Adam, well, he deserved more. *Stop being afraid.* It was time she put her past to rest, and fought for the future she'd longed for. Her fingers curled over his. "Adam . . ."

He flinched.

She shook her head. "No, please, listen." Ah, but she still didn't know what to say. "Shit, Adam, I-I care for you." *Care. Far too weak a word.*

A muscle flexed along his jaw. "Like you care for your friend Sean? Or for Cammie? Or for—"

"No! Look, I worry about you. All the time. I mean, I know you're a freaking dragon and can pretty much kick everyone's ass, but I worry about you. I want to protect you. And I want you. I *want you so much* but I also, dammit, I just want to hold you." She was screwing this up.

A frown lined his brow.

"I like it when you hold me," she whispered and the admission was one of the hardest she'd ever made. "I like it when you smile, even when you get all arrogant and asshole-like on me, I still like it."

His eyes narrowed. "What are you saying?"

Did the man want her to have absolutely no pride? Fine. If that was what he needed, then—"I'm saying I think I love you, dragon."

Savage satisfaction flashed across his face. "Good, because I'm fucking insane for you." His lips took hers, the kiss hard and deep. She could taste his hunger, his lust.

It matched hers perfectly.

But then, Adam had matched her from the beginning.

Dragon.

Warrior.

Lover.

And with a soul as dark as her own.

She wanted to get him somewhere dark and quiet where they could be alone and naked and she could make certain this wasn't some kind of dream.

But first . . . "Hold the thought, Slick," she murmured against his lips. "I got a little bit of business to take care of here."

His head lifted, and he glanced back at the warehouse. "What did the asshole do?"

"Messed with the wrong cop." A good cop, one who just hadn't known how to handle a demon.

"Huh." Adam slowly stepped away from her, but he didn't release her hand. "Then lead the way, sweetheart. We'll take care of him, then I'll take you."

A quiver of excitement heated her blood. "That a promise, dragon?"

"Vampire, think of it more as a guarantee."

Maya smiled at him, reached for her gun, and got ready to kick ass.

It was, after all, one of the things she did best.

*   *   *

It had been a near miss, Adam realized as he stalked be-hind Maya into the darkened building.

She'd nearly escaped him—and left him in the darkness all alone.

But he'd managed to convince her that they had something together, and she was willing to give him a chance.

Willing to give them a chance.

She was still afraid. Maya didn't trust easily, and love for her, well, that would never be easy, either.

But as he'd said, they had plenty of time. Time for him to prove to her that he was exactly the man she needed.

Yes, they had plenty of days. Plenty of nights.

He could be patient.

After all, he'd already waited a thousand years to find her.

He smiled as he watched her kick open a door, shattering wood. The demon was running from her, and Maya was telling him that he had two options.

"Option one," she snarled, "I kick your ass and then watch you drag your sorry carcass out of L.A. *And* you stay away from my cops."

The demon backed into a corner. Its claws were up, but Adam could smell his fear.

Apparently, Maya's reputation had preceded her.

A tough bitch to stake.

An unstoppable killer.

And the woman who could tame a dragon.

"What's the second option?" the L7 asked, voice high.

Maya spared Adam a glance over her shoulder. "My dragon gets to show you how hot his fire burns."

The demon began to shake and then he started making promises, fast. Swearing he'd never so much as look at a cop, or *any* human, again.

Maya's words whispered through his mind. *My dragon.* He liked that. A lot.

Because she was sure as hell his.

A perfect mate.

A woman who could touch the fire and never feel the burn.

Maya Black.

The vampire who held the heart of a dragon in the palm of her hand.

Eternity with her was gonna be one hell of an adventure.

Blood, sex, and fire.

He could hardly wait.

Everyone knows
IT'S HOTTER IN HAWAII,
and in HelenKay Dimon's latest, that doesn't just
mean the weather. . . .

Cassie's head snapped back. "What are you doing?"

The woman asked a *very* good question. "Standing here."

"You were going to kiss me."

For a second there he toyed with the idea, yeah. "Think a lot of yourself, don't you?"

"I know when a man wants to kiss me."

She didn't have to sound so appalled by the possibility. "So, that's a 'yes' on the arrogance thing?"

"Come off it. I saw you."

"Then you need glasses." And a drink. Maybe that would help.

"You're two inches away and swooping in."

"Swooping?" Cal stepped back and well out of swooping range.

Mauling complete strangers was not his style. Neither was making a move on an estranged friend's grieving sister. Make that grieving baby sister. She was somewhere around thirty and hot as hell. Dan probably hadn't slept through the night since Cassie turned fourteen. No sane man who wanted to protect her would.

Cal chalked up the moment of stupidity to the long flight and the shocking news about Dan his brain still refused to compute. Just a heap of pent-up energy with nowhere to go.

Yep. Nothing more than a near miss brought on by low blood sugar . . . or something.

"Reaction." One he insisted had more to do with the heat of the situation than the length of her legs.

"To what?" Those amber eyes narrowed.

"This," he waved his hand back and forth. "Between us. That and the by-product of the gunfire. It's not real."

Her lips twisted into a look of disgust. "Did your head slam against the floor or something?"

Now she was ticking him off. "Give me a break. Are you trying to tell me this only goes one way?"

"Define *this*." She mimicked his hand gesture by waving her hand back and forth between them.

"Interest."

"In you?"

Now she sounded horrified. A guy could get a complex. "Do you see someone else here?"

"No, but I'm not the one who's lost his mind. That seems to be you at the moment."

"You're trying to tell me—"

"Yes."

"You felt nothing when—"

"Exactly."

"At all?"

"Not even a twinge." She topped the response with a smug smile.

Well, hell. Here he thought they both were fighting back a heavy-duty case of adrenaline-fueled lust. Looked like he stood alone on that score.

And try DANGEROUS GAMES
by Charlotte Mede,
available now from Brava. . . .

The Thursday evening salons hosted by Mrs. Hampton had become one of the most coveted invitations in London society, each guest scrutinized by the hostess herself to ensure lively, engaging, and informed debate on the most compelling issues of the day. And while her town house in Mayfair was a modest affair, the company was always of the highest order, along with generous servings of food and drink to satisfy the most discerning guests.

Tonight, the room heaved with conversation, the latest rebellion in India taking center stage, while off to the wings, breathless discussion percolated about the arrival in London of the Koh-I-Noor, the world's largest diamond—destined to be presented to Queen Victoria and Prince Albert upon the opening of the Great Exhibition in under one month's time. Conceived by the prince, the historic occasion would be held in Hyde Park in the spectacularly constructed Crystal Palace, designed to showcase England's and the world's advances in science and industry.

"Not at all, not at all, my dear Mrs. Hampton," Seabourne finally replied, clasping his hands behind his back and away from the tap of her ivory fan. "Your questions are diverting as always but never more so than the woman who poses them."

Lilly inclined her head toward him, raising her low voice slightly to compete with the surging exchanges going on around them. "Well thank you, sir. But you must hasten to answer my question as the buffet will be served quite soon."

John Sydons, the former publisher of the *Guardian*, guffawed, his muttonchops bristling. "And we shouldn't want that, Seabourne. I just saw a spectacular Nesselrode pudding float by along with a platter of oysters swimming in cream. So let's move along. Respond to the lady's query—has the situation settled somewhat this past month?"

Seabourne nodded portentously, the horizontal lines on his forehead deepening. "The political expansion of the British East India Company at the perceived expense of native princes and the Mughal court has aroused Hindu and Muslim animosity alike, a complex situation overall which I do not think will be resolved without a Parliamentary solution."

"A tinderbox is what it is," murmured Lilly.

"Indeed," seconded the man across from her, Lord Falmouth, Member of Parliament. Small and wiry, he barely filled out his impeccably tailored waistcoat and jacket. "It didn't help that our colonial government, in its boundless wisdom, furnished the Indian soldiers with cartridges coated with grease made from the fat of cows and of pigs. Ignorance and incompetence in one fell stroke. Amazing."

"The first sacred to Hindus and the second anathema to Muslims." Lilly splayed her fan in barely concealed annoyance. "We have an ineffectual and insensitive Governor and of course, an historic series of blunders, beginning with the Kabul massacre, that slaughter in the mountain passes of Afghanistan. I have heard it said that of the sixteen thousand who set out on retreat, only one man survived to arrive in Jalalabad."

"It was actually believed that the Afghans let him live so he could tell the grisly story—such a severe blow and bitter humiliation to British pride." Lord Falmouth jutted out his rather weak chin. "Reports from the forty-fourth English Regiment are dismal. The troops kept on through the passes but without food, mangled and disoriented, they are reported to have knocked down their officers with the butts of their muskets. St. Martin is one of the few to have survived, if survive is the word one would choose to use."

"He's quite the loose cannon, or so one hears from the Foreign Office," added Seabourne. "Has publicly resigned his post, whatever it was, something to do with statecraft, certainly."

"You mean spycraft, surely," Lord Falmouth corrected.

"A shadowy figure one would assume and now one not to be trusted, given his precarious mental state," continued Seabourne. "The trauma and so on."

"My goodness. How clandestine and mysterious," said Lilly, frowning, only vaguely familiar with the St. Martin name. "One never knows what resentments these types of horrific experiences may nurture. I infer from your comments that loyalty is at question for these individuals who find themselves one moment at the service of their country and at the next entirely disengaged or worse . And what of his family? The St. Martins do have a seat in the House of Lords, if I'm not mistaken."

"The parents passed away some years ago and his older brother died of smallpox soon after, if I recall correctly. However, St. Martin has never taken up his place in Parliament, having instead disappeared for years to the farthest reaches of the globe. In her majesty's service, one presumes. Although one can presume no longer with his resignation."

And be sure to catch
DEMON CAN'T HELP IT,
Kathy Love's newest book,
coming next month!

Jo breathed in slowly through her nose. What had she just agreed to? Seeing this man every day? She pulled in another slow, even breath, telling herself to shake off her reaction to this man's proximity.

Sure, he was attractive. And he had—a presence. But she wasn't some teenage girl who would fall to pieces under a cute boy's attention. Not that cute was a strong enough word for what Maksim was. He was—unnerving. To say the least.

But she wasn't interested in him. She decided that quite definitely over the past two days. Of course that decision was made when he wasn't in her presence.

But either way, she should have more control than this. Apparently should and could were two very different things. And she couldn't seem to stop her reaction to him. Her heart raced and her body tingled, both hot and cold in all the most inappropriate places.

"So every morning?" he said, his voice rumbling right next to her, firing up the heat inside her. "Does that work for you?"

She cleared her throat, struggling for calm her body.

"Yes—that's great," she managed to say, surprising even herself with the airiness of her tone. "I'll schedule you from eight a.m. to—" she glanced at the clock on lower right-hand of the computer screen, "noon?"

That was a good amount of time, getting Cherise through

the rowdy mornings and lunch, and giving him the go ahead to leave now. She needed him out of her space.

If her body wasn't going to go along with her mind, then avoidance was clearly her best strategy. And she'd done well with that tactic—although she'd told herself that wasn't what she was doing.

"Noon is fine," he said, still not moving. Not even straightening away from the computer. And her.

"Good," she poised her fingers over the keys and began typing in his hours. "Then I think we are all settled. You can take off now if you like."

When he didn't move, she added, "You can go get some lunch. You must be hungry." She flashed him a quick smile without really looking at him.

This time he did stand, but he didn't move away. Instead he leaned against her desk, the old piece of furniture creaking at his tall, muscular weight.

"You must be hungry, too. Would you like to join me?"

She blinked, for a moment not comprehending his words, her mind too focused on the muscles of his thighs so near her. The flex of more muscles in his shoulders and arms as he crossed them over his chest.

She forced herself to look back at the computer screen.

"I—I don't think so," she said. "I have a lot to do here."

"But surely you allow yourself even a half an hour for lunch break."

She continued typing, fairly certain whatever she was writing was gibberish. "I brought a lunch with me, actually." Which was true. Not that she was hungry at the moment. She was too—edgy.

"Come on," he said in a low voice that was enticing, coaxing. "Come celebrate your first regular volunteer."

She couldn't help looking at him. He was smiling, the curl of his lips, his white, even teeth, the sexily pleading glimmer in his pale green eyes.

God, he was so beautiful.

And dangerous.

Jo shook her head. "I really can't."

He studied her for a moment. "Can't or won't. What's the matter, Josephine? Do I make you nervous?"

Jo's breath left her for a moment at the accented rhythm of her full name crossing his lips. But the breath-stealing moment left as quickly as it came, followed by irritation. At him and at herself.

She wasn't attracted to his man—not beyond a basic physical attraction. And that could be controlled. It could.

"You don't make me nervous," she said firmly.

"Then why not join me for lunch?"

"Because," she said slowly, "I have a lot of work to do."

Maksim crossed his arms tighter and lifted one of his eloquent eyebrows, which informed her that he didn't believe her for a moment.

"I don't think that's why you won't come. I think you are uncomfortable with me. Maybe because you are attracted to me." Again the eyebrow lifted—this time in questioning challenge.